A FATAL MISUNDERSTANDING

"I don't want you to think I'm criticising, finding fault or anything like that," Martin Urban said to Finn. "If you don't own your own home these days, it's pretty difficult to find anywhere to live, let alone anywhere decent. And to buy somewhere you don't just have to be earning good money, you need a bit of capital as well. What I'm trying to say is, when my mother told me the way Mrs. Finn was living, I thought maybe I could do something to change all that, to sort of benefit you both."

Finn finished his drink. He said nothing.

"I'll come to the point." Martin Urban said in a lower voice, "I could manage to let you have ten thousand pounds. I'm afraid I can't make it more than that. You'd have to go outside London, of course."

Finn was overwhelmed by the munificence of this offer. His own fame had indeed spread before him, and it wasn't his fame as a plumber and decorator. He said, "It's a lot of money."

"You wouldn't do it for less."

Finn did a rare thing for him. He smiled. He spoke one word. "When?"

"When you like. As soon as possible. You're going to accept then?"

"Oh, yes. Why not?"

"Good. That's splendid. I'm very happy you don't feel you have to put up any show of refusal, that sort of thing." Martin Urban seemed to become doubtful and his expression took on its former shade of mystification. "I have made myself plain? You have understood me?"

Rather impatiently Finn said, "Sure. You can leave it to me. . . ."

The
Lake of Darkness

Ruth Rendell

BANTAM BOOKS

TORONTO · NEW YORK · LONDON · SYDNEY · AUCKLAND

All of the characters in this book are fictitious,
and any resemblance to actual persons, living
or dead, is purely coincidental.

*This low-priced Bantam Book
has been completely reset in a type face
designed for easy reading, and was printed
from new plates. It contains the complete
text of the original hard-cover edition.*
NOT ONE WORD HAS BEEN OMITTED.

THE LAKE OF DARKNESS
*A Bantam Book / published by arrangement with
Doubleday & Company, Inc.*

PRINTING HISTORY
*Doubleday edition published July 1980
A Selection of Detective Book Club February 1980
Bantam edition / September 1981
2nd printing . . . January 1987*

*Bantam Books are published by Bantam Books, Inc. Its trademark,
consisting of the words "Bantam Books" and the portrayal of a
rooster, is Registered in U.S. Patent and Trademark Office and in
other countries. Marca Registrada. Bantam Books, Inc., 666 Fifth
Avenue, New York, New York 10103.*

PRINTED IN THE UNITED STATES OF AMERICA

O   0 9 8 7 6 5 4 3 2 1

Nero is an angler in the lake of darkness...

KING LEAR

I

Scorpio is metaphysics, putrefaction and death, regeneration, passion, lust and violence, insight and profundity; inheritance, loss, occultism, astrology, borrowing and lending, others' possessions. Scorpians are magicians, astrologers, alchemists, surgeons, bondsmen, and undertakers. The gem for Scorpio is the snakestone, the plant the cactus; eagles and wolves and scorpions are its creatures, its body part is the genitals, its weapon the Obligatory Pain, and its card in the Tarot is Death.

Finn shared his birthday, November 16, with the Emperor Tiberius. He had been told by a soothsayer, who was a friend of his mother's whom she had met in the mental hospital, that he would live to a great age and die by violence.

On the morning of his birthday, his twenty-sixth, one of Kaiafas' children came round with the money in a parcel. He knocked on Finn's door. Someone downstairs must have let him into the house. They didn't know it was his birthday, Finn realised that. It was just a coincidence. He undid the parcel and checked that it contained what it should contain—£2,500 in ten-pound notes. Now it had arrived he had better get on with things, he might as well start now.

It was too early to go up to Lena. She liked to sleep late in the mornings. Not that she would mind his waking her on his birthday; she would like it, she would expect it almost. But he wouldn't just the same. He tucked the money safely away and went downstairs.

Finn was very tall and thin and pale. He was near to being an albino but was saved by the watery grey colour that stained the pupils of his eyes. It was remarkable that eyes of such an insipid shade should be so piercing and so bright, like polished silver. His hair, when he was a child, had been white-blond but had now faded to the neutral greyish-beige of cardboard. He had a face that was quite ordinary and unmemorable, but this was not true of his eyes. Under a longish PVC jacket he wore blue denims, a checked Viyella shirt, a black-velvet waistcoat, and round his neck one of those scarves that Greek women wear, black and triangular and sewn along one side with small gold coins. He carried a tool box of laminated blue metal. Finn had a smallish head on a thin, delicate-looking neck and his wrists and ankles and feet were

1

small, but his pale hands were almost preternaturally large with an extravagant span.

His van, a small, pale grey, plain van, was parked in front of the house in Lord Arthur Road. You might call it Kentish Town or Tufnell Park or Lower Holloway. There were some curious houses, mini-Gothic with step gables, fat Victorian red brick, great grey barns with too many bays for grace or comfort, and small, narrow, flat-fronted places, very old, and covered in a skin of pale green peeling plaster. Finn wasn't interested in architecture, he could have lived just as easily in a cave or a hut as in his room. He unlocked the van and got in and drove up past Tufnell Park Station, up Dartmouth Park Hill towards the southernmost part of Hampstead Heath.

It was nine-fifteen. He drove under the bridge at Gospel Oak Station, up into Savernake Road, which skirted Parliament Hill Fields, and on the corner of Modena Road he parked the van. From there he could keep the house Kaiafas owned under observation. He sat at the wheel, watching the three-storey house of plum-coloured brick.

The Frazers were the first to go out. They left together, arm in arm. Next came Mrs. Ionides, five minutes afterwards. Finn didn't care about them, they didn't count. He wanted to be sure of Anne Blake, who quite often took a day off and had told Finn she "worked at home."

However, she emerged from the front door at exactly nine-thirty and set off the way the others had for the station. As a trusted handyman Finn was in possession of a key to the house in Modena Road, and with this he let himself in. His entering as the agent or servant of the landlord was perfectly legitimate, though some of the things he intended to do there were not.

Kaiafas' sister had the ground-floor flat and the Frazers the next one up. The Frazers had accepted £2,000 from Kaiafas and had agreed to move out at the end of the month. Mrs. Ionides would do anything Kaiafas told her, and now he had told her she must go back to nurse their aged father in Nicosia. With vacant possession, the house would sell for sixty, maybe seventy thousand pounds. Kaiafas had asked estate agents about that, and he had watched prices rising and soaring as houses just like his had been sold. The one next door, identical to his, had fetched sixty in August. The house agent smiled and shook his head and said that had been vacant possession, though, hadn't it? Kaiafas had told Finn all about it, that was how he knew.

He let himself into Mrs. Ionides' hall and thence into her living room where one of the window sash cords had broken a day or so ago. He fitted a new sash cord, and then he went upstairs to see what could be done about the coping over the bay window that Mrs. Frazer said let water in. This occupied him till lunchtime.

He had brought his own lunch with him in an earthenware pot. Not for him the black tea and hamburgers and chips and eggs and processed peas of the workmen's cafe. In the pot was fruit roughly cut up with bran and yoghurt. Finn ate a piece of dark brown bread and drank the contents of a half-pint can of pineapple juice. Pineapple was not only his favourite fruit but his favourite of all flavours.

After lunch he sat cross-legged on the carpet and began his daily session of meditation. Presently he felt himself levitate until he rose almost up to the ceiling from where he could look through the top of the Frazers' window at the bright green escarpment of Hampstead Heath rising against a cold, sallow, faintly ruffled sky.

Meditation always refreshed him. He could feel a wonderful sensation of energy streaming down his arms and crackling like electricity out of his fingertips. His aura was probably very strong and bright, but he couldn't see auras like Lena and Mrs. Gogarty could, so it was no good looking in the glass. He took his tool box and climbed the last remaining flight of stairs. Unlike the Frazers and Mrs. Ionides, Anne Blake had given no permission for Kaiafas or his agent or servant to enter her flat that day, but Kaiafas made a point of retaining a key. Finn unlocked Anne Blake's front door, went in and closed it after him. The hall walls were papered in a William Morris design of king-cups and water hawthorn on a blue ground, and the carpet was hyacinth-blue Wilton. Anne Blake had been living there since before Kaiafas bought the house, ten or twelve years now, and she wouldn't leave even for a bigger bribe than Kaiafas was giving the Frazers. She had told Kaiafas she wouldn't leave for twenty thousand and he couldn't make her. The law was on her side. He could have the flat, she said, over her dead body.

Finn smiled faintly in the dimness of the hall.

He opened the cupboard between the bathroom door and the door of the living room and took out a pair of light-weight aluminium steps. They were so light that a child could have lifted them above his head on one hand. Finn took them into the bathroom.

The bathroom was small, no more than eight feet by six, and over one end of the bath, in the ceiling, was a trap-door into the loft. But for this trap-door, Finn would have had to choose some

3

other method. He set up the steps and then he went into the bedroom. Here was the same blue carpet, the walls painted silver-grey. There was no central heating in the house in Modena Road and each tenant had his or her own collection of gas and electric heating appliances. Anne Blake had an electric wall heater in her kitchen, a gas fire in her living room, a portable electric fire in her bedroom, and no heating at all in her bathroom. Finn plugged in the portable electric fire, switched it on, and when he saw the two parallel bar elements begin to glow, switched it off again and unplugged it.

He climbed the aluminium steps and pushed up the trap-door, a torch in his left hand. The loft housed a water tank and a good deal of the sort of discarded equipment that has become unusable but cannot quite be called rubbish. Finn had been up there before, once when a pipe had frozen and once to get out on to the roof itself, and he had a fair idea of what he would find. He was observant and he had a good memory. He trod carefully on the joists, shining his torch, searching among the corded bundles of the *National Geographic* magazine, the ranks of glass jars, an aged Remington typewriter, rolls of carpet cut-offs, flatiron and trivet, chipped willow pattern dinner plates, until he found what he was looking for. An electric ring.

There was no plug on its lead. It was dirty and the coiled element had some kind of black grease or oil on it. Finn brought it down the steps and set about attaching a 13-amp plug to it. When this was plugged in, however, nothing happened. Never mind. Mending something like that was child's play to him.

The time had come to check up on her. He didn't want her coming home because she was starting a cold or her boss had decided to take the afternoon off. She had been unwise enough to tell him where she worked that time he had been in to mend the pipe, just as she had also told him she always took a bath the minute she got in from work. Finn never forgot information of that sort. He looked up the number in the phone book and dialled it. When he had asked for her and been put through to some extension and asked to hold and at last had heard her voice, he replaced the receiver.

An old, long-disused gas pipe ran up the kitchen from behind the fridge into the loft. This Finn intended to utilize. He cut a section out of it about six inches from the floor. Then he returned to the loft, this time with a 100-watt light bulb on the end of a long lead. He soon found the other end of the gas pipe and pro-

4

ceeded to cut off its sealed end. While he worked he reflected on the cowardice of human beings, their fears, their reserve.

Finn had a sense of humour of a kind, though it was far from that perception of irony and incongruities which usually goes by the name, and he had been amused that Kaiafas, in all their dealings, had never directly told him what he wanted doing. It was left to Finn to understand.

"Feen," Kaiafas had said, "I am at my wits' end. I say to her, 'Madam, I give you five thousand pounds, five thousand, madam, to quit my house.' 'Please,' I say, 'I say please on my knees.' What does she say? That it is a pity I ever come away from Cyprus."

"Well," said Finn. "Well, well." It was a frequent rejoinder with him.

A look of ineffable slyness and greed came into Kaiafas' face. Finn had already guessed what he was after. He had done jobs for Kaiafas and others before, the kind of thing a professional hit man does in the course of his work, though nothing of this magnitude.

"So I think to myself," said Kaiafas, "I make no more offer to you, madam, I give you no five thousand pounds. I give it to my friend Feen instead."

That had been all. Finn wasn't, in any case, the sort of person to invite confidences. He had merely nodded and said, "Well, well," and Kaiafas had fetched him another pineapple juice, handing over the key to the top flat. And now the first instalment of his fee had come. . . .

He had inserted a length of electric flex into the pipe from the loft end, its frayed tips protruding ever so little from the cut-out section behind the fridge but apparent only to a very acute observer. The other end of the flex reached as far as the trap-door and with a further two yards to spare. Finn was more or less satisfied. Once he might have done the deed without all this paraphernalia of wires and gas pipe and trap-door, without clumsy manual effort. He looked back wistfully to his early teens, his puberty, now a dozen years past, when his very presence in a house had been enough to begin a wild *poltergeist* activity. It was with a yearning nostalgia that he remembered it, as another man might recall a juvenile love—bricks flying through windows, pictures falling from the walls, a great stone out of the garden which no one could lift suddenly appearing in the middle of Queenie's living-room carpet. The power had gone with the loss of his innocence, or perhaps with the hashish which a boy at school had got him on to. Finn never smoked now, not even tobacco, and he drank no alcohol. It wasn't worth it if you meant to become an adept, a man of power, a master.

He checked that in the electric point behind the fridge there was a spare socket. A certain amount of the black fluffy dirt which always seems to coat the inside of lofts had fallen into the bath. Finn cleaned it with the rags he carried with him until its rose-pink surface looked just as it had done when he arrived. He re-placed the aluminium steps in the cupboard and put the electric ring into a plastic carrier bag. It had been a long day's work for every minute of which Kaiafas was paying him handsomely.

The Frazers would return at any moment. That was of no im-portance provided Finn was out of Anne Blake's flat. He closed her front door behind him. By now it was dark but Finn put no lights on. One of the skills in which he was training himself was that of seeing more adequately in the dark.

The air was strangely clear for so mild an evening, the yellow and white lights sparkling, dimming a pale and lustreless moon. As Finn started the van he saw Mrs. Ionides, dark, squat, dressed as always in black, cross the street and open the gate of the house he had just left. He drove down Dartmouth Park Hill, taking his place patiently in the traffic queueing at the lights by the tube.

The house where Finn lived was a merchant's mansion that had fallen on evil days almost from the first, and the first was a long time ago now. He climbed up through the house, up a wider staircase than the one in Modena Road. Music came from behind doors, and voices and cooking smells and the smell of cannabis smoked in a little white-clay pipe. He passed the door of his own room and went on up. At the top he knocked once at the first door and passed without waiting into the room.

It was a room, not a flat, though a large one, and it had been partitioned off into small sections—living room, bedroom, kitchen. Finn had put up two of the partitions himself. You entered by way of the kitchen, which was a miracle of shelving and the stowing of things on top of other things and of squeezing a quart into a pint pot. In the living room, nine feet by eight, where a thousand little knickknacks of great worth and beauty to their owner were displayed upon surfaces and walls, where a gas fire burned, where a small green bird sat silent in a cage, was Lena consulting the pendulum.

"Well," said Finn, going up to her and taking her free hand. They never kissed. She smiled at him, a sweet vague smile as if

6

she couldn't quite see him or was seeing something beyond him. He sat down beside her.

Finn could do nothing with the pendulum, but Lena had great ability with it just as she had with the divining rod. This was very likely one of the consequences of what those people at the hospital called her schizophrenia. The pendulum was a glass bead suspended on a piece of cotton, and when Lena put it above her right hand it revolved clockwise and when she put it above her left hand it revolved widdershins. She had long since asked it to give her signs for yes and no, and she had noted these particular oscillations. The pendulum had just answered yes to some question which hadn't been revealed to Finn, and Lena sighed.

She was old to be his mother, a thin, transparent creature like a dead leaf or a shell that has been worn away by the action of the sea. Finn thought sometimes that he could see the light through her. Her eyes were like his but milder, and her hair, which had been as fair as his, had reverted to its original whiteness. She dressed herself from the many second-hand clothes shops in which the district abounded and derived as intense a pleasure from buying in them as a Hampstead woman might in South Molton Street. Mostly she was happy, though there were moments of terror. She believed herself to be a reincarnation of Madame Blavatsky, which the hospital had seized upon as a case-book delusion. Finn thought it was probably true.

"Did you buy anything today?" he said.

She hesitated. Her dawning smile was mischievous. It was as if she had a secret she could no longer keep to herself and she exclaimed with shining eyes, "It's your birthday!"

Finn nodded.

"Did you think I'd forgotten? I *couldn't*." She was suddenly shy and she clasped her hands over the pendulum, looking down at them. "There's something for you in that bag."

"Well, well," said Finn.

In the bag was a leather coat, black, long, double-breasted, shabby, scuffed, and lined with rotting silk. Finn put it on.

"Well," he said. "Well!" It was like a storm trooper's coat. He fastened the belt. "Must be the best thing you ever got," he said.

She was ecstatic with pleasure. "I'll mend the lining for you!"

"You've had a busy day," he said. The coat was too big for the room. With every movement he made he was in danger of knocking over little glass vases, Toby jugs, china dogs, pebbles, shells, and bunches of dried flowers in chutney jars. He took the coat off carefully, with reverence almost, to please Lena. The green bird began to sing, shrill and sweet, pretending it was a canary. "What did you do this afternoon?"

"Mrs. Urban came."

"Well!"

"She came in her new car, a green one. The kind of green that has silver all mixed up in it."

Finn nodded. He knew what she meant.

"She brought me those chocolates and she stayed for tea. She made the tea. Last time she came was before you put up the wall and made my bedroom."

"Did she like it?"

"Oh, yes!" Her eyes were full of love, shining with it. "She *loved* it. She said it was so compact."

"Well, well," said Finn, and then he said, "Ask the pendulum something for me. Ask it if I'm going to have a good year."

Lena held up the string. She addressed the pendulum in a whisper, like someone talking to a child in a dark room. The glass bead began to swing, then to revolve clockwise at high speed.

"Look!" Lena cried. "Look at that! Look what a wonderful year you'll have. Your twenty-seventh, three times three times three. The pendulum never lies."

II

On the broad gravelled frontage of the Urbans' house were drawn up the Urbans' three cars, the black Rover, the metallic-green Vauxhall, and the white Triumph. In the drawing room sat the Urbans drinking sherry, oloroso for Margaret, amontillado for Walter, and Tio Pepe for Martin. There was something of the Three Bears about them, though Baby Bear, in the shape of twenty-eight-year-old Martin, was no longer a resident of Copley Avenue, Alexandra Park, and Goldilocks had yet to appear.

Invariably on Thursday evenings Martin was there for dinner. He went home with his father from the office just round the corner. They had the sherry, two glasses each, for they were creatures of habit, and had dinner and watched television while Mrs. Urban did her patchwork. Since she had taken it up the year before as menopausal therapy she seemed to be perpetually accompanied by clusters of small floral hexagons. Patchwork was beginning to take over the house in Copley Avenue, chiefly in the form of cushion covers and bedspreads. She stitched away calmly or with suppressed energy, and her son found himself watching her while his father discoursed with animation on a favourite subject of his, Capital Transfer Tax.

Martin had a piece of news to impart. Though in possession of it for some days, he had postponed telling it and his feelings about it were now mixed. Natural elation was mingled with unease and caution. He even felt very slightly sick as one does before an examination or an important interview.

Margaret Urban held out her glass for a refill. She was a big, statuesque, heavy-browed woman who resembled Leighton's painting of Clytemnestra. When she had sipped her sherry, she snipped off a piece of thread and held up for the inspection of her husband and son a long strip of joined-together red and purple hexagons. This had the effect of temporarily silencing Walter Urban, and Martin, murmuring that that was a new colour combination, he hadn't seen anything like that before, prepared his opening words. He rehearsed them under his breath as his mother, with the artist's sigh of dissatisfaction, rolled up the patchwork, jumped rather heavily to her feet and made for the door, bent on attending to her casserole.

"Mother," said Martin, "wait here a minute. I've got something to tell you both."

Now that the time had come, he brought it out baldly, perhaps clumsily. They looked at him in silence, a calm, slightly stunned silence into which gratification gradually crept. Mrs. Urban took her hand from the door and came slowly back, her eyebrows rising and disappearing into her thick, blue-rinsed fringe.

Martin laughed awkwardly. "I can't quite believe it myself yet."

"I thought you were going to tell us you were getting married," said his mother.

"Married? Me? Whatever made you think that?"

"Oh, I don't know, it's the sort of thing one does think of. We didn't even know you did the football pools, did we, Walter? Exactly how much did you say you'd won?"

"A hundred and four thousand, seven hundred and fifty-four pounds, forty-six pence."

"A hundred and four thousand pounds! I mean, you can't have been doing the pools very long. You weren't doing them when you lived here."

"I've been doing them for five weeks," said Martin.

"And you've won a hundred and four thousand pounds! Well, a hundred and five really. Don't you think that's absolutely amazing, Walter?"

A slow smile was spreading itself across Walter Urban's handsome, though somewhat labrador-like, face. He loved it, the consideration of how to make it multiply, how (with subtle and refined legality) to keep it from the coffers of the Inland Revenue, and he loved the pure beauty of it as an abstraction on paper rather than as notes in a wallet. The smile grew to beaming proportions.

"I think this calls for some sort of congratulation, Martin. Yes, many congratulations. What a dark horse you are! Even these days a hundred thousand is a large sum of money, a very *respectable* sum of money. We've still got that bottle of Piper-Heidsieck from our anniversary, Margaret. Shall we open it? Wins of this kind are free of tax, of course, but we shall have to think carefully about investing it so that you don't pay all your interest away to the Inland Revenue. Still, if a couple of accountants can't work it out, who can?"

"Go and get the champagne, Walter."

"Whatever you do, don't think of paying off the mortgage on your flat. Remember that tax relief on the interest on your mortgage repayments is a concession of H. M. Government, of which a single man in your position would be mad not to take advantage."

"He won't keep that flat on, he'll buy himself a house."

"He could become an underwriting member of Lloyd's."

"There's no reason why he shouldn't buy a country cottage *and* keep the flat."

"He could buy a house and have the maximum twenty-five thousand mortgage...."

"Do go and get the champagne, Walter. What *are* you going to do with it, dear? Have you made any plans?"

Martin had. They weren't the kind of plans he considered it would be politic to divulge at the moment, so he said nothing about them. The champagne was brought in. Eventually they sat down to the casserole, the inevitably overdone potatoes, and a Black Forest cake. Martin offered his parents ten thousand pounds which they graciously but immediately refused.

"We wouldn't dream of taking your money," said his father. "Believe me, if you're lucky enough these days to get your hands on a tax-free capital sum, you hang on to it like grim death."

"You don't fancy a world cruise or anything?"

"Oh, no, thank you, dear, there really isn't anything we want. I suppose you'd really rather we didn't tell anyone about it, wouldn't you?"

"I wasn't thinking of telling anyone but you." Martin observed his mother's look of immense gratification, and this as much as anything prevented him from adding that there was one other person he felt obliged to tell. Instead he said, "I'd rather keep it a secret."

"Of course you would," said Walter. "Mum's the word. You don't want begging letters. The great thing will be to live as if nothing whatsoever out of the way had happened."

Martin made no reply to this. His parents continued to treat him as if he had earned the hundred and four thousand pounds by the expending of tremendous effort or by natural genius instead of the merest chance. He wished they had felt able to accept a present of some of it. It would somewhat have eased his conscience and helped him over the guilt he always felt on Thursday nights when he had to say good-bye to his mother and go home. She was still after nine months inclined to ask, plaintively if by now rhetorically, why he had seen fit to move out of Copley Avenue and go far away to a flat on Highgate Hill.

Into this flat, 7 Cromwell Court, Cholmeley Lane, he now let himself with the feeling of deep satisfaction and contentment he always had when he entered it. There was a pleasant smell, a mixture, light and clean, of new textiles, furniture polish, and herbal bath essence. He kept all the interior doors open—the rooms were impeccably neat—so that when you walked through the front door the impression was rather as of entering the centrefold of a colour supplement of *House and Garden*. Or so he secretly hoped, for he kept such thoughts about his flat to himself, and when showing it to a newcomer merely led him through the living room to exhibit from the picture window the view of London lying in a great well below. If the visitor chose to comment on the caramel Wilton, the coffee table of glass set in a brass-and-steel frame, the Swedish crystal, or the framed prints of paintings from the Yugoslav naïve school, he would look modestly pleased, but that was all. He felt too deeply about his home to enthuse publicly, and along with his gratitude to goodness knows whom, a certain fear about tempting Providence. There were times when he dreamed of its all being snatched away from him and of his being permanently back in Copley Avenue.

He switched on the two table lamps which had white shades and bases made from blue-and-white ginger jars. The armchairs were of rattan with padded seats, and the sofa—or French bed as the furniture-shop man had called it—was really only a divan with two bolsters at the back and two at the sides. Now he had won that large sum of money he would be able to replace these with a proper suite, perhaps one in golden-brown hide.

From the coffee table, between the ashtray with the Greek key design round its rim and the crystal egg with the goat for Capricorn—his birth sign—etched on it he picked up and studied the list he had made on the previous evening. On it were four names: Suma Bhavnani, Miss Watson, Mr. Deepdene, Mr. Cochrane's sister-in-law. Martin inserted a question mark after this last. He wasn't sure of her eligibility for his purpose, and besides he must find out what her name was. Some doubt also attached to Mr. Deepdene. But about Suma Bhavnani he was quite sure. He would call on the Bhavnanis tomorrow, he would call on them after he had seen Tim Sage.

Martin went over to the window. The temples and towers of London hung black and glittering from the sky like the backdrop to some stage extravaganza. He pulled the cord that drew together the long dark green velvet curtains and shut it out. Tim Sage. For days, ever since, in fact, he had heard that he was to benefit from a fifth share in the Littlewoods Pool's first dividend, he had avoided thinking about Tim Sage, but he was going to have to think about him now because tomorrow Tim was coming into the office to talk about his income tax. It would be the first time he had seen Tim for a fortnight, and before three tomorrow he had to decide what to do.

What to do? He had suppressed that remark to his mother about being obliged to tell one other person, but that was because he had been unwilling to hurt her, not because he was in doubt as to the right way to act. As soon as he allowed himself to think of Tim he knew without a doubt that Tim must be told. Indeed, Tim ought to have been told already. Martin's gaze travelled speculatively over towards the gleaming dark green telephone. He ought to phone Tim now and tell him.

Martin's father always said that one should never make a phone call after ten-thirty at night or before nine in the morning—except, that is, in cases of emergency. This was hardly an emergency and it was ten to eleven. Besides, Martin felt strange about phoning Tim at home. He had never done so. From Tim's own veiled accounts, his home was a strange one, not to mention his domestic arrangements, and who, anyway, would answer the phone? Tim didn't live in a place like this where everything was open and above-board as well as immaculate in a more literal sense.

He turned his back on the phone and switched off the ginger-

12

jar lamps. On second thoughts he helped himself to a small whisky from the glass, brass-and-steel cabinet. It would be silly to phone Tim now when he was going to see him tomorrow. As he drank his whisky he reflected that, of course, it was because he was going to see Tim tomorrow that he hadn't troubled to phone him before.

Martin was a well set-up healthy man of medium height with rather too-broad shoulders. In an overcoat he looked burly and older than his age. He had a big square forehead and a strong square chin, but otherwise his features were shapely and refined, his nose being short and straight and his mouth the kind that is sometimes called chiselled. His dark brown curly hair was already beginning to recede in an M-shape from the broad and prominent forehead. He had greeny-blue eyes, a curious shade, very bright and clear, and even white teeth for the attainment of whose regularity Walter Urban had paid large sums to orthodontists in Martin's early teens.

Following in his father's footsteps, he always wore a suit to work. To wash the dishes he put on an apron. Martin wouldn't have worn an ordinary apron, that would have been ridiculous, but the joke kind made of oilcloth were trendy and amusing and perfectly suitable for men. His mother had given him this one which was orange and brown and represented a gigantic facsimile of a Lea and Perrins Worcester Sauce label. He changed the sheets on his bed, a regular Friday morning task, but he did no other housework because Mr. Cochrane was due at half-past eight.

That his cleaner was a mister and not a missus was due to the Sex Discrimination Act. When Martin put his advertisement in the *North London Post* he had been obliged by law not to state that he required female help, and when Mr. Cochrane turned up similarly obliged not to reject him. He was lucky to get anyone at all, as his mother pointed out.

Mr. Cochrane usually arrived just after the postman and before the newspaper delivery, but this morning the newsboy must have been early—it was unthinkable for Mr. Cochrane to be late—and Martin had already glanced at the front pages of the *Post* and the *Daily Telegraph* before his help rang the doorbell. Always at this moment he wished that he was about to admit a large motherly charwoman, an old-fashioned biddable creature who, if she didn't exactly call him sir, might nevertheless treat him with respect and show some consideration for his wishes. He had read about such people in books. However, it was pointless to indulge in day-

13

dreaming with Mr. Cochrane outside the door and likely to appear outside the door every Friday for the next ten years. He liked his jobs, of which he had several, in Cromwell Court.

Martin let him in.

Mr. Cochrane was about five feet two and spare and wiry with a little scrap of dust-coloured hair fringing a bald pate. His face was exactly like a skull with lampshade material stretched tightly over it and ornamented with a pair of bi-focals. He carried the cleaning gear he didn't trust his employers to provide about with him in a small valise.

"Morning, Martin."

Martin said good morning. He no longer called Mr. Cochrane anything. He had begun by calling him Mr. Cochrane and had been called Martin in return, whereupon he asked his christian name which Mr. Cochrane, flying into one of his sudden rages, had refused to give. It was about this time that a neighbour and fellow-employer told him of his own experience. He had suggested that Mr. Cochrane call him by his surname, to which he had received the reply that it was a disgrace in this day and age to expect an elderly man, a man nearly old enough to be his grandfather, to call him Mr. It was sheer fascism, as if he, Mr. Cochrane, hadn't done enough kow-towing all his miserable downtrodden life. He had been, apparently, a manservant to some more or less aristocratic person in Belgravia. A butler, said one of Martin's neighbours who also employed him, but this Martin didn't believe, for to him butlers were less real a bygone race than dodos.

As a cleaner, he was wonderful. That was why Martin, and presumably the others, kept him on in spite of the familiarity of address and the rages. He cleaned and polished and scrubbed and did ironing all at high speed. Martin watched him open his suitcase and take out of it the khaki canvas coat—like an ironmonger's—he wore for work, the silver-cleaning cloths, and the aerosol can of spray polish.

"How's your sister-in-law?" said Martin.

Mr. Cochrane, wearing red rubber gloves, had begun taking the top of the stove apart. "She'll never be better till she gets another place, Martin. The blacks was bad enough, and now they've got the pneumatic drills." He was a ferocious racist. "She'll never be better stuck up there, Martin, so you may as well save yourself the trouble of enquiring. Three hours' pneumatic drills in the mornings she gets and three hours' in the afternoons. The men themselves can't keep it up more than three hours, and that tells you something. But it's no use moaning, is it, Martin? I say that

14

to her. I say to her, what's the good of moaning at me? I can't do nothing, I'm only a servant."

"What's her name?"

"Whose name?" said Mr. Cochrane, wheeling round from the sink in the sudden galvanic way he had. "You're always wanting to know folks' names. My sister-in-law's name? What d'you want to know that for? It's Mrs. Cochrane of course. Naturally it is. What else would it be?"

Martin forebore to ask the address. He thought that, from Mr. Cochrane's persistent descriptions of the North Kensington block of flats and its geographic location, he could discover it for himself. If he still wanted to. Ten minutes in his cleaner's company only made him feel there must be many far more deserving candidates for his bounty than the Cochrane family—Suma Bhavnani, Miss Watson, Mr. Deepdene. He pocketed the list lest Mr. Cochrane should find it and pore over it paranoidally.

As usual he left for work at ten past nine, taking the route by way of the Archway and Hornsey Lane. Sometimes, for the sake of variety, he drove up to Highgate Village and down Southwood Lane across the Archway Road into Wood Lane. And once or twice, on beautiful summer mornings, he had walked to work as he had done on the day he met Tim in the wood.

The offices of Urban, Wedmore, Mackenzie and Company, Chartered Accountants, were in Park Road, in the block between Etheldene Avenue and Cranley Gardens. Walter Urban was the expert on matters relevant to the Inland Revenue, Clive Wedmore the investment specialist, while Gordon Tytherton had all the complexities of the Value Added Tax at his fingers' ends. Martin didn't specialise, he called himself the general dogsbody, and his room was the smallest.

He knew he would keep at this job for the rest of his life, yet his heart wasn't in it. Although he had tried, he had never been able to sum up that enthusiasm for manipulating cash in the abstract which his father had, or even understand the fascination which the stock market exerted over Clive Wedmore. Perhaps he should have chosen some other profession, though the leanings and longings he had had while still at school had been hopelessly impractical—novelist, explorer, film cameraman. They were not to be seriously considered. Accountancy had chosen him from the first, not he it. Sometimes he thought he had passively let himself be chosen because he couldn't bear to disappoint his father.

And the safety of it, the security, the respectability, satisfied him. He wouldn't have cared for a job or a life style such as

15

Tim's. He was proud of the years of study that lay behind him, of the knowledge acquired, and was always determined not to let a lack of enthusiasm lead to omissions or oversights. And he liked the room he had here which looked out across the tree tops to Alexandra Park, the park and the trees which he had known as a child.

Martin had no clients to see that morning and no phone calls to make or receive. He spent nearly three hours unravelling the zany and haphazard accounts of a builder who had been in business for fifteen years without paying a penny of income tax. Walter looked in to beam on him. The news of the pools win was making him behave towards his son much the way he had done when Martin got his A-Levels and then his degree. After he had gone Martin asked Caroline, who was their receptionist and whom Gordon and he shared as secretary, to bring him Mr. Sage's file.

He opened it without really looking at the statements and notices of coding and Tim's own accounts which lay inside. In just over two hours' time Tim would be sitting there opposite him. And he hadn't made up his mind what to do. That firm decision of last night had been—well, not reversed but certainly weakened by the sight of the *North London Post*. He had to decide, and within the next couple of hours.

Martin usually had lunch in one of the local pubs or, once a week, at a Greek place in Muswell Hill with Gordon Tytherton. Today, however, he drove alone up to the Woodman. It seemed the right and appropriate place in which to be for the solving of this particular problem.

It was far too cold, of course, and far too late in the year to take his sandwiches and lager out into the Woodman's garden. There, in summer, one was made very aware, in spite of the thunderous proximity of the trunk road roaring northwards, of the two woods that nestled behind these divergent streets. To the north was Highgate Wood, to the east Queen's Wood where, walking under the pale green beech leaves, he and Tim had encountered each other on a May morning. Now, in November, those groves appeared merely as throngs of innumerable grey boughs, dense, chill, and uninviting.

But Tim . . . Was he going to tell Tim or was he not? Didn't he have a duty to tell him, a moral obligation? For without Tim he certainly wouldn't have won the hundred and four thousand pounds, he wouldn't have done the pools at all.

16

III

Martin had first known Tim Sage at the London School of Economics. They had been friendly acquaintances, no more, and Tim had left after a year. Martin hadn't seen him again until that morning in Queen's Wood, eight years later.

It was the kind of morning, misty and blue and gold and promising heat to come, when the northern reaches of London look as if Turner had painted them. It was the kind of morning when one leaves the car at home. Martin had walked over Jackson's Lane and into Shepherd's Hill, entering the wood by the path from Priory Gardens. The wood was full of squirrels scampering, its green silence pierced occasionally by the cry of a jay. Underfoot were generations of brown beech leaves and above him the new ones, freshly unfolded, like pieces of crumpled green silk. It had been a strange experience, even rather dramatic, walking along the path and seeing Tim appear in the distance, over the brow of the hill, the idea that it might be Tim gradually deepening to certainty. When they were fifty yards apart Tim had run up to him, stopping sharply like a reined-in horse.

"It has to be Dr. Livingstone!"

Why not? Journalist meets explorer in a wood . . .

It was odd the amount of emotion there seemed to be generated in that moment and the intensity of pleasure each felt. They might have been brothers, long-separated. Was it because the meeting took place on a summer's morning and under the greenwood tree? Was it the unlikelihood of the wood as a meeting place? Martin had never quite been able to understand why this chance encounter had brought him a sensation of instant happiness and hope, and why there had come with it a prevision of lifelong friendship. It was almost as if what he and Tim had experienced for each other, spontaneously and simultaneously, had been love.

But with the utterance of that word to himself Martin had felt both excited and very frightened. Before parting from him, Tim had briefly put an arm round his shoulder, lightly clapping and then gripping his shoulder, the sort of thing a man may do to another man in comradely fashion but which no man had ever before done to him. It left him feeling confused and shaken, and two days later, when Tim phoned, it took him a few seconds to find his normal voice.

Tim had only wanted to know if he could consult him as an accountant. He was worried about the tax he had to pay on his free-lance earnings. Martin agreed at once, he couldn't help himself, though he had mental reservations.

It was a maxim of Walter Urban's that one man cannot tell if another is attractive. He can only judge in respect of the opposite sex. Martin thought about this and it troubled him. In his case now it wasn't true, and what kind of a man did that make him?

Tim was very handsome, beautiful even, except that that wasn't a word one could use about a man. He had an actor's beauty, dashing, rather flamboyant. One could imagine him as a duellist. His hair was black, short by current standards (though not so short as Martin's), and his eyes a vivid sea-blue. There was something Slavonic about his high cheekbones and strong jaw and lips that were full like a woman's. He was tall and very thin, and his long thin hands were stained leather-coloured down the forefingers from nicotine. He had been smoking in the wood, and he lit a Gauloise the moment he entered Martin's office.

Tim's affairs were in considerably less of a muddle than Martin was accustomed to with new clients. It impressed him that, as he studied the columns of figures, Tim was able to repeat them perfectly accurately out of his head. He had a photographic memory. Martin promised to arrange things so as to save him money and Tim had been very gratified.

Were they going to see each other again, though? Were they going to meet socially? Apparently, they were. Martin could no longer remember whether it was he who had phoned Tim or the other way about. But the upshot had been a pub lunch together, then a drink together one Friday evening, encounters at which Martin had been uneasy and nervous, though extraordinarily happy as well with a curious tremulous euphoria.

After that Tim had become a fairly frequent visitor at the flat in Cromwell Court, but what Martin had dreaded during their first few meetings had never happened. Tim had never touched him again beyond shaking his hand, never tried to take him in his arms as had sometimes seemed so likely, so imminent, just before their partings. Yet Tim must be homosexual, for what other explanation could there be for his obvious fondness for him, Martin? What else could explain why he continued to find Tim so attractive? For he did find him attractive. He had wrenched this confession out of himself. Normal men probably did find certain homosexuals attractive if they were honest with themselves. Martin was sure he had read that somewhere, in a book about the psychology of

18

sex probably. The fact was that he liked watching Tim, listening to the sound of his deep yet light voice, as one might like watching and listening to a woman.

It came to him at last that what he really wanted was to *fight* Tim, to engage with him, that is, in some kind of wrestling match. Of course it was quite absurd. He had never done any wrestling and he was sure Tim hadn't. But he thought a lot about it, more, he knew, than was good for him, and such a wrestling figured sometimes in his dreams. It was part of these fantasies that in real life he should actually provoke Tim to a fight, and that might not be so difficult for, in spite of his affection for Tim, he knew he wasn't really a nice person. Long before the wrestling fantasy began, he had seen in Tim signs of ruthlessness, egotism, and cupidity.

Tim lived in Stroud Green. To this address Martin had sent business letters, but he had never phoned Tim on his private number and he had never been there. This wasn't for want of being asked. It was the way Tim had looked and the tone he had used when asking that had set Martin so determinedly against ever visiting those rooms or flat or half a house or whatever it was. Tim had said to come and see his "menage," smiling and raising his somewhat satanic eyebrows, and at once Martin had understood—Tim was living with a man. Martin had never actually been in company with two men living together in a sexual relationship, but he could more or less imagine it and the fearful embarrassment he would feel in such a situation.

He had returned a polite refusal—he always had an excuse ready—and after a time Tim seemed to understand, for there were no more invitations. But had he really understood? Martin hoped Tim hadn't thought he wouldn't come because he disliked the idea of slumming down in Stroud Green.

Tim seemed impressed by the flat in Cromwell Court. At any rate, he listened and admired when Martin showed him some new item he had bought, and he enjoyed sitting on Martin's balcony on summer evenings, drinking beer and admiring the view. Martin, like his father, often mixed business with relaxation, and it was on one of these evenings, when Tim had expressed his envy of those who own their homes, that he suggested he too should buy a flat. He should do so as much for the tax relief on a mortgage as for security.

"With your income and the increasing income you're getting from these short stories, I'd say you can't afford not to."

"My income, as you call it," said Tim, lighting his twentieth cigarette of the evening, "is the lowest rate the NUJ allows the *Post* to pay me. *You* know what my income is, my dear, and I haven't got a penny capital." Martin almost shivered when Tim called him "my dear." "The only way I'd ever get the money to put down on a house is if I won the pools."

"You'll have to do them first," said Martin.

The blue eyes that could sometimes flame were lazy and casual. "Oh, I do them. I've been doing them for ten years."

That had surprised Martin. He had supposed doing football pools to be an exclusively working-class habit. He was even more surprised to find himself agreeing to do them too, just to have a go, what had he to lose?

"I wouldn't know how to start."

"My dearest old Livingstone," said Tim, who sometimes addressed him in this way, "leave it to me. I'll work out a forecast for you. I'll send you a coupon and a copy, and all you've got to do is copy the same one every week and send it off."

Of course he had had no intention of copying it out and sending it off. But it had come and he had done so. Why? Perhaps because it seemed unkind and ungrateful to Tim not to. Martin supposed he had been to a great deal of trouble to work out that curious pattern on the chequered coupon, a pattern that he found himself religiously copying out each successive week.

Five times he had filled in and sent off that coupon, and the fifth time he had won a hundred and four thousand pounds. He had won it on the permutation Tim had made for him. Tim, therefore, was something more than indirectly responsible for his having won it. Shouldn't he then have gone straight to the phone as soon as the news came to him to tell Tim?

Martin drove back to Park Road by way of Wood Lane. The wood was a crouching grey mass on either side of the road, crusted underfoot with brown leaves. If he had taken the car that morning in May or if he had walked along Wood Vale instead of Shepherd's Hill, or if he had been five minutes earlier or five minutes later, he would never have met Tim and therefore never have won that huge sum of money. In an hour's time he would once more be confronting Tim; Tim was coming at three.

The purpose of his visit was to bring his tax return for the previous financial year and the fees statements from the various magazines that had used his stories. It wouldn't have crossed Martin's mind to keep the news of his win from Tim if Tim hadn't been a journalist. Once tell Tim and the story of his acquisition of wealth would be all over the front page of next week's *North*

London Post. Suppose he asked Tim not to use it? It was possible Tim might agree not to, but Martin didn't think it likely. Or, rather, he thought Tim would give a sort of half-hearted undertaking and then drop a hint to another reporter. And this story would be even better when he began on his philanthropy. . . .

Martin thought deeply about any major action he took, and about a good many minor ones too. He meant to conduct his life on a set of good solid principles. To perform every action as if it might form the basis of a social law, this was his doctrine, though he couldn't of course always live up to it. Plainly, he ought to tell Tim. He owed Tim thanks, and no consideration that publicity would make life uncomfortable for him for a few weeks should be allowed to stop him. Suppose he received a few begging letters and phone calls? He could weather that. *He must tell Tim.* And perhaps also—a new idea so alarmed him that he was obliged to stop scrutinising Mrs. Barbara Baer's investments and lay the file down—*offer* him something. It might be incumbent on him to offer Tim some of the money.

Tim received the lowest possible salary the National Union of Journalists permitted his employers to pay him. He couldn't buy a house because he had no capital. Ten thousand pounds would furnish a deposit for Tim to put down on a house, and ten thousand, Martin thought, was the sum he ought to give him, a kind of 10 per cent commission. He found the idea not at all pleasing. Tim wasn't a deserving case like Miss Watson or Mrs. Cochrane. He was young and strong, he didn't *have* to stay working on that local rag. At the back of Martin's mind was the thought that if Tim wanted to get capital, he shouldn't smoke so much. He had an idea too that Tim was a fritterer. It would be awful to give Tim ten thousand pounds and then find he hadn't used it to get a home for himself but had simply frittered it away.

Martin continued to present the two sides of this question to himself until three-fifteen. Tim was late. His inner discussion had led to nothing much, though the notion of telling Tim had come to seem rash almost to the point of immorality. At twenty past three Caroline put her pale red Afro round the door.

"Mr. Sage is here, Martin."

He got up and came round the desk, thinking that if Tim asked, if he so much as mentioned the football pools, he would tell him. But otherwise, perhaps not.

Tim was never even remotely well-dressed. Today he was wearing a pair of black cord jeans, a dirty roll-neck sweater that had presumably once been white, and a faded denim jacket with one of its buttons missing. Such clothes suited his piratical looks. He lit a Gauloise the moment he came into the room, before he spoke.

"Sorry I'm late. A court case that rather dragged on."

"A story in it?" said Martin, using what he hoped was the right terminology.

Tim shrugged. His shoulders were very thin, and his hands and his narrow, flat teen-ager's loins. He looked hard like an athlete until he coughed his smoker's cough. The only soft fleshy thing about him was his full red mouth. He sat down on the arm of the chair and said, "Humanity treads ever on a thin crust over terrific abysses."

Martin nodded. He was struck by what Tim had said. That was exactly how he had felt that morning while recalling all the chances there had been against the meeting in the wood happening at all. "Is that a quotation?"

"Arnold Bennett."

"Humanity treads ever on a thin crust over terrific abysses. . . ." Of course there weren't inevitably abysses, sometimes only shallow ditches, Martin thought. Novelists were very prone to exaggeration. "Let's have a look at all this bumf then, shall we?" he said.

"I've had a demand for nearly five hundred pounds tax. That can't be right, can it?"

Martin got out Tim's file. He had a look at the demand. Tim wanted to know if he could get an allowance for the use of his car and if a library subscription he had taken out was tax-free. Martin said no to the car and yes to the subscription and asked Tim some questions and said he would lodge an appeal with the inspector against the five hundred demand. There wasn't really anything more to say, as far as business went. Tim was on his second cigarette.

"And how's life been treating you, love?" said Tim.

"All right," said Martin carefully. It was coming now. He felt nervous, he couldn't imagine saying it, couldn't bear to think of Tim's initial disbelief, his dawning wonder, his gleeful congratulations. He said in a tone that sounded in his own head artificially bright, "I had that carpet laid in the flat, the one I told you I thought I'd have."

"Fantastic."

Martin felt himself redden. But Tim's expression was quite serious, even interested and kind. "Oh, well," he said, "I don't lead a very exciting life, you know."

22

"Who does?" said Tim. He sat silent for a moment. It seemed to Martin that his silence was *expectant*. Then he stubbed out his cigarette and got up. Martin found that he had been holding his breath, and he let it out in what sounded like a sigh. Tim looked at him. "Well, I mustn't keep you. I'm having a party tomorrow week, Saturday the twenty-fifth. Any chance you might be free?"

This caught Martin unprepared. "A party?"

"Yes, *you* know," said Tim, "a social gathering or entertainment, a group of people gathered together in a private house for merry-making, eating and drinking, et cetera. A feast. A celebration. In this case we shall be celebrating my thirtieth birthday, thirty misspent years, my Livingstone. Do come."

"All right. I mean, of course I will. I'd like to."

"The place is unsavoury but the food won't be. About seven?"

Martin felt a lightness and a relief after Tim had gone. He hadn't asked. He hadn't so much as mentioned football or gambling, let alone the pools, and he had hardly mentioned money. Probably he had forgotten ever having introduced Martin to the pools. How absurd I've been, thought Martin, telling myself he would be bound to ask and I would be bound to reward him. As if I could give money to Tim, as if I could even offer it. All the time Tim had been there he had felt as if he were walking on that fragile crust over that chasm, and yet he hadn't really—the ice had been inches thick and perfectly safe to skate on.

Caroline came in with a request from Clive Wedmore for the Save as You Earn literature he had lent Martin the day before.

"Mr. Sage is very attractive, isn't he?" said Caroline. "He reminds me of Nureyev, only younger."

He wouldn't be much good to you, my dear, were the words that sprang immediately into Martin's head. The vulgarity of this thought was enough to make him blush for the second time that afternoon. "Be a good girl and take that ashtray away, would you?"

"It smells like being in France."

She bore the ashtray away, sniffing it as appreciatively as if it had been a rose. Martin wrestled with the builder's tax for another hour or so and then set off down Priory Road to the tobacconist and newsagent's kept by the Bhavnanis. He felt rather excited. He tried to put himself in Mrs. Bhavnani's shoes, imagining how she was going to feel in five minutes' time when she understood that someone cared, that someone was going to give her son life and health and a future. Possibly she would cry. Martin indulged in a full-blown fantasy of what would happen when he made his offer, only breaking off when he remembered that one should do good by stealth so that the right hand knoweth not what the left hand doeth.

It was an old-fashioned little shop. When he opened the door a bell rang and from the back regions appeared Mrs. Bhavnani in a green sari with a bright blue knitted cardigan over it. Her face looked dark and wizened and full of shadows in contrast to these gay colours, and when Martin said he wanted to speak to her privately it grew grim. She turned the sign on the shop door to Closed. Martin stammered a little when he explained to her why he had come. She listened in silence.

"You are a doctor to operate on Suma?" she said.

"No, no, certainly not. It's just that—well, my mother told me about him, and what I'm saying is that if it's a fact you can get this operation on his heart done in Sydney—well, I could help pay for things."

"It will cost a lot."

"Yes, I know that. I mean, *I* could pay. I *will* pay. I'd like you to let me pay for you and him to fly to Sydney and for your accommodation there and for the operation, that's what I mean."

She looked at him, then lowered her eyes and stood passively before him. He knew she didn't understand. Was her husband in? No, not at present. Martin asked the name of their doctor.

"Dr. Ghopal," she said, "at Crouch End." The dark mournful eyes were lifted once more and Mrs. Bhavnani said, as if he were some importunate intruder, if that munificence had never been offered, "You must go now, the shop is closed. I am sorry."

Martin couldn't help laughing to himself, and at himself, once he was out in the street. So much for the philanthropist's reward. Of course it would have been far more sensible and business-like to have got Dr. Ghopal's name in the first place and to have written to him rather than make that romantic direct approach. He would write to him tonight. He would also, he thought as he began the drive home, make the preliminary manoeuvres in his project for using half the money. Suma Bhavnani was merely a sideline. The really serious business was his scheme for giving away fifty thousand pounds.

He could concentrate on that now that Tim Sage was off his conscience.

IV

Dear Miss Watson,

I don't know if you will remember me. We met last Christmas at the house of my aunt, Mrs. Bennett. I have since then been told that you have a housing problem and that when your employer goes to live abroad next year you expect to be without a home. The purpose of this letter is to ask if I can help you. I would be prepared to advance you any reasonable sum for the purchase of a small house or flat preferably not in London or the Home Counties. You could, if you would rather, regard this sum as a long-term loan, the property eventually to revert to me by will. I should then be able to look on this money in the light of an investment. However, please believe that my interest is solely in helping you solve this problem, and I hope that you will allow me to be of assistance.

Yours sincerely,
Martin W. Urban.

Dear Mr. Deepdene,

You will not have heard of me, but I am a friend of the Tremletts who, I believe, are friends of yours. Norman Tremlett has explained to me that the local authority which is your landlord intends to pull down the block of flats in which you are at present living and to rehouse you in a flat which will be of inadequate size to accommodate your furniture, books, etc. The purpose of this letter is to ask if I can be of any help to you. I would be prepared to advance you any reasonable sum for the purchase of a small house or flat preferably not in London or the Home Counties. If you would care to get in touch with me as soon as possible, we might meet and discuss this, whether you feel you can accept the money as a gift or would prefer to think of it as a lifetime loan, whether you feel able to consider living outside London, and so on.

Yours sincerely,
Martin W. Urban.

Dear Mrs. Cochrane,

You may have heard of me through your brother-in-law. He

has told me that you are suffering considerable hardship owing to your housing conditions and are anxious to move. The purpose of this letter . . .

Martin had found these letters very difficult to write. He abandoned temporarily the one to Mrs. Cochrane because he still hadn't found out her address. Dr. Ghopal must have had his letter by now, though he hadn't yet replied to it. It was pleasant to think of the incredulous delight of those two elderly people when the post came on Monday morning. They would understand without resentment, wouldn't they, what he meant by asking them to choose homes away from London? If he was to benefit four or five people, he couldn't rise to London property prices. He posted the letters on his way to have his usual Saturday lunchtime drink with Norman Tremlett in the Flask.

Dr. Ghopal phoned him at the office on Monday morning. He would be seeing Mrs. Bhavnani that day and then he hoped to be in touch with the great heart surgeon in Australia. The accented voice that always sounds Welsh to English ears cracked a little as Dr. Ghopal said how moved he had been by Mr. Urban's more than generous offer. Martin couldn't help feeling gratified. His mother had said Suma was reputedly good at his schoolwork. Suppose, as a result of his, Martin's, timely intervention, the boy should grow up himself to be a famous surgeon or a musician of genius or a second Tagore?

Gordon Tytherton came in in the middle of this daydream to say that he and his wife had a spare dress circle seat for *Evita* on Saturday night and would Martin like it and come with them? Martin accepted with alacrity. He passed the rest of the day on the crest of a wave, and it was some time before it occurred to him that perhaps he ought to have asked for Dr. Ghopal's discretion in the matter of the source of the money. Still, you could hardly imagine a doctor, a general practitioner, telling the press a thing like that. He thought very little more about it until Thursday when, as he came in from lunch, Caroline told him Mr. Sage had phoned and would call back.

Had Tim found out, maybe from the Bhavnanis? Not that Martin had said anything about the source of his wealth to Dr. Ghopal, but Tim was no fool. Tim would put two and two together. If Tim wanted a story for the *Post* tomorrow, this would be just about his deadline, Martin calculated. He pictured the headlines in thirty-six point across the front page . . .

"If he does call back, tell him I'm not available, will you?"

"What, even though you're really here?"

"I'll be too busy to talk to him this afternoon."

Caroline shrugged and pouted her shiny, blackberry-painted mouth. "Okay, if that's the way you want it. He's got a lovely voice on the phone, just like Alastair Burnet."

Whether Tim had phoned again Martin didn't bother to enquire. It would now, in any case, be too late for this week's *Post*. He went alone to the house in Copley Avenue, his father having an engagement with a client in Hampstead, and on an impulse told his mother about his £50,000 charity and his offer to Suma Bhavnani. She listened, drinking oloroso, and Martin could see that she was torn between admiration for his magnanimity and a natural maternal desire to see him spend the whole hundred and four thousand on a house for himself.

"I suppose I shouldn't ask why," she said.

It would have been embarrassing to give his reasons, that life had been extraordinarily kind to him, that he felt he owed the world a living and a debt to the fates. He didn't answer. He smiled and lifted his shoulders.

"What does Dad say?"

"I haven't told him—yet."

They exchanged a glance of veiled complicity, a glance which implied that while they could they would keep this, to him highly disconcerting, information from Walter Urban. Martin refilled their sherry glasses. Later, after they had eaten, Mrs. Urban said:

"You know, when you said what you were going to spend that money on I couldn't help thinking of Mrs. Finn."

"Who's Mrs. Finn?"

"Oh, *Martin*. You remember Mrs. Finn. She was my cleaner. It must have been—oh, while you were still at school, when you were a teen-ager. A very thin fair woman, looked as if a puff of wind would blow her away. You must remember."

"Vaguely."

"I've made a point of keeping in touch with her. I go there regularly. She lives in such a dreadful place, it would break your heart. A room smaller than this one divided into *three*, and where the bathroom is goodness knows. I was dying to spend a penny last time I was there, but I didn't dare ask. There are such strange people in the house. It's a real warren. There's a son who's a bit backward, I think, and he's got a room downstairs. He's a plumber or a builder's labourer or something. Of course, Mrs. Finn herself has had mental trouble. The misery and squalor they live in, you can hardly imagine it."

There was a good deal more of this and Martin put on a show of listening attentively, but he felt that since Mrs. Finn had a son whose responsibility she was, she hardly qualified for his bounty. Besides, he had two elderly women on his list already. Wouldn't it be better to complete it with perhaps a young couple and a baby?

It surprised him that he hadn't yet heard from either Miss Watson or Mr. Deepdene. There was nothing from them in the morning. Mr. Cochrane and the newspapers arrived simultaneously, and Martin leafed quickly through the *North London Post,* looking for a story about Suma Bhavnani or, worse, about Suma Bhavnani in connection with himself.

"I said it was a nice morning, Martin," said Mr. Cochrane severely, putting on his ironmonger's coat. "I said it was considerably warmer than it has been of late. I suppose you don't think it's worth answering the pleasantries of a mere servant." His eyes bulged dangerously in their bony sockets.

"I'm sorry," Martin said. The newspaper made no mention of the Bhavnanis or himself. Its front page was devoted to the murder of a girl in Kilburn, a story which carried Tim's by-line. "It *is* a nice day. You're quite right, it's a lovely day." He saw that he had just managed to deflect Mr. Cochrane's incipient rage. It was like looking at some kind of meter on which, when oil or water is poured into the appropriate orifice, a needle oscillates, wavers and finally sinks away from danger level. "How's your sister-in-law?"

"Much the same, Martin, much the same." Mr. Cochrane, applying silver polish to the tea and coffee spoons, seemed to brood with suspicion on this question. When Martin came back with his overcoat on he said sharply, "I don't know what accounts for your interest, Martin. She's not a nubile young lady, you know. She's not one of your pin-up girls. Just a poor old woman who went out into service when she was fourteen. You wouldn't trouble to pass the time of day with the likes of her, Martin."

If it hadn't been for the fact that he knew Mr. Cochrane, by the time he left at noon, would have made the flat more immaculate than even the house in Copley Avenue, would have ironed with exquisite finesse seven shirts, cleaned three picture windows, and polished a whole canteen of cutlery, Martin would have booted him out on the spot. He only sighed and said he was off now.

"Good-bye, Martin," said Mr. Cochrane in the tones of a headmaster taking end-of-term farewell of a pupil whose conduct has been idle, slovenly, violent, and rude.

It was rare for Mr. Cochrane to leave him messages but if he did, his notes were in the same disapproving and admonitory style as his conversation. Martin found one waiting for him when he came home just before six. *Dear Martin, A Mr. Sage phoned 2 mins after you left. I said I was only the cleaner and could not account for you going off so early like that. W. Cochrane.* Martin screwed the note up and threw it into the emptied, and apparently actually polished, wastepaper bin. As it struck with a faint clang the side of this, in fact, metal container, the phone began to ring. Martin answered it cautiously.

"How elusive you are," said Tim's voice. "You have quite an army of retainers to protect you from the press."

"Not really," said Martin rather nervously. "And what can I— er, do for the press now it's found me?"

Tim didn't answer that directly. There was a silence in which Martin guessed he must be lighting a cigarette. He braced himself for the question and was very taken aback when Tim said,

"Just to remind you you're coming over here tomorrow night, love."

Martin had forgotten all about the party. It had gone so far out of his head that he had accepted Gordon's invitation to the theatre. Suddenly he realised how much he hated, and had always hated, Tim calling him "love." It was much worse than "my dear." "I'm sorry," he said, "I'm afraid I can't. I've arranged to do something else."

"You might have let me know," said Tim.

Martin said it again. "I'm sorry," and then, rather defensively, "I didn't think it was necessary for that sort of party."

If it were possible to hear someone's eyebrows go up, Martin felt he would have heard Tim's then. "But what sort of party, Martin?" the drawly, now censorious, voice said. "This is going to be a dinner party. Surely you understood that when I said to come at seven? Just eight of us for dinner." There was a long, and to Martin awful, pause. "It was to be rather a special celebration."

"I'm sure my not being there won't spoil the evening."

"On the contrary," said Tim, now very cold. "We shall be desolate."

The receiver went down. No one had ever hung up on Martin before. He felt unfairly persecuted. Of course he had always refused in the past to go to Tim's, but this time, if it had been made plain to him from the first that this wasn't going to be a noisy drunken get-together in uncomfortable darkened rooms, he wouldn't have forgotten about it and he would have gone. If Tim had something to celebrate, why hadn't he told him so when he had invited him last Friday? Martin felt a sudden, almost fierce, dislike of Tim. When he heard from the tax inspector he would write him a formal letter, not phone this time. He had had quite enough of Tim for the time being. Let a few weeks go by, then maybe at Christmas he'd give him a ring.

But that night he dreamed of Tim for the first time for many weeks. They were in the house in Stroud Green which Martin, in waking reality, had never visited. Tim had spoken of it as unsavoury, and in the dream it was more than that, Dickensian in its grotesque squalor, a series of junk-crowded rat-holes that smelt of rot. He and Tim were arguing about something, he hardly knew what, and each was provoking the other to anger, he by a kind of contrived pomposity, Tim by being outrageously camp. At last Martin could stand it no longer and he lunged out at Tim, but Tim parried the blow and together, clutching each other, they fell on to a deep, red, dusty, velvet settee that filled half the room. There, though still locked together, elbows hooked round each other's necks, it was impossible to continue struggling, for the red velvet which had become damp and somehow soggy, exerted an effect of sucking and seemed to draw them into its depths. Or to draw Martin into its depths. Tim was no longer there, the red velvet was Tim's mouth, and Martin was being drawn down his throat in a long devouring kiss.

It was the kind of dream from which one awakens abruptly and to a kind of rueful embarrassment. Fortunately, it was half-past eight when Martin awoke as he could hardly have remained comfortably in bed after visions of that sort. Once recovered, he saw the day floating invitingly before him, a rather-better-than-usual Saturday. It was warmish, a damp, misty November day with the sun like a little puddle of molten silver up there over the dome and cupolas of St. Joseph's, jade green and gleaming in that sun's pale glow.

By lunchtime the mist had melted and the sun brightened and Martin wondered whether to walk to the Flask for his drink with Norman Tremlett. It took him about a quarter of an hour to walk there, two or three minutes to drive—but walking there meant walking back too. He often thought of that in the weeks to come, that if he had decided to walk he wouldn't have been there when the doorbell rang and he would never have met Francesca. Why hadn't he? There had been no reason but laziness. A spurt of energy had prompted the walk that led to his meeting Tim; laziness had cancelled the walk that would have prevented the meeting with Francesca. He felt there must be some significance in this, though he was never able to say what it was.

He thought his caller must be Miss Watson. She had never called on him before, but he had never offered to buy her a home before, and he was convinced it must be she. He opened the door, a kindly and welcoming smile already on his lips.

Outside stood a boy holding a bunch of enormous bright yellow incurved chrysanthemums. The boy had thick smooth black eyebrows and big dark brown eyes and very pink cheeks. He was wearing jeans and a kind of tunic of dark blue cotton or canvas and a close-fitting woolly cap that covered all his hair.

He said, "Mr. Urban?" in a voice that sounded to Martin very like a woman's.

"Yes, that's right," said Martin, "but those can't be for me."

"You are Mr. Martin W. Urban and this is 12 Cromwell Court, Cholmeley Lane, Highgate?"

"Yes, of course, but I still can't . . ."

"They certainly are for you, Mr. Urban." The woolly cap was suddenly snatched off to release a mass of long glossy wavy hair. The hair was dark brown and nearly two feet long and its owner was definitely a woman, a girl of perhaps twenty. She had a rather earnest voice and she spoke slowly. "It's really warm today, isn't it? I don't know why I put this on. Look, you can see on the label they're for you."

He forced himself to stop staring at her hair. "Please come in, I didn't mean to keep you standing there." She came in rather shyly, it seemed to him, hesitated between the open doorways, not knowing which to enter. "In here," he said. "People don't send flowers to men unless they're ill, do they?"

She laughed. In here, where the big window made it very light, he was a little taken aback to see how pretty she was. She was tallish and very slim and delicately made and with a beautiful high colour in her face, a rose-crimson that deepened with her laughter. How awful if he had betrayed to her that at first he had taken her for a boy! It was her slimness, those strongly marked eyebrows, her earnest look, the boyishness in fact about her, which only made her more attractive as a woman. He was suddenly aware of the strong, aggressive, bitter scent of the chrysanthemums.

"Is there a card with them?" He took the flowers from her and found the card, wired on to the bunch of coarse damp stems. The message on it was printed, the signature an indecipherable scrawl. "'Thanks for everything,'" he read aloud, "'I will never forget what you have done.'"

"The name is just a squiggle. I expect whoever it is came into the shop and wrote that themselves." She looked distressed. "Could it be Ramsey or Bawsey? No? I could try and check if you like."

He was standing by the window and he could see the van she had come in parked on the drive-in to the flats. It was a dark blue van lettered on its side in pink: Bloomers, 416 Archway Road, N. 6.

"Is that your shop on the corner of the Muswell Hill Road? I pass it every day on my way to and from work."

"On weekdays we don't close till six. You could call in on Monday."

"Or I could phone," said Martin. It would be difficult to park the car, one of the worst places he could think of. Was it his imagination that the girl looked slightly hurt? You're twenty-eight, he told himself, and you're fussing like some old pensioner about where you're going to park a car two days hence. He could put it in Hillside Gardens, couldn't he? He could walk a hundred yards. "I'll come in about half-past five on Monday," he said.

From the window he watched her drive away. The mist had gone and the puddle of sun and the sky had become leaden. It was twenty-five to one. Martin put on his jacket and went off to the Flask to meet Norman Tremlett. When he got back the first thing he had to do was put those flowers in water. He didn't know anyone called Ramsey or Bawsey or anything like that; he didn't think he knew anyone who would send him flowers.

There were far too many chrysanthemums for one vase, there were too many for two. He had to use a water jug as well as the Swedish crystal vase and the Copenhagen china jar with the spray of brown catkins on a blue ground. Fleetingly, he thought of not putting them into water at all but of taking them with him as a gift for Alice Tytherton. And have Alice think he had chosen them? It seemed awful to say so, but they were very ugly flowers. Martin had always believed that flowers were beautiful, all flowers as by definition, and his feeling about these slightly shocked him. But it was no use pretending. They were very ugly, hideous, more like vegetables than flowers really, like a variety of artichoke. You could imagine them cooked and served up with butter sauce.

He began putting them into water and in doing so looked again at the card. Not Ramsey—but, yes, surely, Bhavnani! What more likely than that Mrs. Bhavnani should send him flowers as a token of her gratitude. As an Indian she wouldn't know it wasn't the custom in England to send flowers to men, and she might see flowers with different eyes too. The eye of an Oriental might not see these great spherical blooms as monstrous and coarse. But if she were the sender, it was an oddly colloquial message she had sent: "Thanks for everything. I will never forget what you have done." And why would she come all the way to the Archway Road when there was a flower shop in her own block in Hornsey? It was just as likely that Miss Watson who lived in Highgate, in Hurst Avenue, was the mysterious donor.

His living room was transformed, and somehow made absurd, by an embarrassment of chrysanthemums, chrome yellow, incurved, smelling like bitter aloes. All the time he was arranging them Martin had been searching his memory for what incident in the past that scent brought back to him. Suddenly he knew. A dozen years ago and chrysanthemums arriving for his mother from some friend or recent guest. Those chrysanthemums had been fragile-looking, pale pink with frondy petals, but the smell of them had been the same as these. And what Martin remembered was going into the drawing room where a pale frail woman called Mrs. Finn was crying bitterly because she had dropped and smashed a cut-glass vase. The pink flowers lay about in little pools of water and Mrs. Finn wept as if it were her heart and not a vase that had broken.

The extraordinary things one remembers, thought Martin, and evoked by so little. He could still see Mrs. Finn as she had been that afternoon, weeping over the broken glass or perhaps over her own cut finger from which the blood fell in large dark red drops.

V

His window gave on to the back of a house in Somerset Grove. There were strips of untended garden between and tumbledown sheds and even a green-house in which all the glass was broken. But unless he looked down all he could see was the yellow brick back of the other house, its rusty iron fire escape, and its bay windows. In one of these bays a woman stood ironing.

Finn stared at her, exercising his powers on her, trying to bend her to his will. He bore her no malice, he didn't know her, but he willed her to burn her finger just slightly on the iron. Pressing his body against the glass, he concentrated on her, piercing her with his eyes and his thought. He wanted her to feel it in her head, to stagger, bemused, and graze her trembling hand with the burning triangle.

The iron continued to move in steady, sweeping strokes. Once she glanced up but she didn't see him. All magicians long to discover the secret of making themselves invisible, and Finn wondered if he had found it. He stared on, forcing his eyes not to blink, breathing very deeply and very slowly. The woman had set the iron up on end now and was folding a rectangle of something white. He could have sworn she brushed the tip of the iron with her hand, but she didn't wince. And now, suddenly, she was staring back at him with indignation, looking at him full in the face. If he had been invisible, he was no longer. He saw her move the ironing board away from the window to another part of the room, and he turned back to what he had been doing before, screwing the cover back on the hot plate.

His room was on the second floor. It contained a single mattress, a three-legged stool, and a bookcase. There had once been more furniture but gradually, as he mastered himself and his energies increased, he had disposed of it piece by piece. He hung his clothes from hooks on the wall. No curtains hung at the window and there was no carpet on the floor. Finn had painted the ceiling and the walls a pure, radiant white.

He had no means of cooking anything, but he seldom ate anything cooked. On the floor stood a stack of cans of pineapple and pineapple juice and in the bookcase were the works of Aleister Crowley, *Meetings with Remarkable Men* and *Beelzebub's Tales to his Grandson* by Gurdjieff, Ouspensky's *A New Model of the Universe,* and *The Secret Doctrine* of Helena Blavatsky. Finn had picked them up in second-hand bookshops in the Archway Road.

As he was coiling the flex round the hot plate and putting it into a carrier bag, Finn heard Lena pass his door and go on up the stairs. She had been out all the morning at a shop in Junction Road called Second Chance, spending two ten-pound notes Finn had given her from the initial Anne Blake payment. Her movements were uneasy. He could tell by ear alone, by the sound of her feet on the stairs, her footsteps pattering across the landing, whether she was happy or afraid or whether there was a bad time coming. There hadn't been a bad time for nearly two years now. Finn looked on her strangeness quite differently from the way most people did, but the bad times were another matter. The bad times had been brought into being by himself.

He took off the white cotton robe he wore for studying or meditating or just being in his room and hung it on one of the hooks. Finn had no mirror in which to see his long body, hard and white and thin as a root. The clothes he put on, jeans, a collarless grandad shirt, the velvet waistcoat, and the scarf with the coins on, had all been acquired by Lena, as had the pearl-handled cut-throat razor with which he now began to shave. He could see his face reflected in the window pane which, if he stood back a little, the opposing brick wall made into a passable looking glass. Nevertheless, he cut himself. Finn, with no pigment anywhere except in those water-grey pupils, sometimes thought it strange his blood should be as red as other people's.

Lena's tiny living room was draped all over with her purchases, a mauve silk dress with a fringe round the hem, a man's grey morning coat, a bunch of scarves, a pair of lace-up girl's can-can boots, and several little skirts and jumpers. The budgerigar, temporarily manumitted, surveyed all this array from its perch on an art nouveau lamp standard. In a day or two Lena would sell all these clothes to another shop, retaining perhaps one garment. She nearly always lost by these transactions, but sometimes she made a tiny profit. When she saw Finn she recoiled from him, alarmed, inordinately distressed as always by even a pinhead drop of blood.

"You've been cut!" as if it had been done to him by someone else.

"Well, well," said Finn, "so I have. Let's cover it up, shall we?"

She gave him a lump of cotton wool that might have come out of a pill bottle or been the bedding of a ring. Finn stuck it on his chin. It smelt, like Lena's clothes, of camphor. She had brought in with her, he saw to his annoyance, a local paper, the *Post*, and he knew at once the cause of her uneasiness. Her eyes followed his.

"There's been a girl murdered in Kilburn."

He opened his mouth to speak, guessing what was to come. She came up even closer to him, laid her finger on his lips, and said in a hesitant, fearful voice,

"Did you do it?"

"Come *on*," said Finn. "Of course I didn't." The bird flew down and clung to the hem of the mauve dress, pecking at its fringe.

"I woke up in the night and I was so afraid. Your aura had been all dark yesterday, a dark reddish-brown. I asked the pendulum, and it said to go down and see if you were there, so I went down and listened outside your door. I listened for hours but you weren't there."

"Give it here," said Finn. He took the paper gently from her.

"She wasn't killed in the night, see? She wasn't killed yesterday. Look, you read it. She was killed last Wednesday week, the fifteenth."

Lena nodded, clutching on to his arm with both hands like a person in danger of drowning clutches a spar. The bird pecked little mauve beads off the dress and scattered them on the floor.

"You know where we were that Wednesday, don't you? The day before my birthday it was. All afternoon and all evening we were in here with Mrs. Gogarty, doing Planchette. You and me and Mrs. Gogarty. Okay? Panic over?"

Ever since the Queenie business, which had also marked the onset of her trouble, Lena had supposed every murder committed north of Regent's Park and south of Barnet to have been perpetrated by her son. Had supposed it, at any rate, until Finn proved it otherwise or someone else was convicted of the crime. From time to time there came upon her flashes of terror in which she feared his arrest for murders committed years ago in Harringay or Harlesden. It was for this reason, among others, that Finn intended to make his present enterprise appear as an accident. Had he known what he was doing in those far-off days, had he not been so young, he would have done the same by Queenie and thus saved poor Lena from an extra anguish.

"Panic over?" he said again.

She nodded, smiling happily. One day she might forget, he thought, when he took her with him to India and they lived in the light of the ancient wisdom. She had begun rummaging through the day's horde of treasures, the budgerigar perched on her shoulder. A cushion, falling out, was caught between an octagonal table and a wicker box. Few objects could fall uninterruptedly to the floor in Lena's flat. She surfaced, grasping something yellow and woollen.

"For you," she said. "It's your size and it's your favourite colour." And she added, like any mother who fears her gift won't be appreciated as it should be, "It wasn't cheap!"

Finn took off his waistcoat and pulled on the yellow sweater. It had a polo neck. He got up and looked at himself in Lena's oval mirror with the blue-velvet frame. The sleeves were a bit short and under the left arm was a pale green darn, but that only showed when he lifted his arm up.

"Well, well," said Finn.

"It does suit you."

"I'll wear it to go out in."

He left her noting down her new stock in the book she kept for

36

this purpose. Finn had once seen this book. When Lena couldn't describe a garment she drew it. He went down into his own room and collected his tool box and the hot plate in its carrier and his PVC jacket. It was just gone two. He went in the van but not all the way, leaving it parked in a turning off Gordonhouse Road at the Highgate end.

Finn had waited to do the deed until after the departure of the Frazers. They had moved out the previous Friday. Sofia Ionides always spent Monday evening baby-sitting for her brother and his wife in Hampstead Garden Suburb. Finn didn't mind being seen entering the house in Modena Road, but he would have preferred not to be seen leaving it. By then, however, it would be dark. What most pleased him was the turn for the worse that the weather had taken. From Saturday afternoon it had grown steadily colder, there had been frost this morning, and as he drove up Dartmouth Park Hill a thin snow had dashed against the windscreen. If the weather had stayed as warm as it had been on Saturday morning he might have had to postpone his arrangements.

Anne Blake's flat was clean and tidy and very cold. One day, Finn thought, when he had developed his theta rhythms, he might be able to generate his own bodily heat, but that day was not yet. It would be unwise to use any of Anne Blake's heating appliances, he must just endure it. He attached a 13-amp plug to the flex which protruded from the gas pipe behind the fridge and plugged it in to the point next to the fridge point. Then he put up the steps and climbed into the loft, carrying the hot plate. Up there it was even colder. Finn joined the flex on the hot plate to the flex, some five or six yards of it, that came out of the gas pipe. Down the steps again to test if it worked. It did.

Watching the coiled element on the electric hot plate begin to glow red, Finn checked over his plan for the perfect accident. She would come in at six, turn on the heaters, including the electric fire in her bedroom, maybe have a drink of some sort, then her bath. She might bring the electric fire into the bathroom or she might not, it mattered very little either way. Finn would be lying up in the loft on the joists between the trap-door and the water tank. When he heard her in the bath he would lift up the trap-door and drop the hot plate down into the water. Electrocution would take place instantaneously. The hot plate he would then dry and replace among the glass jars and the *National Geographic* magazines. Once more broken and unusable, what more suitable place for it? When all the arrangements of flex and plug had been dismantled, nothing remained but to plug Anne Blake's bedroom electric fire into the bathroom point, switch it on and toss it into the bath water. Accidental death, misadventure, the fire had very obviously (a complaisant coroner would say) slipped off the tiled shelf at the end of the bath.

Finn felt no compunction over what he was about to do. There was no death. He would simply be sending Anne Blake on into the next cycle of her being, and perhaps into a fleshly house of greater beauty. Not for her, this time, the human lot of growing old and feeble, but a quick passage into the void before giving her first cry as a new-born child. Strange to think that Queenie too was a child somewhere now, unless instead her unenlightened soul still wandered aimlessly out there in the dark spaces.

Clambering across the loft, he peered out through a gap between roof strut and tile to watch the fluttering snow. In the wind on the top of Parliament Hill grey trees waved their thin branches as if to ward off the cloudy blizzard. The sky was the hard shiny grey of new steel.

It was because he was at the extreme edge of the roof, lying down to look under the eaves, that he was able to hear nothing in the depths of the house below him. Soft-soled shoes treading the carpeted stairs made sounds too low to reach him. He heard nothing at all until there came the scrabbling of a key in the front door lock.

Finn might just have managed to pull the steps up in time and close the trap-door, but he wouldn't have been able to push the fridge back against the kitchen wall or remove his open tool box from the middle of the kitchen floor. She had come home more than two hours early. He came across the loft and looked down through the aperture in the ceiling as Anne Blake opened the bathroom door and stood looking up, startled and annoyed. There were snowflakes on her bushy dark grey hair.

"What on earth are you doing up there, Mr. Finn?"

"Lagging the pipes," said Finn. "We're in for a freeze-up."

"I didn't know you had a key. It's the first I've heard of it."

Finn didn't answer, he never went in for pointless explanations. What now? She would never have her bath with him up there, otherwise he might have proceeded as planned. He must try again tomorrow. Nevertheless, it wouldn't be quite safe to leave that mysterious lead proceeding from the gas pipe still plugged in. Finn descended. He wrenched off the plug, went back into the loft and disconnected the hot plate. It would be a good idea actually to lag those pipes, an excuse for being in the roof again tomorrow.

He would go down and tell her he would return tomorrow with fibreglass wrap for the pipes.

Finn put the hot plate with the iron and trivet, packed up his tool box and came down the steps, pulling the trap-door closed behind him. He was sitting on the side of the bath, about to close the lid of the box when, across the blue-and-yellow papered hall, through the open doorway to the bedroom, he saw Anne Blake crouched down, her back to him, as she struggled to pull open the lowest drawer of a tallboy. Lying on the top shelf of the box was the largest and heaviest of his hammers. How easy it would be now! In just such a manner had he struck Queenie down.

He shut the box, slipping the hammer into his right-hand pocket. Then the box was on the bathroom floor and Finn was moving swiftly across the blue carpet towards her.

VI

She was on her feet, clutching to her the two or three garments she had been groping for in the drawer, before Finn had so much as entered the bedroom. He stood still on the threshold and she seemed to find nothing untoward in his looks or his behaviour. She said rather ungraciously,

"Have you finished whatever you were doing up there?"

Finn nodded, fixing her with his pale eyes. He knew she was uneasy in his presence, but there was nothing new in that, most people were. Quite alone in the house with him for the first time, she was probably afraid of rape. Finn smiled inwardly. He wasn't much interested in sex. It was more than a year since he had had anything to do with a woman in that way, and then it had been very sporadically.

He put the steps away and got into his jacket. It was still only four-thirty, but twilight. Anne Blake had turned some lights on and gone into the kitchen. The gas fire, just lighted, burnt blue in the living room grate. Finn still had the hammer in the pocket of his jeans. He went into the kitchen to tell Anne Blake about coming back tomorrow with the fibreglass, and while she talked to him, asking him what right Kaiafas had to a key to her flat and scolding him about knocking over something when he moved her fridge, he closed his hand round the hammer handle and thought, how easy, how easy . . . and how easily too he would be found out and caught afterwards, not to mention Lena's terror.

She forgot to ask him to relinquish the key or perhaps she thought he had better keep it since he was coming back the next day. It was still snowing when he got down to the street, but the snowflakes were now the big clotted kind that melt and disperse as soon as they touch a solid surface. Finn walked along Mansfield Road and under the railway bridge at Gospel Oak and got into the van.

Immediately, it seemed, that he had closed the door the blizzard began. The wipers on his windscreen weren't what they had been and Finn decided to stay put until the snow stopped. It flopped on to the roof and windows of the van and streamed as water down its sides.

After about twenty minutes the snow had almost ceased but there was a big build-up of rush-hour traffic headed for Highgate West Hill. Finn couldn't stay parked where he was and he couldn't turn round, so he started the van and drove back the way he had walked. It was dark now but the street lamps were all on, and as he passed the end of Modena Road he saw Anne Blake leaving the house, holding a pagoda-shaped umbrella in one hand and a plastic carrier in the other. She turned in the direction of Hampstead Heath.

Finn turned right at the next turning into Shirlock Road and came out into Savernake Road by the great porridge-coloured pile of All Hallows' Church. Anne Blake had just reached the corner of Modena Gardens and Savernake Road and was now crossing the road towards the footbridge. Finn parked the van among all the other parked cars and vans. The snow had changed to a thin sleety rain.

It was very dark, though not yet half-past five. Finn supposed that Anne Blake had gone to call on some friend who lived on the other side of the railway line in Nassington Road maybe or Parliament Hill. She wouldn't go shopping that way. Besides, the carrier had looked full. He debated whether to go back into the house in her absence. She would very likely be absent for a couple of hours.

He wondered if she had had her bath. There had been quite enough time for her to have had it, but would she go out into the cold immediately after having had it? She might intend to have it immediately she got in. It would only take him a few minutes, say ten, to reconnect those plugs. But if she had already had her bath he might find himself stuck up there in the loft all night.

Perhaps a dozen people, coming singly or in pairs, had appeared from the approach to the footbridge while he sat there. Its only use really was to take one on to the Heath or into those streets to the east of South End Road. No one living here would use Hampstead Heath Station when Gospel Oak was just as near. She hadn't gone to the station.

At last Finn got out of the van, crossed the road and let himself once more into the house in Modena Road. The rain had begun lashing down by the time he got there. He went upstairs without turning any lights on, and at the top, he entered Anne Blake's flat in darkness. A street lamp lit the living room and so, with a richer orange glow, did the gas fire which she had left on. She wouldn't have done that, Finn thought, if she had intended to be out for long.

He went into the bathroom and ran his hand along the inside of the bath. It was wet and so was one of the towels that hung on the chromium towel rail. There was no point in his remaining. He padded softly, although there was no one to hear him, across to the bedroom window. The rain was now coming down in the kind of deluge that no one would venture out in unless he had to. Finn had to. He opened one of the doors of Anne Blake's wardrobe. Inside, among her clothes, were two or three garments still sheathed in the thin polythene covers in which they had come back from the dry-cleaners. Finn selected one of these, slipped it off the hanger and the long black evening dress it covered, and pulled it over his head, splitting its sides open a little way down for his arms to go through. It made a kind of protective tunic, impervious and transparent.

The rain began to let up a little as he came up to Savernake Road. There was no one about. He felt drawn by the Heath, by its wide green emptiness, and he walked up the steps and on to the footbridge. A single lamp, raised up high, illumined the bridge, but you couldn't see the railway line, the walls were built up too high for that. To prevent suicides, thought Finn. He gazed across the smooth slope of Parliament Hill Fields to Highgate on the horizon, the emerald domes of St. Joseph's gleaming colourless and pearly against a sky which the glow of London made velvety and reddish. The backs of the houses in Tanza Road were as if punctured all over with lights, but the glittering screen of rain prevented much of that light from being shed on the path. It seemed to Finn that the whole area to the left of the footbridge and immediately above the railway embankment was extraordinarily dark. He could barely see where the turf ended and Nassington Road began.

He came down the steps on the Parliament Hill side of the

bridge. A train rattled underneath as he passed. The rain was running in streams down his plastic covering, though now it was lightening again, setting in evidently for a night of torrents with short drizzly remissions. In the dark hollow where the path ran under trees to link with the end of Nassington Road, Finn picked his way between the puddles. Now he could see why it was so dark. The lamp at the end of Nassington Road had gone out or never come on.

Finn liked the solitude and the silence. The train and its noise had long gone down the deep cutting to Gospel Oak. No one was venturing out into the rain. A strange tall figure in a shining glassy robe, Finn stood under the trees viewing the grey and rain-washed plain, feeling one with the elements, a man of power, a conqueror.

Someone was coming down Nassington Road, he could just hear the footfalls, though they were deadened by the wetness of the pavement. He stepped a little aside, behind the trunk of a tree. He could see her clearly now, passing under the last lighted lamp, the pagoda umbrella up, the carrier in her other hand empty or nearly so. She had waited to leave for home until the rain lifted a little. He could tell she was nervous because the lamp was out. She looked to the left past where he was standing and to the right, towards the bridge, and then she came on into the lake of darkness.

Finn no more intended to move forward and strike than he had intended to move forward and strike Queenie. It happened, that was all. It happened without his volition or his desire in the same way perhaps as the stone had moved and the pictures fallen. At one moment he was standing, watching with those night-seeing eyes of his, at the next the hammer was in his hand and he had fallen upon her. Queenie had made terrible sounds. Anne Blake made none but a throaty gasp, falling forward from the knees as he struck her again and again, now using the wide, flat side of the hammer.

In the dark he couldn't tell which of that dark fluid that spread everywhere was water and which blood. He pulled her away from the path and round the side of the nearest tree. There was no pulse, she was dead. Already she had passed into the unknown and was in possession of what was beyond. He almost envied her.

There was no Lena this time to come in and witness what he had done. He must keep this from Lena, wash himself clean of all the blood that so terrified her, deny her newspapers. Finn picked up Anne Blake's umbrella and furled it. He felt inside the carrier and found there a small suede handbag in which he found twenty-six pounds in notes, a cheque-book, and two credit cards. He took these and the money with him.

In the light on the bridge he could tell blood from water by running his fingers down his body and then holding up his hands. The lamplight robbed everything of colour, but the fluid was dark that ran from his hands. Someone was coming from the Parliament Hill side. Whoever it was had passed Anne Blake's body. Finn took refuge at the foot of the switchback slope that was designed for those who didn't want to or couldn't use stairs. Footsteps passed across the bridge and went on towards Savernake Road. The rain had returned now to all the force of its former intensity.

Finn stepped out into it and let it wash him clean.

He also washed the hammer in the rain. Once back in the van, he stripped off his plastic tunic and rolled it up into a ball. Underneath he was perfectly clean and fairly dry. He replaced his hammer in the tool box and fastened the lid. The gas fire would still be on in Anne Blake's flat, might very likely remain on all night, but it wouldn't burn the house down.

The problem was to get rid of the contents of the handbag, particularly the cheque-book and the credit cards. Finn drove home. It was still only seven, the rain falling steadily as if, having at last found a satisfactory rhythm, it meant to stick to it. Because of the rain he put the van away in the garage he rented in Somerset Grove, an old coach-house with bits of rotting harness still hanging on the walls.

With Lena was Mrs. Gogarty, the friend who had predicted for Finn a violent death in old age. The two of them were intent upon the pendulum. A white-and-pink baby's shawl with a scalloped edge had been thrown over the bird-cage. Mrs. Gogarty was as fat as Lena was thin, with abundant hair dyed a stormy dark red.

"Well, well," said Finn, "you *are* cosy. Can I have a lend of a pair of scissors?"

Lena, looking in the mauve dress and yards of stole like the appropriate one of the Three Fates, handed him the Woolworth scissors with which she picked and snipped at her daily finds.

"He's a lovely boy, your boy," said Mrs. Gogarty, who made this remark every time the three of them met. "The picture of devotion."

Finn managed to palm his mother's reading glasses off the top of a chest of drawers where they nestled among some half-burnt candles and incense sticks and pieces of abalone shell. He went

43

down to his own room where he cut up the notes and the cheque-book and the credit cards into very small pieces. The tin from which he had eaten pineapple chunks at lunchtime was now quite dry inside. Finn put the pieces of paper and card into the empty tin and applied a match. It took several more matches to get it going and keep it going, but at last Anne Blake's twenty-six pounds and her Westminster Bank cheque-book were reduced to a fine black ash. The American Express and Access cards were less destructible, but they too went black and emitted a strong chemical smell.

Re-entering his mother's room, Finn dropped the glasses and trod on them. This made Mrs. Gogarty scream out and jump up and down, jerking her arms, which was what she did whenever anything the slightest bit untoward happened. Lena was too much occupied in calming her down to say anything about the glasses; she diverted her with the pendulum as one diverts a child with a rattle.

Finn promised to get the glasses repaired as soon as he could. He would go into the optician's first thing tomorrow, he said. In the meantime, had she noticed the rain coming in over her gas stove? Better put a bowl there, and the first moment he got he'd be out on that roof.

"Devotion itself," gasped Mrs. Gogarty.

The pendulum rotated, widdershins and swiftly.

VII

The snow, which had been falling for most of the afternoon, had changed to rain when Martin drove across the Archway Road and began searching for a place to park. Southwood Lane was hopeless and so was the narrow congested curve of Hillside Gardens. He finally left the car in one of the roads up behind Highgate Police Station and walked back to the crossroads, wondering if he might be too late to catch Bloomers open, although it was only ten to six.

During the week-end he had asked himself several times why he should bother to call at the shop when he was sure it must have been the Bhavnani family who had sent those flowers. Anyway, did it matter particularly who had sent them? Of course, if he knew, he could write a note of thanks or phone. Dr. Ghopal had phoned the office during the afternoon to say that the great heart

44

specialist was prepared to operate in the week immediately preceding Christmas. No further time should be wasted when a condition like Suma's was in question. Would Martin buy the air tickets himself and arrange a hotel for Mrs. Bhavnani? Martin had agreed to do this, but he had felt unable to make enquiries about the flowers, especially as he was going to see the pretty dark-haired girl that evening.

He saw her when he was still on the other side of the road, outside the post office. She was taking in boxes of cut flowers and poinsettias in pots from the pavement. He waited for the lights to change and then crossed the street. The shop, which was very small, had a red bulb in one of its hanging lights, and the orangey glow, the mass of fresh damp glistening foliage, the red-velvet long-leaved poinsettias, gave to the place a festive air, Christmasy, almost exciting. It was dark and bleak outside. The shop was alight with reds and yellows and jungle greens, and the girl stood in the middle of it, smiling, her arms full of carnations.

"Oh, I was so sure you wouldn't come!"

She checked herself, seeming a little embarrassed. The colour in her cheeks had deepened. It was as if—he couldn't help feeling this—she had actually looked forward to his coming and had then resigned herself to—disappointment? She turned away and began putting the carnations in water. He said in a voice he recognised as typically his, a hearty voice he disliked,

"Did you happen to find out who was the kind person who sent my bouquet?"

It was a little while before she turned round. "There, that's all done." She wiped her hands on the brown-and-white-checked apron she wore. "No, I'm awfully afraid we couldn't. You see, the person who came in didn't give her name. She just wrote that card and paid for the flowers."

"You wouldn't know if it was an old woman or a young one, I suppose, or if she was—well, white or Indian or what?"

"I'm afraid not. I didn't see her, you see. I *am* so sorry." She took off her apron, went into the little room at the back and reappeared wearing a red-and-blue-striped coat with a hood. "If you're worrying about thanking them," she said, "I'm sure you needn't. After all, the flowers were to thank *you*, weren't they? For something you'd done. You can't keep on thanking people for thanking you backwards and forwards, the next thing would be they'd have to thank you for your thank-you letter." She added, the pink once again bright in her cheeks, "Of course, it's nothing to do with me. I don't mean to interfere."

45

"No, you're quite right." He went on quickly, "If you're going to close the shop now—I mean, if you're leaving, can I give you a lift anywhere? I have my car."

"Well, you can. Oh, *would* you? But you're going home and I have to go to Hampstead. I always go to see my friend in Hampstead on Monday evenings, and you've no idea how awful it is getting from here to Hampstead if you haven't got a car. You have to go on the 210 bus, and they either don't come at all or they hunt in packs."

Martin laughed. "I'll go and get the car and pick you up in five minutes." To make it as fast as that he had to run. When he pulled up at the lights she was waiting, scanning the street, looking lost.

"You're very very kind," she said.

"Not at all. I'm glad I happened to mention it." He was already aware that she was the kind of girl who makes a man feel manly, protective, endowed with virile power. Sitting beside him, she smelt of the flowers she had been with all day. She pushed back her hood and felt in her hair to release some slide or comb which held it confined, and the dark silky mass fell down over her shoulders like a cape.

At Highgate High Street, waiting in the traffic queue to turn up past the school, he turned to speak to her. She had been talking artlessly, charmingly, about transport difficulties between Highgate and Hampstead, how there ought to be a new tube line under the Heath, a station called the Vale of Health. He didn't speak. He was suddenly conscious that she was not pretty but beautiful, perhaps the only truly beautiful person who had ever been in his car or sat beside him. Except, of course, for Tim Sage.

She told him her name as they were driving along the Spaniard's Road.

"It's Francesca," she said, pronouncing it in the Italian way. "Francesca Brown."

It turned out that the friend, who had a flat in Frognal, wouldn't yet be home from work. Martin suggested a drink in the Hollybush. The rain was lashing against the windows of the car, but Martin had an umbrella on the back seat. He put up the umbrella and held it out over her but, to his surprise and slightly to his confusion, she put her arm through his and drew him towards her so that they were both protected from the rain. There weren't yet many people in the bar. As he came back to her, carrying their drinks, he saw her big dark glowing eyes fixed on him and slowly she broke into

46

a somehow joyful smile. His heart seemed to beat faster. It was eight before either of them realised how much time had passed and even then she lingered for another half-hour.

"Would you have dinner with me tomorrow night, Francesca?"

He had parked the car at the top of Frognal in front of the big houses in one of which Annabel had her flat. Francesca hesitated. The look she turned on him was intense, unsmiling, no longer joyful.

"What's the matter?" he said. "Is something wrong?"

She said carefully, "No," and then in a shy voice but as if she couldn't hold the words back, "we must meet again, I know that."

"Then tomorrow?"

Her answer was a vehement nod. She got out of the car. "Call for me at the shop."

The grey rain, blown by sharp gusts of wind, swallowed her up. It went on raining most of the night. On the radio at breakfast there was an announcement of a murder that had taken place in Hampstead the evening before. Martin shivered a little to think that while he had been sitting and talking with Francesca a woman had been murdered less than a mile away, her body left lying out in the teeming rain.

He called for Francesca at the shop at a quarter to six. They had drinks at Jack Straw's Castle and then dinner at the Villa Bianca. Francesca didn't smoke or drink more than a glass of wine, and for an aperitif she had orange juice. When the time came for her to go home she wouldn't let him drive her. They were standing by his car, arguing about it, Martin insisting that he must drive her and she declaring in her earnest fashion that she wouldn't dream of allowing it, when a taxi came along and she had hailed it before he could stop her. The taxi bore her away down Hampstead High Street and turned into Gayton Road which was what it would have done whether her home had been to the north of Hampstead or to the east or even possibly to the west. Tomorrow night, he thought, he would ask her point blank where she lived. Why hadn't he done that already? He felt almost ashamed when he reflected that he had spent most of their time together talking about himself while she had listened with the attention of someone already committed to a passionate interest in the speaker. Of course, he wasn't used to that kind of companionship. It was laughable to think of his parents or Gordon or Norman Tremlett hanging breathlessly on his words. But it hadn't been laughable in Francesca. It had been enormously flattering and gratifying and sweet, and it had made him feel very protective towards her—and it had distracted him from asking her any questions about her own life. However, he would ask her tomorrow.

Not the shop this time but the foyer of the Prince of Wales theatre. This was the way he had conducted his previous and rather brief unsatisfactory relationships with girls, dinner one night, theatre the next, cinema the next, then dinner again. What else was there? Francesca looked so beautiful that he blurted out his feelings once they were in their seats.

"You look absolutely beautiful. I can't stop looking at you."

She was wearing a softly draped dress of rose-coloured *panne* velvet, and round her neck on a ribbon a tiny pink rosebud. Her hair was piled like a Japanese lady's in mounds and coils, fixed with long tortoiseshell pins. The unaccustomed make-up she wore made her seem a little strange, remote, and violently sexually attractive. She winced a fraction at the compliment.

"Don't, Martin."

He waited until the play was over and they were walking towards his car, parked in Lower Regent Street. Then he said gently and with a smile,

"You shouldn't make yourself look like that if you don't like compliments."

His tone was light but hers serious and almost distressed. "I know that, Martin! I know I'm a fool. But I couldn't help it, don't you see? I did want you to think I looked nice."

"Of course. Why shouldn't you?"

"Oh, let's not talk about it," she said.

When they were driving up Highgate West Hill he said he was going to drive her home and where did she live? If he would drop her here, she said, she would get a taxi. He pulled into Gordonhouse Road by the Greek Orthodox Church, switched off the engine, turned to look at her.

"Have you got a boy friend that you're living with, Francesca?"

"No, of course not. Of course I haven't." And she added, "Not a *boy friend*. Not that I'm *living* with." He was quite unprepared for what she did next. She opened the car door and jumped out. He followed her, but not fast enough, and by the time he reached the corner a taxi carrying her was starting off up the hill.

That night he asked himself if he could possibly, after only three days, be in love, and decided that he couldn't. But he slept badly and could think of nothing and no one but Francesca until he had phoned Bloomers at nine-thirty and spoken to her and been told she would see him again in the evening.

They went to a little restaurant she knew at the top of the Finchley Road. He didn't ask her why she had run away and she volunteered no explanation. After the meal he asked her if she would come back to Cromwell Court with him and he would make coffee. And in saying this he felt shy and awkward with her, for invitations of that kind to girls he supposed always carried the implication of a sexual denouement. He had had a secret half-ashamed conviction since last night that she might be a virgin.

She agreed to come. The yellow chrysanthemums were still alive, fresh and aggressive as ever, only their leaves having withered.

"They are *immortelles,*" said Francesca.

After half an hour she insisted on leaving. He helped her into her coat, she turned to him, and they were so close that he brought his face to hers and kissed her. Her lips were soft and responsive and her hands just touched his upper arms. He put his arms round her and kissed her passionately, prolonging the kiss until suddenly she broke away, flushed and frightened.

"Darling Francesca, I couldn't help it. Let me take you home."

"No!"

"Then say you'll see me again tomorrow."

"Will you come down with me and find a taxi?" said Francesca.

It was a damp rather misty night, the last of November. From every bare twig hung a chain of water drops. They walked out into Highgate Hill. There were plane and chestnut leaves underfoot, slippery and wet and blackened.

"Shall I call for you at the shop tomorrow?" He had hailed the taxi and it was already pulling in towards them. So many of their dramas, he was later to feel, had been associated with taxis. She took his hand.

"Not tomorrow."

"When, then? Saturday?"

She gasped, put up her hands to her face. "Oh, Martin, never!" And then she was gone.

If his car had been at hand he would have followed that taxi. But it was two hundred yards away in the Cromwell Court car park. He walked back, dizzy with panic, with near-terror, that he had lost her. Because of that kiss? Because he had pressured her about her private life? He was sitting desolate in his living room when the phone rang. The reprieve of her voice made him sink back with a kind of exhaustion.

"I shouldn't have said that, Martin, I didn't mean it. Only you do understand, don't you, that I can't see you this week-end?"

49

"No, I don't understand, but I'll accept it if you say so."

"And we'll meet next week, we'll meet on—Tuesday. I'll explain everything on Tuesday and it'll be all right. I promise you it'll be all right. Trust me?"

"Of course I trust you, Francesca. If you say it'll be all right, I believe you." He hadn't meant to say it, he hadn't been quite sure until this moment that he felt it, and it should be said for the first time face to face, but, "I love you," he said.

"Martin, Martin," she said and the phone clicked and the dialling tone began.

It was a strange empty feeling knowing he wasn't going to see her for four whole days. Instead, his parents' house tonight to make up for his absence on Thursday, drinks tomorrow with Norman in the Flask, dinner with Adrian and Julie Vowchurch, Sunday a long gloomy void. . . . The postman came early, at ten past eight, bringing the phone bill and an envelope addressed in an unfamiliar elderly hand.

The letter inside was signed Millicent Watson. She addressed him as Mr. Urban, "Dear Mr. Urban," though he remembered having been introduced to her as Martin and hearing her call him by his christian name. She hadn't quite understood his letter, she wrote. Was he sure he wasn't mistaking her for someone else? If he was under the impression that she was a client of his firm and had investments, this was not so. She couldn't take on the responsibility of owning property. Moreover, she would never be in a position to repay any money which Urban, Wedmore, Mackenzie and Company might advance her. She had never in her life owed anyone a penny and didn't want to begin now. His letter had worried her a lot; she hadn't been able to sleep for worrying.

Martin was reading this in some dismay when Mr. Cochrane arrived. He was carrying a six-foot long cane with a green-nylon brush attached to the head of it. This implement, designed for sweeping the ceilings, had once before been brought into the flat, transported very ill-temperedly by Mr. Cochrane on the bus from his home in the Seven Sisters Road. Martin had said he would gladly buy a ceiling brush to save his cleaner so much trouble and inconvenience, but Mr. Cochrane, getting angrier and angrier, had replied that it made him sick to hear people who had never known the meaning of want talk of throwing money about like water, spending pounds like pence; Martin would want to buy a dustette next, he supposed, or an electric polisher—and so on.

This morning he omitted any greeting. Positively hurling himself into his ironmonger's coat, he plunged into a rather incoherent account of his sister-in-law's latest dramas—and thereby imparted to Martin information that otherwise would have been hard to get. The green-nylon brush rasped and whisked across the ceiling.

"On the verge of total nervous collapse, Martin, according to the doc. He's put her on eight Valiums a day—no, I tell a lie—twelve. I was round there at number twenty, up with her half the night, Martin, and I don't mind telling you . . ."

"Number twenty?" hazarded Martin.

"Number twenty, Barnard House. Top of Ladbroke Grove, isn't it? How many times do I have to tell you? Might as well talk to a brick wall. Now mind out or you'll get cobwebs down on that expensive suit. Beautiful, them chrysanths, aren't they? Must have cost a packet. And here today, as you might say, Martin, and tomorrow to be cast into the oven."

If only that were true, Martin thought, but the yellow chrysanthemums still looked aggressively fresh on Monday morning. On his way to work he posted the now completed letter to Mrs. Cochrane. He drove by way of Highgate High Street and Southwood Lane so that he passed the flower shop, but at twenty past nine it wasn't yet open. He waited till ten and then he phoned her at Bloomers. The other girl answered, the one who owned the shop. Martin asked to speak to Miss Brown and wondered why he sensed a sort of hesitant pause before the girl said she would fetch Francesca. Again he felt that quickened heartbeat when her voice came soft and serious, faintly apologetic, on the line. Yes, she was going to see him tomorrow, she was looking forward to it, she could hardly wait, only she had to wait, and would he call for her at the shop?

He had lunch with Gordon Tytherton in Muswell Hill. Gordon had invented a new system of taxation. There was, of course, no question of its ever being implemented, it was purely academic, but Gordon was immensely proud of it, being certain that if put to use, it would solve all the nation's economic problems. He talked about it all the time. His little short-sighted eyes lit up and occasionally his voice trembled with emotion as might another man's when he spoke of a woman or a work of art. Martin parted from him at the foot of the hill and went into the travel agency where he collected the air tickets for Mrs. Bhavnani and Suma. Should he take them to the Bhavnanis' shop or send them? After a protracted inner debate he decided to send them to Dr. Ghopal.

Francesca phoned him at twenty-five to ten on Tuesday morning to say she couldn't see him and not to come to the shop.

"It's not possible, Martin, and something awful's happened! Martin, do you see the *Post*?"

He heard it as the post, the mail. "What post?"

"The local paper, the *North London Post*. I know you do, I saw it when I was in your flat. Martin, promise me you won't look at it when it comes on Friday. Please, Martin. I'll see you on Friday and I'll explain everything."

After she had rung off he thought how, if she left her job, he would have no means of knowing where to find her, she would be lost to him. He was in love with someone whose life was a total mystery to him, who might live, for all he knew, in Golders Green or Edmonton or Wembley, with her parents, in a hostel, in her own flat. She was like one of those heroines of a fairy story or an Arabian Nights tale who comes from nowhere, who vanishes into a void, and who threatens to disappear forever if her lover attempts to lift the veil that conceals her secrets.

In her absence, the week passed with a dreary plodding slowness. She dominated his thoughts. Why had she asked for his promise not to look at the local paper? He hadn't given it. Had he done so he would have adhered to his promise, but he hadn't and she, strangely enough, hadn't insisted. It occurred to him that the truth might be she really wanted him to see the *Post*, half-feared it, half-desired it, because it was to contain some story about herself, flattering to herself. Francesca was very modest and diffident. Could it be that she was shy of his seeing praise of her? She might have been taking part in some contest, he thought, or succeeding with honours in some examination. And he indulged in a little fantasy in which a photograph of Francesca covered the paper's front page with a caption underneath to the effect that this was London's loveliest flower seller.

The postman and Mr. Cochrane arrived simultaneously. Mr. Cochrane greeted Martin dourly, said nothing about his sister-in-law, got to work at once on the windows with chamois leather and soapy water. Martin opened the letter with the Battersea postmark. It was from Mr. Deepdene. Here was no misapprehension, no paranoia, no getting hold of the wrong end of the stick. Mr. Deepdene wrote that he had never known such kindness in all his seventy-four years, he was overwhelmed, it was unbelievable. At first he had thought of refusing Martin's offer, it was too generous, but now it seemed ungrateful, even wrong, to turn it down. He would accept with a full heart. Martin shut himself in his bedroom, away from Mr. Cochrane, wrote a rapid note to Mr. Deepdene and put into the envelope with it a cheque for fifteen thousand pounds. Then he wrote to Miss Watson, asking her to phone him at his office so that they might make an appointment to meet.

The sun was shining on the white frosted roofs that hung like a range of glittering alps beneath his window. It was going to be a fine day, it was Friday, tonight he was going to see Francesca. He stood at the bedroom window, looking down at the white roofs, the long shadows, the occasional spire of whiter smoke rising through the bright mist. Coming across the car park was the paper boy with his canvas satchel. Martin turned away from the window and went into the living room where Mr. Cochrane was polishing plate glass and the chrysanthemums were as vigorous as ever. He took the vases out into the kitchen. The big yellow blossoms seemed to look reproachfully at him as he thrust them into the waste bin.

"Wicked waste," said Mr. Cochrane, padding up behind him to empty his bowl of water. "Not a withered petal on the lot of them!"

The two newspapers had just come through the letter box. Martin picked them up and looked at the *Post*. The front page lead, for the second week running, was the Parliament Hill Fields murder. This time it was a report of the inquest on Anne Blake, the heading was WOMAN BRUTALLY MURDERED and the by-line Tim Sage's. Martin went through the paper to try and find what had so upset Francesca in anticipation. The *Post* was a forty-page tabloid so this took some time, but he could find nothing, no photograph, no story. It was still only ten to nine. Watched curiously by Mr. Cochrane, Martin began again, working this time more slowly and meticulously.

Because he could no longer bear the scrutiny of pebble eyes through distorting bi-focals he took the paper into the bedroom. There, using a red ballpoint, he went through each page like a proof reader, ticking its lower edge when he had cleared it.

He found what he was looking for on page seven, a mere paragraph in a gossip column called "Finchley Footnotes."

The coming year will be an exciting one for Mr. Russell Brown, 35, whose first book is to be published in the summer. This is an historical novel about the Black Death entitled *The Iron Cocoon*. Mr. Brown, who is an authority on the four-teenth century, teaches history at a north London polytechnic. He lives with his wife, Francesca, and two-year-old daughter, Lindsay, in Fortis Green Lane.

VIII

"Since this is going to be our last meeting," said Martin, "I should have liked to take you somewhere nice." He glanced round the Greek *taverna* in the Archway Road where she had insisted on coming. It smelt of cooking oil, and over the glass-fronted case of raw kebabs trailed the fronds of a plastic tradescantia. "Still, I don't suppose it matters." An unpleasant thought, among so many, struck him. "Where does *he* think you are? Come to that, where did he think you were all last week?"

"He had flu," she said, "and the doctor said to take a week off to convalesce, so he went to his parents in Oxford and took Lindsay with him."

"I can't believe you have a child," he said miserably. "A child of two." The waiter came to their table. Martin ordered lamb kebab, a salad, for both of them. She passed across the table to him something she had taken from her handbag. He looked without enthusiasm, with dismay, at the photograph of a dark-haired, wide-eyed baby girl. "But where is she? What happens to her when you're at work?" It was as if he doubted the very truth of it, as if by questioning her closely, he might break her down and make her confess that she had lied and the newspaper been wrong.

"In a day nursery. I take her there in the mornings and Russell fetches her. He gets home before me."

"I looked him up in the phone book," said Martin. "I take it he's the H. R. Brown at 54 Fortis Green Lane?"

She hesitated momentarily, then nodded. "His first name," she said, "is Harold, only he prefers his second name and Russell Brown sounds better for an author."

"And I used to wonder all the time why you wouldn't let me take you home. I thought you might be ashamed of your home or even have an angry father. I thought you couldn't be more than twenty."

"I'm twenty-six."

"Oh, don't cry," said Martin. "Have some wine. Crying isn't going to help."

Neither of them could eat much. Francesca picked at her kebab and pushed it away. Her deep brown glowing eyes held a kind of feverish despair and she gave a little sob. Up till then he had felt only anger and bitterness. A pang of pity made him lay his own hand gently on hers. She bit her lip.

"I'm sorry, Martin. I shouldn't have gone out with you last week, but I did want to, I wanted some fun. I'm not going to indulge in a lot of self-pity, but I don't have much fun. And then—then it wasn't just fun any more." He felt a tremor of delight and terror. Hadn't she just admitted she loved him? "Russell came home on Friday, and on Monday he'd said he had this phone call from the *Post* about his book. I knew they'd put something in the paper, and I knew you'd see it."

"I suppose you love him, don't you? You're happy, you and Russell and Lindsay and the Black Death?" Wretchedness had brought out a grim wit in him and he smiled a faint ironical smile.

"Let's go," she said. "Let's go back to your place, Martin."

In the car he didn't speak to her. So this is what it's like, he thought, this is what it had been like for all those men he had heard of and read about and even known who had fallen in love with married women. Clandestine meetings, deception, a somehow dirty feeling of being traitorous and corrupt. And at the end of it a bitter parting with ugly recriminations or else divorce and re-marriage in some High Street register office to an experience-ravaged girl with a ready-made family. He knew he was old-fashioned. He had been a schoolboy when the word "square" was current slang, but even then he had known he was and always would be, square. A thickset square-shouldered man with a square forehead and a square jaw and a square outlook on life. Rectangular, tetragonal, square, conventional, conservative, and reactionary. The revolution in morals which had taken place during his adolescence had passed over him and left him as subject to the old order as if he had actually spent a lifetime under its regime. He would have liked to be married to a virgin in church. What he certainly wasn't going to do, he thought as he drove up to Cromwell Court, was have an affair with Francesca, with Mrs. Russell Brown, embroil himself in that kind of sordidness and vain excitement and—disgrace. They must part, and at once. He helped her from the car and stood for a moment holding her arm in the raw frosty cold.

The place looked strangely bare without the chrysanthemums, as a room does when it has been stripped of its Christmas decorations. He drew the curtains to shut out the purplish starry sky and the city that lay like a spangled cloth below. Francesca sat on the edge of her chair, watching him move about the room. He remembered that last week he had thought there was something child-like about her. That had been in the days of her supposed innocence, and it was all gone now. She was as old as he. Under her eyes were the shadows of tiredness and suffering and her cheeks were pale. He glanced down at her hands which she was twisting in her lap.

"You can put your wedding ring on again tomorrow," he said bitterly.

She said in a very low voice, not much above a whisper, "I never wear it."

"You still haven't told me where he thinks you are."

"At Annabel's, the girl who lives in Frognal, the one I see on Mondays. Martin, I thought we could—I thought we could sometimes meet on Mondays."

He went over to the drinks cabinet and poured himself some brandy. He held up the bottle. "For you?"

"No, I don't want anything. I thought Mondays and—and Saturday afternoons, if you like. Russell always goes to White Hart Lane when Spurs play at home."

He almost laughed. "You know all about it, don't you? How many have there been before me?"

She shrank as if he had made to strike her. "There haven't been any at all." She had a way of speaking very simply and directly, without artifice. It was partly because of this, that like him she had no sharp wit, no gift of repartee, that he had begun to love her. Begun, only begun, he must remember that. Caution, be my friend!

"We aren't going to see each other any more, Francesca. We've only known each other two weeks and that means we can part now without really getting hurt. I think I must have been a bit crazy, the way I went on last week, but there's no harm done, is there? I'm not going to come between husband and wife. We'll forget each other in a little while, and I know that's the best thing. I wish you hadn't—well, led me on, but I expect you couldn't help yourself." Martin came breathlessly to the end of this speech, drank down the rest of his brandy, and recalled from an ancient film a phrase he had thought funny at the time. He brought it out facetiously with a bold smile. "I was just a mad impetuous fool!"

She looked at him sombrely. "I shan't forget you," she said. "Don't you know I'm in love with you?"

No one had ever made that confession to him before. He felt himself turn pale, the blood recede from his face.

"I think I loved you the day I brought those horrible flowers and you said"—her voice trembled—"that no one sends flowers to men unless they're ill."

"We're going to say good-bye now, Francesca, and I'm going to put you in a taxi and you're going home to Russell and Lindsay. And in a year's time I'll come and buy some flowers from you and you'll have forgotten who I am."

He pulled her gently to her feet. She was limp and passive, yet clinging. She subsided clingingly against him so that the whole length of her body was pressed softly to his and her hands tremulously on either side of his face.

"Don't send me away, Martin. I can't bear it."

He was aware of thinking that this was his last chance to keep clear of the involvement he dreaded. Summon up the strength now and he would be a free man. But he longed also to be loved, not so much for sex as for love. He was aware of that and then of very little more that might be said to belong to the intellect. His open lips were on her open lips and his hands were discovering her. He and she had descended somehow to the cushions of the sofa and her white arm, now bare, was reaching up to turn off the lamp.

Martin hadn't much experience of love-making. There had been a girl at the L.S.E. and a girl he had met at a party at the Vowchurches and a girl who had picked him up on the beach at Sitges. There had been other girls too, but only with these three had he actually had sexual relations. He had found it, he brought himself to confess to himself only, disappointing. Something was missing, something that books and plays and other people's experiences had led him to expect. Surely there should be more to it than just a blind unthinking need beforehand and afterwards nothing more than the same sense of relief as a sneeze gives or a drink of cold water down a thirsty throat?

With Francesca it wasn't like that. Perhaps it was because he loved her and he hadn't loved those others. It must be that. He had done nothing different, and it couldn't have been any great skill or expertise on her part. She had whispered to him that he was the only man apart from Russell. Before Russell there had been no one and for a long time now Russell had scarcely touched her. She was married and she had a child, but still she was nearly as innocent as Martin would have had her be.

She slept beside him that night. At eleven she phoned Russell and told him she would be staying the night with Annabel because of the fog. Martin heard the murmur of a man's voice answering her truculently. It was only the second time in his life he had been in bed all night with a woman. On an impulse he told her so and she put her arms round him, holding him close to her.

In the morning he looked once more at that copy of the *Post* with its cover photograph of the path from the railway bridge to Nassington Road and, on the inside, the paragraph about Russell Brown. It seemed a hundred years since he had first read it, had underlined that emotive name and inserted, after a feverish scanning of the phone book, the number of her house in Fortis Green Lane. He put the paper on top of the neat pile of tabloids on the floor of the kitchen cupboard and the *Daily Telegraph* on the pile of broadsheets. Later, walking up the hill with Francesca—she refused to let him drive her—he called in to the newsagents and cancelled the *Post*. Why had he ever bothered to take a local paper? Only, surely, because of knowing Tim Sage.

Martin didn't expect to see Francesca again that week-end, he didn't even really mind that, but he had somehow taken it for granted that now they would meet every evening. He was very taken aback when she phoned him on Monday morning to say she wouldn't be able to see him that night, Lindsay had a bad cold, and perhaps they could see each other in a week's time. He was obliged to wait, phoning her every day, very aware of that other life she led with a husband and a little child, yet scarcely able to believe in its reality.

Nothing could have brought that reality more forcefully home to him than Lindsay herself. On the first Saturday afternoon Russell went off to football and she was able to get away she brought Lindsay with her.

"Oh, Martin, I'm so sorry. I had to bring her. If I hadn't I couldn't have come myself."

She was a beautiful little girl, anyone would have thought that. She was dark like her mother but otherwise not much like her, their beauty being of two very distinct kinds. Francesca had a high colour and fine pointed features, hair that waved along its length and curled at its tips, and her eyes were brown. Lindsay's eyes were bright blue, her skin almost olive, her mouth like the bud of a red flower, a camellia or azalea perhaps from her mother's shop. Because her straight, almost black hair was precociously long, she looked older than she was. To Martin it seemed for a moment as if the face beside Francesca's smiling apologetic face was that of an aggressive adolescent. And then Francesca was stripping off coat and woolly scarf and it was a baby that emerged, a walking doll not three feet high.

Lindsay ran about examining and handling the Swedish crystal. Martin's heart was in his mouth, but he scolded himself inwardly for turning so young into an old bachelor. If he was like this now how would he be when he had children of his own, when he and Francesca had children of their own? Lindsay began turning all his books out of the bookcase and throwing them on the floor. It surprised Martin that Francesca kissed him in front of Lindsay and let him hold her hand and sat with her head on his shoulder. It surprised and slightly embarrassed him too, for Lindsay had so far only uttered one sentence, though that frequently and in a calm conversational tone.

"I want to see my daddy."

Martin looked at Francesca to see how she took this, but even when Lindsay had repeated it at least ten times Francesca only smiled vaguely and she continued to give Martin butterfly kisses. It's because she doesn't mind Russell knowing, Martin thought and he felt elated. It's because she knows now that her marriage is over.

Then a rather curious thing happened.

Martin had been saying rather gloomily that he supposed they wouldn't be able to meet much over Christmas.

"No, but I've got something nice to tell you, darling." Francesca's eyes sparkled. "I'll be able to come and stay the whole New Year week-end with you—if you'd like that."

"If I'd like it! It's the most wonderful Christmas present you could give me."

"Russell's taking her to his parents in Cambridge for the week-end."

Lindsay came over and climbed on her mother's knee and put her hand over her mother's mouth and said,

"We'll go home now."

Martin said, "I thought you said his parents lived in Oxford. That week we met I thought you said he had taken Lindsay to his parents in Oxford."

Francesca opened her mouth to speak and Lindsay pinched her lips together. "We'll go home now, we'll go home now," Lindsay chanted. "I want to see my daddy."

Lifting Lindsay, Francesca stood up. "I'll have to take her home, Martin, or we could all go for a walk. Oh, don't do that, Lindsay, don't be so *awful.*" She turned on Martin her direct and transparently honest gaze. "Russell's parents live in Cambridge, Martin. I'm afraid it's you who got it wrong. One always does associate those two places, don't you think? That's why you got confused."

She wouldn't let him drive them home but insisted on a taxi.

On Saturday, December 16, Mrs. Bhavnani and Suma flew to Sydney, and Martin, after drinks in the Flask with Norman Tremlett, did his Christmas shopping. He bought six rose bushes for his father, My Choice, Duke of Windsor, Peace, Golden Showers, and Super Star twice, Rive Gauche eau de toilette, for his mother, a box of handkerchiefs embroidered with blue and yellow flowers for Caroline, and for the Vowchurches, who had invited him on Boxing Day, a macramé hanging plant container. Mr. Cochrane would get a ten-pound note. There was no one else to buy for except Francesca.

This was difficult. He had never seen her wear jewellery, so presumably she didn't like it. He couldn't buy her clothes when he didn't know her size or perfume since he didn't know her taste. At last he found two cut-glass scent bottles with silver stoppers in an antique shop and paid thirty pounds for them.

On Sunday he had lunch with his parents. Secretly, so that his father shouldn't observe them, his mother showed him the current *North London Post*. The front page lead was headed "Miracle Op for Hornsey Boy," and there was a photograph of Mr. and Mrs. Bhavnani with Suma, the three of them posed, evidently several years before, in a very Victorian way in a photographer's studio. Mrs. Bhavnani, wearing a sari, was sitting in a carved chair with the boy standing at her knees and her husband behind her.

"It's some relative told the paper," whispered Mrs. Urban. "Look, it says the money was raised by a customer of the shop who wants to remain anonymous."

Martin saw that the by-line was Tim's. It was a month now since he had seen Tim. Ought he to give him a ring and arrange to see him at Christmas?

He would be going for a drink with Norman Tremlett on Christmas Eve and to supper with Gordon and Alice Tytherton on Christmas Night. Christmas was a time when you made a point of seeing your close friends, and Tim had seemed a closer friend than either Norman or the Tythertons. Had seemed. Martin couldn't remember that there had ever, since that encounter in the wood in May, been such a long time go by without their seeing each other. He had read somewhere that we dislike those whom we have injured, but that seemed absurd to him. Surely we should dislike those who injure us? Perhaps both were true. Anyway, you couldn't say

60

he had *injured* Tim by not going to his dinner party. No, it was *he* who had taken rightful offence at Tim's sarcasm and reproaches. So what if they had made him come to dislike Tim? Tim was a dangerous companion, anyway, and not likely to get on with Francesca.

Mr. Cochrane didn't come on the Friday before Christmas. He phoned, waking Martin up, at five minutes to six in the morning to say his sister-in-law was about to be taken away to what he called a nursing home. He intended to go with her in the ambulance. Martin wondered if this accounted for Mrs. Cochrane's failure to reply to his letter. Perhaps. It couldn't, however, explain why Miss Watson hadn't written again or phoned or why he had had no acknowledgement of his cheque from Mr. Deepdene.

IX

The police came and talked to Finn. He was one of the last people to have seen Anne Blake alive. Her friends in Nassington Road had told them that. Finn said he had left the house in Modena Road at half-past four, soon after she had come in, and had driven straight home. They seemed satisfied. They seemed to believe him. Finn thought how different things might have been if one of the officers, that middle-aged detective sergeant for instance, had happened to have been involved in the investigation into Queenie's death eleven years before. But no one connected the carpenter and electrician of Lord Arthur Road with the fifteen-year-old white-headed boy who had been in the house in Hornsey when another woman was beaten to death. Finn wasn't frightened of the police, anyway. His fear was for his mother.

Lena's reading glasses were ready for her within a week. By that time the Parliament Hill Fields murder had retreated to the inside pages, but Finn was afraid of some old copy of a newspaper falling into her hands. Such a one might be stuffed into the toes of a bargain pair of shoes or used to wrap a scented candle. When Lena set off for the shops, made stout by layers of coats and a lagging of stoles, a Korean straw basket in one hand and a greengrocer's net in the other, he watched her with a pang. He couldn't understand the impulse that had made him slaughter Anne Blake out there in the open, when he might so easily have waited till the next day and achieved an accident. How was he going to master others and control destinies when he couldn't yet master himself?

He had waited in daily expectation for the balance of the payment to come, for one of those olive-faced children to appear with a parcel. It was Christmas before that happened. The eldest boy brought the money wrapped in red paper with holly leaves on it and secured with silver Sellotape. Finn's pale glazed eyes and skeletal frame in a dirty white robe frightened him, he muttered something about Dad having had flu and now pneumonia, and fled.

Finn peeled off the red paper, not much amused by Kaiafas' idea of a joke. Underneath, before he reached the Mr. Kipling jam tart box in which the money was packed, was an inner wrapping of newspaper, the *Daily Mirror*, November 28, with a picture of the path and the grove of trees where Anne Blake had died. Finn tore it to pieces and burnt it as he had burnt Anne Blake's money and cheque-book and credit cards.

The money was correct, two hundred and fifty ten-pound notes. No one would come robbing him, he was the last person. They were wary of him in the neighbourhood since he had roughed up those squatters for Kaiafas. Kneeling on the floor, tucking the money into a plastic carrier under his mattress, he heard Lena pass his door. She was chattering away; there was someone with her. Mrs. Gogarty maybe or old Bradley whose daughter-in-law locked him out of the house while she was at work so that he had to take refuge in the library or with Lena. Finn listened, slightly smiling. She had a host of friends. She wasn't like him, she could love people. She had even loved Queenie...

Lena had been over forty when Finn was born. She had never supposed she would have a child and her husband was dying of Addison's disease. The baby she named Theodore after the dead man, which he was destined never to be called except by school-teachers. For Lena he needed no name, speaking to him summoned a special note into her voice, and to Queenie he was always "dear." They went to live with Queenie when Finn was six months old.

Lena couldn't live alone with a baby. She wasn't strong or self-reliant. Queenie was her first cousin and also a widow, a State Registered nurse who owned her own house and was fat and practical and seemingly kind.

Queenie's house was in Middle Grove, Hornsey, one of a row of neat, narrow houses on three floors under a slate roof. Finn would have liked to sleep in Lena's room, but Queenie said that was silly and wrong when there were four bedrooms. Lena had a small pension from Theodore Finn's employers, but it wasn't enough to live on and keep Finn on, so later she went out cleaning for Mrs. Urban in Copley Avenue, leaving the child at home with Queenie. It was Queenie's aim and desire, though without intentional cruelty, without really knowing what she was doing, to win Finn's love and make him prefer her over his mother. She knew she would be a better influence on him. She read to him out of *Thomas the Tank Engine* and gave him banana sandwiches for tea and wheeled him round the shops, and when people said "your little boy" she didn't contradict them.

Lena observed it all with speechless anguish. There was no fight in her; she could only contemplate the theft of her son in passivity and pain. But there was nothing to contemplate, for Finn was not to be won. He wavered for a while, half-seduced by the reading and the sandwiches, and then he returned quietly to his mother, creeping into her bedroom at night, finding his way in the dark.

When he was thirteen the poltergeists started. Lena, who was psychic, believed that they were spirits, but Finn knew better. Sometimes he could feel the energy coursing through his veins like electricity along wires, charging his muscles and raying out through his finger ends. Lena saw his aura for the first time. It was golden-orange like the rising sun. He was aware of his brain waves, of a surplus of power.

One day all the plates in Queenie's china cupboard rattled down off the shelves and a lot of them smashed. Another time a brick came flying through the kitchen window, and in the same hour the framed photograph of Queenie in her staff nurse's uniform, wearing her SRN badge, fell down off the wall and the glass cracked.

Queenie said Finn was responsible, he was doing it himself, though even she couldn't explain how he had brought into the house a rockery stone no one could lift an inch off the ground. The poltergeists went away soon after he started smoking the hashish, and when they were gone he regretted their loss bitterly, praying for their return to any god or spirit or seer he came across in his reading. But they had deserted him. He decided to kill Queenie.

There were a number of reasons for this. He was afraid of her mockery and alarmed at her distaste for his pursuits. She had burned a book of his about the Rosicrucians. He also wanted to know how it would feel to have killed, and he saw killing as a fire baptism into the kind of life he wanted to lead and the kind of person he wanted to be. Queenie was the obvious choice for victim, ugly, stupid, unsympathetic, one who had never begun to see the light, a young soul. And she had a house which she had said over and over again she would leave to Lena. Brenda, her daughter, who lived in Newcastle, she never saw and got nothing from but a card at Christmas. Finn couldn't understand why his mother wanted a house of her own, but she did want one, and Finn thought she had a better right to one than Queenie.

He carried the dream of killing her about with him for two years, but when he actually did the deed it happened spontaneously, almost by chance. One night Queenie awakened him and Lena, saying she had heard someone in the house downstairs. It was springtime, three in the morning. Finn went down with Queenie. There was no one there, though a window was open and some money, about seven pounds in notes and change, had been taken out of a tin in one of the kitchen cupboards. Queenie was carrying the poker they used for riddling out the slow-burning stove in the living room.

"Give me that," Finn said.

"What d'you want it for?"

"Just to try something out."

She handed it to him and turned her back to look for her rings, the wedding band and the engagement ring, which each night she took off and dropped into a glass dish on the mantelpiece. Finn raised the poker and struck her on the back of the head. She made a terrible sound, an unnerving, groaning wail. He struck her again and again until she was silent and lying in a big, huddled, bloody heap. He let the poker fall and turned round slowly and saw Lena standing in the doorway.

Lena was trembling at the sight of the blood. Her teeth were chattering and she kept making little whimpering whistling sounds. But she took hold of him with her shaking hands and made him wash himself, and she took away his pyjama trousers and his vest, which were all he had been wearing, and stuffed them into the stove among the glowing nuggets of coke. She washed the poker herself. She made Finn put on clean pyjamas and get into bed and feign sleep and then she went out and got the people next door to phone the police. When they came Finn was really asleep. He was never even suspected.

It pushed Lena over the edge of sanity. She had been teetering there for long enough. "Spontaneous schizophrenia" was what Finn heard a doctor say. That was in the hospital where they had taken her after she had been found going into butchers' shops and crying out that they sold human flesh. She went into the shops and then she walked into the Archway Road and lay down in the middle of the road and cried out to the motorists to kill her.

And they hadn't got the house after all. There was no will, so it went to Brenda who let them go on living there for just six months. Finn never went back to school after Queenie died, and in the depths of the winter after his sixteenth birthday they moved into Lord Arthur Road, she into her top floor warren, he into this room.

He stood inside the door, listening to the ascending steps and to Mr. Bradley's thin broken voice croaking over and over, "God bless your kind heart, my darling, God bless your kind heart." After a while Finn went down to the street where he phoned Kaiafas at home from the call box on the corner of Somerset Grove. He needed employment, he hadn't done a job of work since patching up the Frazers' bay.

Kaiafas suggested a meeting at Jack Straw's Castle. That was half-way between their homes, he said, and he coughed piteously into the phone. The meeting was for a long way ahead, two days after Christmas, but Finn couldn't argue, for Kaiafas claimed still to be bed-bound.

The air was charged with frost and the melted snow had frozen again when he went off to Hampstead to keep his date with Kaiafas. Lena wasn't yet back from some trip she had gone on with Mrs. Gogarty. There was a waxing moon that hung up over Highbury, greenish-white in a fuzz of mist, and a fine snow was falling, tiny hard pellets of snow that burned when they touched the skin. Up on the Heath, the highest you could get above London and still be in it, an east wind was blowing and the broken and refrozen ice on the Whitestone Pond made it look like a shallow quarry of granite.

The saloon bar in Jack Straw's was half empty. Finn sat down to wait for Kaiafas. He wasn't going to buy himself a drink, wasting money for form's sake. There was only one person in there that he knew and then only by sight. This was the *Post* reporter, a dark man as thin as himself with black hair and a red mouth, whom Finn had often seen when he had been conducting a one-man investigation into stories of maltreatment and terror-isation of tenants in Lord Arthur Road. The reporter hadn't got very far. The people he interviewed didn't think it worth their while to talk to the police, let alone a newspaper.

Finn watched him. He was talking to a pompous-looking fat man, writing something in a notebook, stubbing out a cigarette. Finn concentrated on him and tried by the power of thought to make him light another cigarette. What hadn't worked on the woman with the iron worked immediately on the reporter. Finn felt pleased with himself. Then Kaiafas came in. Kaiafas had a wrinkled, seamed face like an old leather bag and eyes like muscatels. When out for the evening he always wore pale-coloured suits of some smooth cloth with a glistening sheen to it. Tonight the suit was silvery-blue, but Kaiafas had a black sheepskin coat over it with a black fur collar into which he huddled his paler-than-usual face.

"What will you drink, Feen?"

"Pineapple juice," said Finn. "The Britvic."

Kaiafas began to talk of Anne Blake as if Finn had had nothing to do with her death, as if indeed he might not know of her death, but he did so with numerous nudges and winks.

"The rent she pay me, Feen, she could afford have a car, but no, she must go walking in these lonesome places, in the dark. So here we have the result." Kaiafas had a way of wagging a finger at whomsoever might be his companion. "She have some good furniture. Antiques. Her sister come and take them all away." He sounded regretful.

"Well, well," said Finn.

Kaiafas nudged him. "An ill wind that blows nobody no good, eh?" He chortled a little which made him cough. Finn didn't ask him how he was, it wasn't the kind of question he ever asked of anyone. "Another one of those pineapples?" said Kaiafas.

Finn nodded.

"With a drop of vodka this time, no?"

"No," said Finn. "You know I don't drink."

"So. Now how about you do a nice decorating job for me, Feen? Paint out the house, do the rewire, and put down a nice bit of carpet I got fall off the back of a lorry?"

Finn said he would and drank his second pineapple juice. They talked about it for a while and then Finn left. In Lord Arthur Road he parked the van in the same troughs of frozen grey snow from which he had taken it out. As soon as he entered the house, he knew there was something wrong, he could smell it. He went upstairs in the manner of an animal that keeps climbing though it knows there may be a trap or a predator at the top.

Half-way up the flight between his room and Lena's Mrs. Gogarty was waiting for him. She was bending over the banisters so that he saw her white moon face searching for him, hovering over the deep stairwell, before he reached his own floor. He came on more quickly, and Mrs. Gogarty clutched him, holding fistfulls of his clothes. Her face worked, her voice was a croak, and she could hardly speak. Mrs. Gogarty was afraid of almost everything the natural world held, of enclosed places and open spaces, of spiders and mice and cats, of crowds, of loneliness, of sudden noise, of silence, but she was rather less afraid of insanity than most people are. She had seen so much of it. As they came to the door of Lena's room he managed to get the story out of her.

She and Lena had been to a sale and exchange clothes market in Hampstead, in Fleet Road, and coming away from it to catch a bus, had seen a notice attached to a lamppost which had frightened Lena. Finn wanted to know what sort of a notice and Mrs. Gogarty could only say over and over, "The murder, the murder," but that was enough to make all clear to him. Lena had seen one of the police notices enquiring for information leading to the arrest of the Parliament Hill Fields murderer. No doubt they were posted up all over the area between Hampstead Heath and Gospel Oak stations.

"What happened?" he whispered.

"She shouted out you'd done it. 'Him?' I said. 'Your lovely boy?' But words are wind. There weren't so many people, thank God. A taxi came, I got a taxi, but I don't know how I got her in it. I had to hold on to her in the taxi. She's little but she's strong when she's like that."

"Where is she now?"

"In there," said Mrs. Gogarty, trembling. "Crouched down like a tiger. She said you'd done the murder and then she said not to send her away. I knew what that meant, I promised not *that*."

Finn said, "Wait a minute," and went down and into his own room. From the back of the bookshelf, behind *Beelzebub's Tales* he took a glass jar that contained his hypodermic and his ampoules of chlorpromazine. Give her a big dose, fifty milligrams—or seventy-five? Finn had no friends, but he had acquaintances who could get him anything. Mrs. Gogarty was still outside Lena's door, her face quivering and tears now shining in the corners of her not quite symmetrical blue eyes.

Finn opened the door and walked across the tiny kitchen. He stood in the doorway of the partition he had made. Lena was crouched in the armchair under the budgerigar's cage, her legs flexed under her, her hands up to her head. When she saw Finn she sprang. She sprang at him and at his throat, holding on to his neck and pressing her thumbs in.

Mrs. Gogarty gave a little cry and shut the door and subsided against it like a flung cushion. Finn staggered under his mother's stranglehold. He got his hands under her fingers which had become like steel clasps and he forced her arms down and held her turned from him, one hand holding her wrists, the other arm hooked under her jaw. She was champing now, grinding her teeth, murmuring meaninglessly, "Take me home, I want to go home." Finn didn't dare let her go. He knew she would attack him again, for she no longer knew who she was or he was or where they were. He said to Mrs. Gogarty,

"You do it."

She came fearfully to take the syringe, but she had seen it done often enough before, had had it done to herself. Finn could have used a straitjacket but he balked at anything of the sort. He held her until the drug made her limp, and then he lifted her up and laid her on the bed in the diminutive bedroom.

"The picture of devotion," mumbled Mrs. Gogarty. "The very picture."

"Can you get home on your own okay?"

The big white face quivered in a nod.

"Won't mind the dark?"

"It's been dark," she said, "since four," and she held up for his inspection an amulet she wore round her neck. It wasn't on account of marauders or the glassy pavements that the dark menaced her.

Finn covered Lena up and stayed with her through the night. Before dawn he gave her another injection and she lay quiet and almost without breath as if she were already dead. He didn't know what a doctor would have given her, and he wasn't going to call one. A doctor would want to have Lena committed and he wasn't having that, besides listening curiously to her ravings about murder.

These began again in the morning. It was far too late for Finn to produce any trumped-up proofs to exonerate himself. She didn't know him. He wasn't her son but the fiend who had killed Queenie and who had killed since then a hundred women. She screamed so loudly that one of the people from downstairs came up and said he was calling the police if it didn't stop.

Finn got hot milk with phenobarbitone in it down her throat. Because it didn't work at once he forced brandy into her. He was terrified he might overdo it and kill her, but he had to silence those cries. They had been through so much together, he and she, fighting the world, exploring the unseen, approaching strange spiritual agents. She cried herself to sleep and he sat beside her, looking inscrutably at that pale twisted face, holding her big veined hand in his big hand, the nearest he had ever got to tenderness with a living creature.

68

On the Sunday she walked round and round the room, feeling up the walls with her fingertips as if she were blind, lifting every ornament and feeling it and sniffing it. When she was asleep he took the bird and bird-cage down to his room. She would kill the bird, twist it to death in her strong hands as she had the last one, and then break her heart over its death. He gave her phenobarbitone every day until her eyes focussed again and rested on him and a voice that was more or less normal came out of her cracked and swollen lips.

"Don't let them take me away."

"Come on," said Finn. "Would I?"

She cried and she couldn't stop. She cried for hours, tossing this way and that, burying her face in her hands, throwing her head back and forwards, crying until it seemed that all the madness had been washed away in tears.

X

"Three cheers for the Three Musketeers!" said Norman Tremlett, waving and slightly spilling his gin and tonic.

He had said this every Christmas for the past ten years and probably would say it every Christmas for the rest of his life if given the opportunity. He referred, of course, to himself, Martin, and Adrian Vowchurch. Adrian smiled his thin, tolerant, resigned smile at Norman and handed him a dish of Japanese rice crackers. Although these had been available as cocktail snacks almost as long as Martin (and therefore Norman too) could remember, Norman affected to find them an extremely *avant-garde* novelty, examined them clownishly, and expressed as his opinion that they were really made out of insects. Everyone knew the Japanese ate insects. His own father had been offered chocolate-covered ants while in Tokyo on a business trip.

Norman always behaved like this at parties. Nobody minded because he was basically so kind and good-natured. He and Adrian and Martin had been at school together and each, in his particular field, had later entered his father's firm. Norman was a surveyor and Adrian a solicitor. Norman, as well as his Three Musketeers joke, sometimes called them the Triumvirate. It gave Martin considerable deep pleasure and a feeling of power to think that his closest friends were his solicitor and his surveyor, and he was sure they felt the same about him being their accountant. He handled the Tremlett and Vowchurch financial affairs, and when he had bought his flat, Norman had made the preliminary survey and Adrian had handled the conveyance.

Of the three of them only Adrian had so far married. Because of Francesca, Martin felt closer to him this year than he had done for a long time. Adrian had married a girl with a lot of family money and they lived in a smart little house in Barnsbury. They gave the sort of parties Martin liked, not too many people and nearly all people one knew, proper drinks not plonk, a buffet meal but a real one with courses. There wasn't any loud music or dancing, and the guests stood around in groups talking. Martin couldn't help thinking that Tim would probably be having a Christmas party and that it would be very different from this one, dark, noisy, and with goings-on it was better not to think of. Finding himself briefly alone with Adrian, Martin said on an impulse,

"There's a girl I'd like to bring to meet you and Julie—next time you have a party."

"That'll be for Julie's birthday in March," his thin face taking on the sharp intense look it did when he was pleased. "It's serious?"

"About as serious as could be." Martin looked over his shoulder. "She has to get a divorce, she'll want to . . ." He was breaking their rule about never consulting each other on social occasions. "Well, I'll get her to come along and see you, shall I?"

Adrian said very sympathetically, "Anything I can do to help, you know that. And Martin—congratulations, I'm awfully glad."

Congratulations seemed a bit premature. They had only known each other for a month. But he was sure, he was certain that no one else would ever suit him as Francesca did. And if, before he could get her entirely as his own, there had to be a divorce and sordidness and haggling over property and maybe trouble with his family, well—he must go through it and endure it, knowing it was all worth while with Francesca at the end of it.

Russell was to take Lindsay to Cambridge by train on Friday evening, having first collected her from the nursery. Martin was going to pick Francesca up at the shop. He had wondered several times why he had queried her saying that Russell's parents lived in Cambridge. Of course she must know where her own parents-in-law lived. It must have sounded to her as if he doubted her, as if he thought she had been lying. When he phoned her at the shop he apologised for what he had said, he couldn't imagine why he had thought they lived in Oxford, he didn't want her to think he was accusing her of any sort of deception. Francesca only laughed and said she had forgotten all about it, she hadn't been in the least upset.

The weather had been growing steadily colder since Christmas, it had snowed and thawed and frozen. Mr. Cochrane, wearing a fur hat that made him look like a bespectacled Brezhnev, arrived late for him, at twenty-five to nine, announcing bitterly that he had fallen over on the ice and thought he had broken his arm. However, since he had intercepted the postman and was holding a letter in his right hand and his attaché case in his left, Martin decided he must be exaggerating. Mr. Cochrane made a sling for his arm out of his woolly scarf. He didn't mention his sister-in-law beyond uttering the single word "Terrible!" when Martin asked after her. He made a disgusted reconnaissance of the flat, running his fingers through dust on the woodwork and muttering that some folks were useless when they had to look after themselves. Martin took no notice. He was reading the letter.

Dear Mr. Urban,
I am very sad to have to tell you that my father died on December 11. He seemed quite well and in good spirits the previous evening but was found dead in his armchair when the home help came in at nine. Apparently, he had just been going through his post and your cheque was found beside him. I am at a loss to know why you should have sent my father a cheque for what seems an enormous sum to me, but I am returning it with apologies for not having sent it back sooner.

Yours sincerely,
Judith Lewis.

Martin was horrified. Had he, in effect, killed poor Mr. Deepdene with kindness? It rather looked like it. Mr. Deepdene had been seventy-four and perhaps his heart hadn't been very sound, and although he had known the money was coming, the actual arrival of the cheque would be a different matter from hopeful, perhaps doubtful, anticipation of it. Martin imagined him opening the envelope, taking out the brief one-line note, then the cheque, and his aged tired heart suddenly—what exactly *did* happen in a heart attack?—well, whatever it was, his heart failing and stopping with the wonderful, unbelievable shock of it, his body falling back into the armchair, the cheque fluttering from his lifeless hand . . .

"You want to mind how you go on that ice, Martin," shouted Mr. Cochrane above the vacuum cleaner. "You want to watch

71

your step, it's very treacherous, look at my arm. I reckon I've dislocated something, put something out, so don't be surprised if I don't turn up next week, Martin."

The death of Mr. Deepdene troubled Martin for most of the day. A client, an up-and-coming country singer, took him out to lunch, but he didn't really enjoy himself and he didn't feel he was being very lucid as he tried to explain, over coffee, why the cost of setting up a music room in the singer's Hampstead home might be tax deductible while a swimming pool certainly would not be. He kept imagining Mr. Deepdene, whom he saw as small and bent and frail, reading the sum delineated on that cheque and then the pain thundering up his arm and his chest.

Was he wrong to do what he was doing or attempting to do? Was he playing God without the wisdom and experience essential to a god? All he had done with his philanthropy so far, it seemed to him, was frighten an old woman into insomnia and shock an old man to death. There was, of course, Suma Bhavnani, but for all he knew Suma Bhavnani might have died on the operating table. Yet surely his project was so simple, just to provide homes for a handful of needy people who suffered particularly from London's housing shortage. He wrote a letter of sympathy to Judith Lewis and that made him feel better—or perhaps it was knowing that in an hour he would be with Francesca which made him feel better. Mr. Deepdene, after all, might well have had a heart attack whether he had sent him a cheque or not. He was old, past his three score and ten, and it was what people called a lovely way to go, dying like that in the midst of life . . .

Bloomers was glowing with flame-coloured light, its window banked with pots of pink cyclamen. Francesca came out to him, wearing the rose-velvet dress. She must have just changed, after the other girl had gone, especially for him. If it could be said that Martin disliked anything at all about Francesca, it was her clothes. Most of the time she wore jeans, flounced skirts with hems that dipped, shapeless tunics, "antique" blouses, shawls, big loose cardigans, scarves with fringes. She dressed like the hippies used to, a pair of scuffed seven-league boots poking out under a skirt of wilted flower-sprigged cotton. These things couldn't spoil her beauty, they merely disguised it. But in the rose velvet her beauty was enhanced, you could see the fragile wand-like shape of her, her tiny waist, her long legs, and the rose colour was exactly that of her cheeks. She put her arms round him and kissed him with tenderness.

As soon as they were in the flat he gave her her Christmas

present. The cut-glass bottles with the silver stoppers had come to seem inadequate somehow, so after lunch with the country singer he had bought some Ma Griffe cologne with which to fill them. It was odd, but although she admired the bottles and said they were pretty, beautiful really, she'd never seen anything so delicate, he sensed that she was disappointed. He asked her directly, but she said no, not a bit, it was just that she hadn't got anything for him and she felt bad about that.

After they had had dinner—steaks which he grilled and a salad which she made—he asked her if Russell would expect her to phone him, but she said she and Russell had had a violent quarrel and weren't on speaking terms.

"It was about you, Martin. I told him I was in love with someone else."

Martin held her hands. She came closer to him on the sofa and laid her head on his shoulder. "You're going to leave him and get a divorce and marry me, aren't you?"

"I want to, I don't know..."

"There's nothing to stop you. I love you and you say you love me..."

"I do love you, Martin!"

"You could stay here. We could go up there tomorrow and fetch your things and you need never go back there again."

She said nothing but put her arms round him. Later, in the bedroom, he watched her undress. She seemed to have no self-consciousness about this, no false modesty, and no desire provocatively to show off. She undressed rather slowly and concentratedly, like a young child. Her body was extraordinarily white for someone with such dark hair and eyes, her waist a narrow stem, her ankles and feet finely turned. She managed to be extravagantly thin, yet curvy and without angularity. He thought of fairy girls in Arthur Rackham drawings—and then, laying her clothes on a chair, she turned her left side to him.

Her upper arm was badly bruised and there was a kind of red contusion on her forearm. But that was as nothing to the bruising on her hip, black and blue and swollen, and all down the side of her thigh to her knee.

"Francesca...!"

He could tell she wished he hadn't seen. She tried ineffectively to cover her body with her arms.

"How on earth did that happen to you?" The explanation would never have occurred to him, he had never lived in that sort of world, if he hadn't seen the ashamed misery in her eyes and remembered what she had said about a quarrel. "You don't mean that Russell . . . ?"

She nodded. "It's not the first time. But this—this was the worst."

He took her very gently in his arms and held the bruised body close to his. "You must come to me," he murmured. "You must leave him, you must never go back."

But on the following day she wouldn't let him fetch her things from the house in Fortis Green Lane. At the end of the week-end she must go home again as they had arranged, she must be home before Russell and Lindsay returned. Martin didn't persist. The last thing he wanted was to spoil the three precious days they had together. On Saturday afternoon they went shopping in Hampstead. Martin had never before been round dress shops with a woman and he found it boring and alarming, both at the same time. Francesca admired extravagantly a coat and dress in grey suede, a pair of tapered pants in cream leather, and a dress that seemed quite impractical to Martin, being made of transparent knife-pleated beige chiffon. Francesca didn't notice prices, he knew that, she was naïve about that sort of thing like a child in a toyshop. It crossed his mind to buy her the coat and dress, but then he saw it was three hundred pounds and he didn't have that much in his current account. Besides, what would Russell say— what would Russell *do?*—if she brought something like that home with her? In the end, because she looked so wistful, he asked her to let him buy her the little short-sleeved jumper which was the latest thing to catch her fancy. Martin thought fifteen pounds a ridiculous amount to pay for it, but that didn't matter if it made Francesca happy.

They went to the theatre and then to supper at Inigo Jones. Norman Tremlett called in unexpectedly in the morning at about ten-thirty. Francesca had only just got up and she came out of the bathroom in her dressing gown. It was very obvious she had nothing on underneath it. Martin saw with a good deal of pride and pleasure that Norman's eyes were going round in excited circles like a dog's following the movements of a fly. He stayed for coffee. Francesca didn't bother to go and dress. She was quite innocent of the sensation she was causing and sat there talking earnestly about the play they had seen as if Norman were her brother or she wearing a tweed suit and a pair of brogues.

"You're a dark horse," Norman whispered admiringly as Martin saw him out. "I never would have thought it of you. D'you often do this sort of thing?"

Deep down, Martin rather loved being treated as a Casanova. But it wasn't right to allow it, it was a reflection on Francesca, on her—well, virtue, if that term still had any meaning today.

"We're going to be married."

"Are you? Are you really? That's perfectly splendid." Norman hesitated on the doorstep. "At the wedding," he said, "I suppose—I suppose you'll have Adrian for your best man?"

Martin laughed. "It won't be that sort of wedding."

"I see. Right. That's fine. Only if you do need any—well, anyone, you know what I mean—well, you know where to come."

On New Year's Day Francesca wore the jumper he had bought her. It showed up the bruises on her arm and she wrapped herself in one of her shawls. At four o'clock she said she ought to go. She would pack her things and go and get a taxi in Highgate High Street. Russell and Lindsay would be home by six at the latest.

"Of course I'm going to drive you home, Francesca."

"Darling Martin, there's no need, really, there isn't. It's been snowing again and it's bound to freeze tonight and you might have a skid. You don't want to damage your nice car."

"The taxi might skid and damage nice you. Anyway, I insist on taking you. I'm not going to be put off this time. Russell won't be there to see us arrive if that's what worries you. I'm going to drive you home, and if you try to stop me I shall just put you in the car by force. Right?"

"Yes, Martin, of course. I won't argue any more. You're so sweet and kind to me and I'm a horrid ungrateful girl."

"No, you're not," he said. "You're an angel and I love you."

He had never thought much about the house she lived in, but now that he was going to see it he felt the stirrings of curiosity. He had probably driven along Fortis Green Lane in the past, but he couldn't recall it. It was Finchley really, that area, borders of Muswell Hill. While Francesca was packing her case he looked it up in the London Atlas. There was no telling from that whether the district was seedy terraces, luxury suburban or given over to council housing. She came out and he helped her into the blue-and-red-striped coat with the hood.

"If I'd known it was going to be so cold," she said, "I'd have brought my fur." She gave him one of her serious, very young, smiles. "I've got an old fur coat that was my grandmother's."

"When we're married I'll buy you a mink. It'll be my wedding present to you."

He drove up North Hill and into Finchley High Road. Fortis

Green Lane ran up out of Fortis Green Road towards Colney Hatch Lane. Francesca didn't issue directions, she wasn't that sort of woman. He got the impression, when she was with him, that she was content to let him organise things and steer her life his way. She wasn't so much passive as gracefully yielding. He took a left turn out of Fortis Green Road and they were in the street where she lived.

By now it was growing towards dusk and what daylight remained was clear and blue. Mustard yellow lamps, true opposite in the spectrum to that blue, were coming on in Fortis Green Lane. It was a long wide winding road, disproportionately wide for the small squat houses which lined it. Here and there was a short Victorian terrace, red brick and three storeys high, but the small low houses predominated and eventually took over altogether. They stood in blocks of four, some of brown stucco, some of very pale anaemic-looking brick, with small metal-framed windows and shallow pantiled roofs. In their front gardens snow lay on the grass. They weren't bad houses, they weren't slums, but Martin thought he would go to almost any lengths to avoid living in such a place. He had always, in his heart, despised people who did. Couldn't Russell Brown, who was thirty-five years old and no slouch apparently, a teacher and a writer, have done better for his wife than this? Poor Francesca...

Number 54 was the end house of a block which meant it had a side entrance. It stood on the corner of a side road depressingly called Hill Avenue in which were similar houses stretching away to be lost in the twilight. Their roofs were so low that over the tops of them you could see the branches of trees which Martin guessed must be in Coldfall Wood. He got out of the car and helped Francesca out. There were no lights on in her house. Her husband and child hadn't yet returned. Carrying her suitcase, Martin began to unlatch the small white wrought iron gate.

"You mustn't come in, darling." She had taken his arm and was looking nervously up into his face.

"Would it matter so much if Russell and I were to meet? We're sure to some day. I'm sure he wouldn't do anything to me."

"No, but he might do something to me later."

The truth of this was evident. He had seen the bruises. It wasn't much of a disappointment not seeing the inside of her house. Compared with what he felt about parting from her, not to see her again for perhaps a whole week, it was nothing. He didn't think she would kiss him good-bye with the chance of some neighbour seeing, but she did. Out there in the street she put her arms round

76

his neck and kissed him on the mouth, clinging to him for a moment. But Francesca was like that, too innocent to be aware of the cruelty and malice in other people's hearts.

He got back into the car. She stood there, waving to him, her small bright face made pale by the lamplight, her beautiful hair tucked inside her hood. He turned the car to go back the way he had come and when he looked round again she was gone.

XI

Although Martin had confided to Francesca most of what had happened to him in the past, his present circumstances, and his hopes for the future, he hadn't said anything about the pools win. He didn't quite know why he hadn't. Perhaps it was because she was still living with her husband. He had a vague half-formed idea of Russell Brown as a thorough-going villain, in spite of his education and his talents. Suppose Francesca told Russell that the man she was in love with had won a hundred thousand pounds on a football pool? If he knew that, Russell might try to extort money from him. Martin thought he would only tell Francesca after she had left Russell and was living here with him in Cromwell Court.

After that week-end he didn't see her again, as he had feared, until the following Monday. On the afternoon of that day Dr. Ghopal phoned to say that the operation on Suma Bhavnani had taken place on January 5 and been a complete success. This news had a tonic effect on Martin. Playing God was possible, after all. At lunchtime he had had a sandwich in the Victoria Stakes with Caroline and she had regaled him with a long sad tale about a young couple who were friends of hers and who were paying 60 per cent of their joint wages for the rent of a furnished flat. They had no children and the girl couldn't have children, so they wouldn't get a council place, said Caroline, for five years, if then. The furnished flat was four draughty rooms in Friern Barnet. By telling a few white lies about knowing someone who knew someone who might possibly have an unfurnished flat to let in April, Martin managed to get these people's name and address out of Caroline. That night, after he had taken Francesca to dine at the Cellier du Midi and sent her home to Russell in a taxi, he added this new name to his list. It now read: Miss Watson, Mr. Deepdene, Mrs. Cochrane, Mrs. Finn? Richard and Sarah Gibson. He crossed off Mr. Deepdene's name, put a question mark after Mrs.

Cochrane's. Then he composed a letter to the Gibsons, beginning by mentioning the connection through Caroline Arnold and going on to ask if they would care to meet him one evening in the coming week to discuss accommodation he might be able to offer them. It obviously wasn't a good idea baldly to state in the preliminary letter that he was dispensing money in large quantities. Look what an effect that had had on Miss Watson and Mr. Deepdene. Better meet and talk about it face to face, which was perhaps what he ought to have done and could still do with Miss Watson.

He hadn't said any more to Francesca about leaving Russell. He had hoped she would say something. Perhaps she hadn't liked to, she was such a self-effacing girl. Next time he saw her he would insist on their making definite plans. He went about the flat, thinking what it would be like when she was there all the time. He would buy a three-piece suite, of course, and put that cane stuff in the bedroom. Or they could go out on the balcony; they would be an improvement on his two shabby deck chairs. The bathroom ought to be recarpeted, Francesca would like that, a white carpet with a long pile. And maybe he should buy a wardrobe—the cupboard was full of his own clothes—and a dressing table.

Mr. Cochrane would probably make a terrific fuss once he found out Martin was living with a woman. Martin could just imagine his face and his comments. They could always pretend to be married or, come to that, Mr. Cochrane could be told to go and Francesca do the housework. Martin didn't want her to work in that flower shop or anywhere else once she had left Russell.

It could only have been a couple of hours after he got Martin's letter that Richard Gibson phoned. He was forthright and he sounded suspicious.

"Look, Mr. Urban, Sarah and I have been badly let down about this sort of thing before. If you're really making us a firm offer, that's fine and I'm grateful, but if it's just a possibility or someone else is likely to step in and get the place over our heads—well, we'd rather not know. And I'd better tell you here and now, we can't pay key money or a premium or anything. We haven't got it."

Martin said the offer was firm and there was no question of key money, but he'd rather talk about it when they met. Richard Gibson said any evening in the following week would suit him and the sooner the better, so Martin agreed to go up to Friern Barnet on Monday.

He got back early from the Flask on Saturday because Francesca was coming at two. She got there at five past, wearing the jumper he had bought her and smelling of Ma Griffe. He began at once to tell her of his plans for the flat when she came to live with him. When was she going to tell Russell? When would she leave? He supposed that she would want to bring a lot of her other possessions as well as clothes and they would have to . . .

"I can't come and live *here*, Martin."

She spoke in a small nervous voice and she had begun to twist her hands together in her lap. He stared at her.

"What do you mean, Francesca?"

"I've thought about it a lot. I feel awful about it. But it's not possible. How could we live here? It wouldn't be big enough."

"Not big enough?" He felt stunned. He repeated her words stupidly. "What do you mean, not big enough? Nearly all the people in the other flats are married couples. There's this huge room and a bedroom and a big kitchen and a bathroom. What more do you want?"

"It's not what I want, Martin, you know that. It's Lindsay. Where would we put Lindsay?"

He must have been a fool or totally obtuse, he thought, but it hadn't occurred to him that she would be bringing the child with her. To him Lindsay was a part of Russell, or rather, she and Russell were part of the life lived in Fortis Green Lane. In leaving it behind, Francesca would be leaving behind all that belonged to it, walls, furniture, husband, child. But of course it couldn't be like that. He ought to have known. He ought to have known vicariously if not from experience that a mother doesn't desert her two-year-old child. Lindsay would become his child now. The idea was very disturbing. He lifted his eyes to meet Francesca's mournful eyes.

She would never know what an effort it cost him to say what he did. "She can sleep in here or have a bed in our room."

"Oh, dear, you do make it hard for me. Darling Martin, don't you see it wouldn't be right for the three of us to be living all crowded together like that?" It was hard to tell when Francesca was blushing, her cheeks were always so pink. "She'd—she'd see us in bed together."

"She sees you and Russell in bed together now."

"He's her father. I can't take my little daughter away from her father and her home and her own room and bring her here where she'll have to sleep in a living room or on a couch or something." Her lips trembled. When he put out his arms to her she laid her head against his shoulder and held on to him hard. "Oh, Martin, you do understand?"

"I'll try to, darling. But what alternative do we have? There isn't anywhere else."

His pride was bruised by her rejection of his home and he thought of the little box she lived in. After she had gone he began to feel angry with her. Did she expect him to leave the flat he was fond of and buy a house or something just to accommodate the child she had had by another man? This thought was immediately succeeded by another, that it was his Francesca, his love, that he was using those harsh words about. They would find a way, of course they would. Once Francesca had told Russell she wanted a divorce it might be that he would leave. Surely that was what husbands usually did? Martin wondered if he could possibly bring himself, say for a couple of days each week, to live in the house in Fortis Green Lane.

He got to Friern Barnet at the appointed time of eight on Monday evening. The flat was as nasty as Caroline had led him to believe, with bare stained floorboards, the walls marked all over where other people's posters and pictures had hung. It was furnished partly with Woolworth chipboard and plastic and partly with pre-World War I pitch pine. The Gibsons gave him Nescafé and kept saying how surprised they were that he was young. Sarah Gibson was pale and rather big and dark-haired with a face like Elizabeth Barrett Browning, and her husband was fair and upright and looked like a guards officer, though, in fact, he turned out to be a hospital porter on thirty-seven pounds a week.

When Martin told them—he found it very difficult to do this, he even began to stammer—that his intention was to give them money to buy a flat, they refused to believe him.

"But why?" Sarah Gibson kept saying. "You don't know us. Why should you want to give us money?"

Martin said that he had "come into" a fortune, which was strictly true. He explained his motives. He even described his experiences with Miss Watson and Mr. Deepdene. He had wanted to find a young couple, he said.

"Okay, that's fine for you, but what about us? We'd be under an obligation to you all our lives. We'd be sort of tied to you. Anyway, you must want something out of it."

Martin felt helpless. He couldn't think of any more to say and he wished he hadn't come. Then Richard Gibson said,

"If you're really serious, we'd borrow it from you. I mean, we're both teachers only we can't get jobs. We'd borrow it from you, and when we get proper jobs we'd start paying it back like a mortgage."

That wasn't what Martin had wanted but it was the only arrangement the Gibsons would agree to. He said he would have to do it through a friend of his who was a solicitor. His friend, Adrian Vowchurch, would draw up an agreement for an interest-free loan, and he would be in touch with Richard Gibson in a day or two. Sarah Gibson sat staring at him, bewildered and frowning.

Her husband, seeing Martin out, said, "I honestly don't expect ever to see you or hear from you again. You see, I don't believe you. I can't."

"Time will show," said Martin.

He felt angry. Not so much with the Gibsons as with the world, society, civilisation, so-called, which must be in a pretty terrible state if you couldn't perform an act of altruism without people thinking you were mad. Sarah Gibson had thought he was schizophrenic, he had seen it in her eyes. He drove down across the North Circular Road and into Colney Hatch Lane, passing very near to Francesca's home. But Francesca wouldn't be there now, it was Monday and she had gone to Annabel's, she had told him so on Saturday.

How much he would love to see her now! Maybe the time had come for him to tell her about the money and how he had come by it, or if not that, it would simply be lovely to be with her and talk to her. He was aware of something he never remembered knowing before he had met her—loneliness. It was nearly nine o'clock. Why shouldn't he go to Annabel's place in Frognal and pick her up and drive her home? He didn't know Annabel's surname but he knew the house she lived in. He had parked outside its gate after their second meeting to say good-bye to Francesca. Would she mind his calling for her? He didn't think so. She had met Norman Tremlett at his flat, now it was time for him to begin meeting her friends.

For all his convincing arguments, he felt apprehensive as he drove across Hampstead Lane. Annabel knew of his existence, he told himself, even Russell knew of it. He wasn't doing anything clandestine or dishonourable. He was simply calling at a friend's house for the woman who was going to be his wife. Young men all over London were doing the same. He drove down past the Whitestone Pond into Branch Hill. A little snow still lay in patches on the brown turf of Judge's Walk. There was mist in the air, a damp icy breath. He drew the car into the kerb at the top of Frognal and crossed the road. As soon as he was alone with Francesca he would tell her he intended to put the flat on the market and buy a house for the three of them. Would she consent

81

to live in Cromwell Court with him just until he could do that?

The house outside which he had parked that night in November was large, almost a mansion, with a front garden full of leafless shrubs and small grey alpine plants dripping over steps and the rims of urns. It appeared to be divided into three flats and Martin was rather taken aback to find that there were no names but only numbers to the bells. He had taken very little notice of the house on that previous occasion, but now looking up at its brown bricks and half-timbering, red shingles, and red tiles, seemingly numberless windows of both plain and stained glass, he wondered how any young girl on her own, a friend and contemporary of Francesca's, could afford to live in a place like this. Then, because the top storey seemed the smallest and the least grand, he rang the top bell.

After about a minute a woman opened the door. She was probably forty, a good-looking blonde, very well-dressed but for her footwear which was a fluffy pair of bedroom slippers. Martin apologised for disturbing her. Could she tell him in which of the flats someone with the christian name of Annabel lived? He was calling for his fiancée who was a friend of hers. Martin balked a little at calling someone else's wife his fiancée, yet it had the required respectable ring to it.

"Annabel?" said the woman. "There isn't anyone called that here."

"There must be. A young girl living on her own."

"There's myself and my two sons, we have the top floor. Mr. and Mrs. Cameron have the middle flat. They're elderly and they haven't any children. The ground floor's occupied by Sir John and Lady Bidmead—the painter, you've probably heard of him—and it's them the house belongs to. They own it. I've known them for twenty years and they certainly don't have a daughter."

It had occurred to Martin while she was speaking that Francesca hadn't actually pointed to this house and said Annabel lived there. It was possible she had meant the house next door. He went next door, a slightly smaller place, semi-detached. An elderly man answered his ring. The owner of the house was a Mrs. Frere who occupied the whole of it and whom he referred to as the employer of himself and his wife. Martin called at two more houses but at neither had Annabel been heard of.

The astonishment he felt softened the edge of his disappointment at not seeing Francesca. He tried to remember what had happened on the evening of November 27. She had got out of the car, turned back to say to him, "Call for me at the shop," and then disappeared in the heavy rain. It had been pouring with rain and he hadn't been able to see much, but he knew she had asked him to park here, had said that Annabel lived just here.

Was Annabel an invention then? Had Francesca made her up? There came into his mind the confusion over where Russell's parents lived. She had said Oxford that first time, he knew she had. He went up into the flat and without putting a lamp on, sat at the window, looking down over London. He saw spangled towers drowning in mist, he saw them, yet he saw nothing. He closed his eyes. Annabel as a creation to be presented to Russell for an alibi was feasible—but to *him*? What motive could she possibly have had? Perhaps she lived a fantasy life in a fantasy world; he had heard of people like that. Perhaps none of the people she had told him about existed—but that wasn't true, of course they did. Russell got his name in the papers and there was no doubting the fact of Lindsay. He put the lights on and drew the curtains and poured himself a whisky. What was the matter with him that he doubted her like this and questioned the very foundations of her being? She had small fantasies, that was all. She slightly distorted the truth as some people did to make themselves appear more interesting. That night in November she had told him she had a friend living in an exclusive part of Hampstead to impress him, and later she couldn't go back on what she had said. Russell's parents very likely lived in Reading or Newmarket, but the two great universities had come into her head as more glamorous and intriguing.

He lay awake most of the night, thinking about her and wondering and sometimes feeling rather sick.

Lately he had been in the habit of phoning her every day, but he let the next day and the next go by without speaking to her. Francesca didn't work on Thursdays. She had told him she spent her Thursdays shopping and cleaning the house and taking Lindsay out. Perhaps she did. He wondered if anything she had told him was true. He went to dinner with his parents, the usual Thursday night Three Bears get-together. His mother said a neighbour of hers had seen him shopping in Hampstead with a very pretty dark girl, but Martin shook his head and said she was mistaking him for someone else.

In the morning he phoned Adrian Vowchurch and explained the arrangement he had come to with Richard Gibson. Adrian gave no sign of surprise at hearing that Martin had fifteen thousand pounds to lend or that he proposed to lend it free of interest.

Martin had an appointment with a client at eleven. It was while he was talking to this man that Francesca phoned. He had to promise to call her back in half an hour, and for that half-hour endeavour to quiet his excitement and his fear while he explained to the client how, if he would spend thirty days out of the country on business each year, he might get thirty-three hundred and sixty-fifths of his income free of tax. When he was alone his hand actually trembled as he picked up the receiver.

The explanation of the Annabel affair was so simple and obvious that he cursed himself for doubting her and for his three days of self-torture.

"Darling, Annabel moved away just after Christmas. She lives in Mill Hill now."

"But they hadn't even heard of her in any of those houses I called at."

Her voice was soft and sweetly indulgent. "Now you called at the house where the old lady lives?"

"I just said so, and at the next two down."

"But you didn't call at the fourth down?"

"Is *that* where she lives?"

"Lived, Martin," said Francesca. "Oh, Martin, did you really think I'd been lying to you and deceiving you? Don't you trust me at all?"

"It's because we're not really together," he said. "It's because I hardly ever see you. Days and days go by and I don't see you. It makes me wonder all the time about what you're doing and your other life. Francesca, if I put my flat up for sale and buy a house for you and me and Lindsay, would you come and live with me just till the sale went through?"

"Martin, darling . . ."

"Well, would you? It needn't be for more than three months and then we could all go and live in the house. Say you will."

"Let's not talk about it on the phone, Martin. I'm wanted in the shop, anyway."

He would have sent her flowers but that would have been coals to Newcastle, corn in Egypt. Instead, he took her a box of hand-made chocolates when he went to call for her at the shop on Monday. He parked the car in Hillside Gardens at a quarter to six and walked down through the cold misty dark to the shop. The grey fog in which its orange light gleamed fuzzily gave it the mysterious look of an enchanted cavern. Francesca wasn't alone. Lindsay was with her, perched up on the counter and occupied in pulling the fronds off a head of pampas grass.

"The nursery was closed," Francesca said. "Their heating's broken down. I thought of phoning you—but I did want to see you even if it couldn't be for long."

He held her in his arms. "You've had a hard day. Come to me and you needn't work, you can be at home with Lindsay all the time. I'll buy us a house."

"Listen," she said, "I had a long talk with Russell. He says he'll divorce me after two years' separation, but the trouble is Lindsay. Russell adores her. You have to understand that. And he says—he says"—her lips trembled and she had difficulty in bringing out her next words—"that if I—take her to live with you—he'll ask the divorce judge for custody of—of her—and—and—he'd get it!"

"Francesca, I think that's nonsense. Why would he?"

"He knows about these things, Martin. He's studied the law."

"I thought he was a history teacher."

"Well, of course he is, but he's studied the law as well. He says he's been as much a mother to Lindsay as I have, fetching her from the nursery and getting her tea and putting her to bed, and he says the judge would see he could look after her on his own like he often has, and he'd be leading a normal life while I'd be taking her to live in two rooms with my lover!"

Lindsay threw the pampas grass on to the floor and began whimpering. Francesca started to say more about what Russell would do if she took his child to live under Martin's roof, but Lindsay stamped across the counter and pinched her mother's lips together. She said to Martin, though not in a friendly way,

"We're going home in a taxi."

"Francesca, let me drive you home. You'll never get a taxi out there, and the fog's getting thicker."

"Really, no, Martin." Francesca struggled and mumbled like Papageno with his padlock. "Stop it, Lindsay, I'll put you on the floor."

"But why won't you let me drive you? We'll be there in ten minutes." Martin hesitated. "Anyway, think of me, it would give me ten minutes of your company."

"I want to see my daddy," said Lindsay.

"Is it Russell seeing me that worries you? I promise to drop you a hundred yards from the house. How's that?"

"All right, Martin," said Francesca in the sweet meek voice he loved. "You drive us home. I don't mean to be ungrateful, it's very very kind of you."

XII

The drive took much longer than ten minutes because of the dense fog. The sky itself, smoky, choking, gloomy white, seemed to have fallen through the dark on to the upper reaches of Highgate. Each car was guided by the tail lights of the one in front, lights that looked as if their feeble glow came through cloudy water.

Lindsay sat on Francesca's knee, helping herself to chocolates out of the box Martin had brought. She liked most of the flavours but not violet cream or liqueur cherry, and when she had taken a bite out of these she pushed the remains into Francesca's mouth. Silver paper went all over the floor of Martin's nice clean car.

Francesca could see Martin was offended at this cavalier treatment of his present, but she didn't care about that. He didn't like Lindsay and he showed it, and to Francesca this was so monstrous that whenever she felt like giving the whole business up and just getting out or telling the truth, she thought of how he looked at and spoke to Lindsay and she hardened her heart and went on. He was looking at her like that now while they were stopped at a red traffic light. It was the kind of look a polite host gives to a guest's uninvited dog.

"You see, Martin, she'd soon make a mess of your lovely tidy flat."

"Maybe, but things would be different if we had a house. We could have a big kitchen and a playroom; we'd have a garden. Look, I can see that's valid, what you said about it's not being right to let your child sleep on a couch in the living room. So suppose I put the flat on the market tomorrow and start to look for a house for the three of us and you stay with Russell just until the house is ready to move into. How does that sound?"

"I don't know, Martin."

"Well, darling, will you think about it? Will you, please, because I ask you and I want it so much? You see, I don't know what else to suggest. You do *want* to come and live with me, don't you?"

It was so cold and foggy and she had a long awkward journey ahead of her. She hadn't the nerve to say no. She touched his arm and smiled.

"Well, then. You won't live with me at the flat and you won't come and stay there with me till we can get a house, so I'm asking you to think about this idea. Will you think about it, darling?"

"I really don't think I'll ever..." Francesca started to say when Lindsay clamped a chocolate-smeary hand over her mouth. She didn't have to finish because Martin was parking the car. They had arrived.

She put Lindsay out on to the pavement and got out herself. It was very cold and wet out there, rain penetrating the fog in large icy drops. Martin wanted her to kiss him so she put her head back in through the window and held up to him red lips that a raindrop had already splashed.

"I'll phone you in the morning, Francesca."

"Yes, do," said Francesca vaguely. She was holding on to Lindsay with one hand and clasping the chocolate box against herself with the other. Lindsay was pulling and stamping.

"And you'll have come to a decision? You'll decide it's yes, won't you?"

Francesca had more or less forgotten what she was meant to be deciding. Again she said she didn't know, but she managed a radiant smile, keeping her options open. Martin drove off waving, though with that hurt look on his face which so exasperated her.

When the car was out of sight she started to walk along Fortis Green Lane in the opposite direction to that which Martin had followed. He had put them down outside number 26 and when they reached 54, Francesca stopped for a moment and looked curiously at the house. It was unlit. On its doorstep was a bottle of milk with a cover over it to stop birds pecking at the cream.

"Mummy carry," said Lindsay.

"Must I?"

"Must. Lindsay carry sweeties."

"That's an offer I can't refuse."

Francesca picked her up and Lindsay gave her a wet sticky kiss on the cheek and waved the chocolate box about. Perhaps it would be a good idea to turn up Hill Avenue? Francesca rejected it and tramped on. The pavement was coated with greyish-black, soupy, liquid mud that splashed up her legs. She realised that what she had thought was rain was in fact condensed fog dripping from the tall bushes in front gardens. She felt like one of those women who abound in Victorian fiction, women who are discovered at the beginning of a chapter wandering over heaths or stumbling along city streets at night and in the most inclement weather with a child in their arms. Very likely she looked like one of them too in her lace-up boots and long skirt and woolly shawl wound round her head and her grandmother's old fur coat, spiky and dewed with drops of fog. In spite of the cold and the heavy weight of the little girl and her own tiredness, Francesca suddenly laughed out loud.

"Not funny," said Lindsay crossly.

"No, it isn't, you're quite right, it isn't a bit funny. You'll find out when you're grown-up that we don't always laugh just because things are funny. There are other reasons. I must be mad. Why did I let him bring us up here, Lindsay? I suppose I was so utterly pissed-off with seeing that look on his face. One thing I do know, I'm not going to see him any more. I'm not going on with it, this is the end, this is it. And Daddy can go—go jump in a pond!"

"Lindsay wants Daddy."

"Yes, well, he won't get home till after we do even at this rate, so shut up. I want my daddy, I want my daddy, you're a real pain sometimes."

"I want my daddy," said Lindsay. She screwed up a chocolate paper and threw it into someone's garden.

"We're going to have a bus ride first. You'll like that, you never go on buses. Come on, hoist up a bit. Can't you sort of sit on my hip?"

Lindsay replied by dropping the box and pinching Francesca's lips together. Francesca picked up the box which was now much splashed with mud and growled through Lindsay's fingers and pretended to bite. Lindsay screamed with laughter, took her hand away an inch and clamped it back again.

"Come on, you crazy kid, we'll freeze to death."

By now they had come out into Coppetts Road and Francesca was looking about her for bus stops when a taxi, which had perhaps dropped an inmate or a visitor, came out of the gates of Coppetts Wood Hospital with its light on. The driver didn't seem to know the whereabouts of Samphire Road, N4, even when Francesca said it wasn't far from Crouch Hill Station, but he agreed to let her direct him. Lindsay started screaming that she'd been promised a bus, she wanted a bus, and she made so much noise that Francesca could tell, by the back of his neck, that the driver was wincing. She stuffed Lindsay with more chocolates to shut her up and then they played the growl and snap game most of the way home. The fare was two pounds which Francesca could ill afford.

The pavements here were even stickier and more slippery than in Finchley. It was a depressed, semi-derelict region to which the taxi had brought them, a place where whole ranks of streets had been demolished to make way for new council building. Acres of muddy ground stood bare between half-dismantled ruins, and some of the streets had become mere narrow lanes running between temporary fences ten feet high. Even in the driest weather the roadways were muddy, smeared with clay from the tyres of tractors and lorries. There was an air of impermanence, of dull, unhopeful expectancy, as of the squalid old giving place to a not much more inviting new.

But Samphire Road was sufficiently on the borders of this resurgent neighbourhood for it and the streets which joined it and ran parallel to it, to be left alone. Samphire Road, with its rampart-like houses of cardboard-coloured brick, its grave-sized front gardens, its ostentatious treelessness, was to be allowed to live out its century undisturbed and survive until at least 1995. Sulphur-coloured lamplight turned the fog into just such a pea-souper as Samphire Road had known in its youth.

Francesca unlocked the front door of number 22, painted some years before the shade of raw calves' liver, and let herself and Lindsay through an inner door into the hall of the ground floor flat. Inside it was as cold as only an old house can be that has no central heating and has been empty for ten hours, and when the month is January. It was damp as well as cold, with a damp to make you cringe. Francesca put lights on and humped Lindsay into the kitchen where she lit the gas oven and switched on an electric wall heater. Breakfast dishes were still stacked in the sink. She unwrapped Lindsay's layers of clothes and then her own layers, spreading her fur coat over the back of a chair to dry. The two of them squatted down in front of the open oven and held out their hands to the pale bluish-mauve flames.

After a while Lindsay said her feet were cold, so Francesca went to look for her furry slippers. In the hall it was as cold as out in the street. There were only two other rooms in the flat, the front room where there were two armchairs and a dining table and a piano and a sofa that converted into a double bed, and the bedroom at the back where Lindsay slept. Francesca drew the curtains across the huge, draughty, stained-glass french windows and lit the gas fire. The gas fire had to be on for at least an hour before she could put Lindsay to bed in that ice box. The slippers were nowhere to be seen, so Francesca went into the other room (known as the sitting room but where no one could have borne to sit between November and April) and found the slippers under the piano. The bed wasn't made. It hadn't been made for several days and it hadn't been used as a sofa more than half a dozen times since Lindsay was born.

Lindsay said, "Where's my daddy?"

"Gone to some meeting about historic Hornsey."

"I'm not going to bed till my daddy comes."

"Okay, you don't have to." Francesca made her scrambled eggs and buttered fingers of brown bread. She sat at the table drinking tea while Lindsay plastered chocolate spread on bread and biscuits and even on to a piece of Swiss roll. Lindsay adored chocolate spread, they had had to take sandwiches of it for their lunch. Francesca wiped it off Lindsay's chin and the tablecloth and the wall where a blob of it had landed. She was thinking about Martin. It was like heaven being in the flat in Cromwell Court and in that warm car and eating in the Villa Bianca. She loved comfort and luxury and longed wistfully after them, perhaps, she thought, because she had never known them, had been too busy living to look for them before. That week-end with Martin had shaken her, the warmth and ease, so that, in spite of the boredom, she had actually thought of becoming the girl he thought she was. Not just sweet and obedient and passive and clinging and Victorian, but the girl who was going to get a divorce and marry Martin and live with him forever...

"There's my daddy," said Lindsay.

The front door banged and there was a sound of feet being wiped on the doormat. Francesca didn't get up, and though Lindsay did, bouncing off her chair, she wasn't going to venture into that freezing passage, not even to greet her long-awaited father. He opened the kitchen door and came in, throwing back a lock of wet black hair out of his eyes.

"Hi," said Francesca.

"Hi." He picked up the little girl, held her in the air, then hugged her to him. "And how's my sweetheart? How did you get on in Mummy's shop? I bet they made you manageress." He sang to the tune of the Red Flag, "The working class can kiss my arse, I've got the boss's job at last!"

"Oh, Tim," said Francesca, "we've had an awful evening out in the sticks. Wait till you hear!"

XIII

"So I just don't see the point of carrying on with it," said Francesca. She and Tim confronted each other across the kitchen table and across the greasy pieces of paper and copy of the *Post* which had wrapped the fish and chips brought in by Tim for their supper.

The kitchen was now very warm and smoky, the windows running with condensation. Lindsay had been put to bed ten minutes before. "Can I have another cigarette, please? I can't smoke when I'm with him—it doesn't go with the image and it nearly kills me, I can tell you."

Tim gave her a cigarette. He frowned a little, pushing out his red lips, but he spoke quite lightly in his usual faintly ironic drawl. "Yes, but, honey, why suddenly throw your hand in now? Why *now* when everything is going so extremely well? I mean, even in our wildest fantasies we didn't foresee he'd fall for you quite so heavily. Or has he?" Tim's eyes narrowed. "Maybe mah honey chile wasn't being strictly truthful when she said Livingstone wanted to marry her."

"Well, I'm not always absolutely truthful, Tim, you know that. Who is? But I don't tell pointless lies. Oh, dear, I nearly came a cropper over Annabel, though, didn't I?" Francesca giggled and her eyes met Tim's blue eyes and she giggled even more. "Oh, dear. Now we must be serious. What I mean is, I don't see the point of carrying on with it because it's not getting us anywhere. All it'll do is lose me my job. If he takes to coming into the shop after me, I'll have to leave to get away from him. What did we think we'd get out of it, Tim? I can't even remember."

"Of course you can remember. Money, Prospects, Opportunities." Tim lit a Gauloise. "And, incidentally, my little revenge."

"Isn't it a funny thing? He says he loves me and all that, but he doesn't exactly confide in me. He's never said a word about winning the pools, and I don't believe he has."

"You don't believe in your Uncle Tim's total recall? I tell you, if I died and they opened me up they'd find the perm on that pools' coupon written on my heart. Of course, there's just the weeniest chance Miss Urban didn't send it in. But if Miss Urban did send it in, then sure as fate is fate, she's won herself the first dividend, all or part of, the lucky, lucky girl."

Tim always referred to Martin as Livingstone or, when his camp mood was on him, as Miss Urban. Francesca, for reasons she didn't understand but thought might be sick reasons, found the camp mood almost unbearably sexy. Tim, when he was that way, made her go weak at the knees and she didn't want that happening now, she wanted to be serious.

"Well," she said, "when you sent those awful yellow chrysanths you said to get in his good graces and get him to take me out a bit because he'd got wads of money and hadn't got a girl friend. You said he might let me have the money to start my own florist's, or at least give me some big presents. But nothing like that's happened. He just fell right in love with me. He's not even that interested in sex—well, not *very* I mean, you'd have raped me if I'd gone on with you the way I have with him. But he's in love. It's not just wanting to screw me, it's real love. And the only place it's going to get me is living with him in his flat or some house he wants to buy. And what's the use of that? What's the use of going on with it, Tim, if I only get to where I have to run away and hide to avoid living with him?"

"One would think, wouldn't one," said Tim thoughtfully, "that Livingstone would have given you something more by now than those very strange decanters or whatever they are. Five grand is nothing, but nothing, to spend on a ring, say, or a bracelet in these inflationary times. What about furs? An' mah honey chile shiverin' in her ole coonskin."

"He did say something about a mink," said Francesca, giggling, "when we're married." She groped about under the fish and chip papers. "He did give me some chocolates tonight only Lindsay's gobbled most of them. Here you are."

"She's a chip off the old block all right, she's only left the nougats and the coconuts."

"The latest is he wants to sell his flat and buy a house for him and me and Lindsay, so I suppose he must have money."

"Now she tells me. Francesca, what d'you think Krishna Bhavnani told me today? That it was Livingstone put up the money for his kid's operation."

"Are you going to put something about it in the *Post?*"

"If you're quitting, yes. If you're keeping on, no. Just as untruths have been known to appear in the *Post*, so have truths sometimes been suppressed."

Francesca laughed. She came behind Tim and put her arms round his shoulders and stroked the Nureyev face. "Tim, I could keep it up a little bit longer. I could see him on Wednesday, if you really think it's worth while. Now I know about the Indian boy, I could have a go at getting a fur coat. Or a ring. We could sell a ring."

Tim rubbed his face against her hands, making purring noises. "Did you switch our blanket on?"

He had bought them an electric blanket for Christmas. "When I took Lindsay to bed," she said.

"Then why don't you take me to bed and tell me all about the times you've misbehaved yourself with Dr. Livingstone?"

"Miss Urban," said Francesca somewhat breathlessly.

"Mah honey chile should tak' shame talking like dat befo' her Uncle Tim, Lawd God!"

Francesca and Tim had been living together for three years. Tim had moved into the flat in Samphire Road instead of just spending nights there, when Francesca found she was pregnant with Lindsay. They had never really considered getting married and couldn't have done anyway since Francesca was still married to Russell Brown. After Tim had met Martin Urban in the wood he had several times invited him to Samphire Road but Martin always refused, Tim hadn't known why. He had been wounded by it, Francesca thought, though Tim never showed that he could feel pain. Then had come the Saturday in November when Tim checked his pools and found, as usual, that he had won nothing while the formula he had given Martin must have scooped the first dividend.

It had disturbed Francesca to see Tim waiting for Martin to phone. Her placid happy-go-lucky nature was ruffled by Tim's intense neurotic anxiety. The days had passed and there had been nothing. As taut as a bowstring, Tim had gone to that interview at Urban, Wedmore, Mackenzie and Company, but still Martin hadn't spoken. The worst thing for Tim had been Martin's refusing to come to the party. Getting a party organised at Samphire Road was no mean feat. They had cancelled it at the last minute because there was nothing to celebrate and no point in opening the champagne.

"I fear," Tim had said, camping it up, pretending, "she's keeping it all the darkest because she doesn't want to have to give any to poor me. Though what I've done I never will know, save be friendly and helpful. Maybe I wasn't quite friendly enough, which some girls, you know, can resent."

Francesca couldn't hazard an opinion on that, but she knew Tim had hoped for something from Martin, even a loan to help them buy a place that would be a cut above Samphire Road. He walked up and down shouting that he would be revenged. He would get hold of some of that money by hook or by crook. After that it was a short step for Francesca to go round with the flowers and—hang on hard.

She was a good-tempered easy-going girl and nothing put her out for long. Tim had once told her that one of the things he liked about her was that she had no morals and no guilt. This made playing the part of Martin's Francesca, the moral and guilty Francesca, rather difficult at first, but Tim had instructed her and even

93

set her a course of reading, Victorian and early twentieth-century fiction mainly, with suitable heroines. She had worked hard at moulding herself according to these models and sometimes after meetings with Martin she felt quite tired. She spent a lot of the time in his company silent and apparently raptly listening, while in fact she was concentrating on how to escape in a taxi and get out of being driven up to Finchley. Now she was faced with the additional problem of how to make Martin believe she loved him and wanted to live with him while refusing to submit to any plan for their living together he might make.

Accordingly, the next time he phoned she said that she would hate to think of him selling his flat in order to buy a house. She knew how much he loved his flat.

"But I'll have to sell it one day, darling. When you're free and we can get married we'll need a house."

"I'd much rather you waited till then, Martin."

"Yes, but that doesn't solve the problem of how we're going to live *till* then, does it?"

That lunchtime Francesca went across the Archway Road and sold the two cut-glass scent bottles for seventeen pounds fifty. All those taxis were making inroads into her resources and if Martin was taking her to dinner at the Mirabelle, as he had promised, on Wednesday, she ought to have a new dress. She ought to try and rake up enough to buy the burgundy crepe Kate Ross, who owned the flower shop, had for weeks been trying to sell for twenty-five pounds.

Martin had got into the habit of ringing the shop every morning at ten. At two minutes to ten on Wednesday he phoned, sounding excited, and said he had had a wonderful idea which he would tell her about that night. Francesca went into the room at the back and tried on the burgundy crepe which Kate had brought in with her and got Kate to agree to take twenty-three pounds fifty for it.

It started to snow at about five, great flakes like goose feathers. Kate always went home at half-past because she didn't have a day off or Saturday afternoon. Martin gasped at the sight of Francesca in the dark red dress with her hair piled up and a dark red-and-white speckled orchid tucked into a curl. He stared at her adoringly. These transports of his, though she knew they were sincere, always irritated Francesca. She preferred a lecherous reaction, which was what she had had from Russell Brown and those other men who had preceded Tim and which she had, in his own individual way, most satisfactorily from Tim. But she smiled and looked rather shy and said quietly,

94

"Do I look nice?"

"Francesca, you look so beautiful. I don't know what to say. I wish I was more articulate; I should like to write poems to you."

"I just hope I'm going to be warm enough," said Francesca, her mind on mink coats, but Martin assured her she would be exposed to the open air for no longer than it took to cross the pavement. "So what's this wonderful idea?" she said when they were in the car. Martin said he wasn't going to tell her until they were eating their dinner.

Francesca had an enormous appetite and a hearty capacity for alcohol. She and Tim were both the sort of very thin people who can eat as much as they like without putting on weight. But she never ate and drank anywhere near as much as she wanted when with Martin, it didn't fit the image. Tonight, however, she was going to start off with *quenelles* of lobster, *quenelles* of anything being among her favourite food. To precede it, a brandy and soda would have gone down well. Francesca asked for a dry sherry.

Martin's shyness and awkwardness increased during the meal. He had become almost tongue-tied by the time Francesca started on her roast pheasant, and although this suited her well enough, she couldn't help speculating as to what it might be about the wonderful idea that was so inhibiting. Then, suddenly, like a man confessing a sin that has long been on his conscience, he began. Fascinated, she watched the slow process of the blush spreading across his face.

"I haven't told anyone this except my parents. In November I won a hundred and four thousand pounds on the football pools. No, don't say anything, let me finish. I decided I'd keep half and give half away: You can imagine my reasons for wanting to do that."

Francesca couldn't at all, but she said nothing. She felt a curious breathless excitement as if she were on the brink of enormous revelations. Yet he was only confirming what Tim had said all along.

"You see, I felt grateful to—well, to fate or God or something for having had such a fortunate sort of life. I made up my mind to help people who were having housing difficulties, but I haven't got very far with that. It's much harder than you'd suppose to get people to accept money. All I've managed to do so far really is pay for a boy to have a heart operation."

"That's not housing difficulties," said Francesca.

"No, that was to be the one exception. Apart from that, I'm considering my cleaner's sister-in-law who's having a nervous breakdown because of noise in the place where she lives, and I've managed to get a young couple on very low wages to accept a loan."

He was smiling tentatively at her, leaning forward, waiting for her approval. Francesca looked blankly at him. It occurred to her that he might actually be off his head. But, no, he was just innocent, he didn't know he was born... Suppose she were to throw herself on his mercy, tell him who she was and that Tim was her lover and Lindsay's father and that they were doomed to live in worse conditions than maybe any of those people he had talked about? She couldn't do it. It was impossible. He refilled her wine glass and said,

"So now I've told you. I don't want to have any secrets from you." As if he'd just confessed to some weird perversion, thought Francesca. "But the point of telling—well, I've been a complete fool. I've been worrying about buying homes for other people and worrying about where you were going to live when you left Russell, but it never occurred to me till last night that I don't have to sell my flat or get a mortgage. Apart from what I'm going to give away, I've got fifty thousand of my own. I've got my own half-share of the win."

"So what's the wonderful idea?" said Francesca carefully.

"To buy a flat for you and Lindsay to live in." He paused but she said nothing. "I mean, that solves everything, doesn't it? Lindsay can have her own room, Russell can't possibly accuse you of corrupting her, and after two years when you've got your divorce we can sell both flats and buy a house. How does that suit you? I'm not going to make any conditions, Francesca"— Martin smiled and reached across the table for her hand—"only I hope I can come and stay sometimes, and I'll be the happiest man on earth if you'll choose a flat that isn't far from mine."

"So we're going house-hunting on Saturday. He's out on Cloud Nine already, planning colour schemes and fussing about something called cubic footage."

"Miss Urban was always house-proud. She'll make some lucky chap a wonderful wife one of these days. What did you have to eat?"

"Lobster *quenelles,* roast pheasant, and roast potatoes and calabresse and *sauteed* mushrooms *and* asparagus, and a sort of chartreuse soufflé with cream."

"You should have asked for a paper bag and said you wanted to take some home for your aged relative."

Francesca giggled. She sat on Tim's lap and took the cigarette out of his mouth and put it in her own. "But, seriously, Tim, what's the future in letting him buy a flat for me to live in? I shan't live in it. But I can't think of any way of getting out of it, short of flatly saying I won't leave my husband."

"Suppose I said give it just two weeks more? Just till Monday, the twelfth of Feb.? If he's going to buy mah honey chile a love nest, he's got to furnish it, hasn't he? In these scandalous times five grand is the least, but the leastest, he can expect to spend on furnishings."

"He said I could have the cane chairs out of his living room."

"What a miscreant he is!" said Tim. "Still, you won't stand for that, will you? Not a girl of spirit like you. You'll ask for five thousand to splash about in Heal's."

"Oh dear," said Francesca with an enormous yawn, "I'll try, I'll do my best, but not a minute more after Feb. the twelfth."

XIV

Francesca didn't know whether to fix on the first flat they saw so that she could go home early, or pretend to find nothing to please her so that things would have progressed no further by the time her deadline came. In the event, she did neither, for as soon as they were really doing something together, conducting practical business, Martin made clear his belief in man as the master. In this, as in all matters on a higher level than that of deciding what she should wear or perhaps what they should eat, he took it for granted he made the decisions, asking for her approval only as a matter of courtesy.

During the two days since their dinner at the Mirabelle he had been in touch with estate agents, had made himself familiar with the specifications of every flat for sale in the area of Highgate and Crouch End, and had already viewed several. This led to his making of a short list and from it a shorter list which by Saturday afternoon had fined down to one. The flat in question wasn't quite as near Cromwell Court as he would have liked, but it was in other respects so suitable that he thought they must overlook that small defect.

Francesca hadn't expected to react with either enthusiasm or dislike to the prospect before her. She had expected to be bored. Her feelings on entering the flat surprised her very much. She had never lived anywhere very spacious or elegant or even ordinarily attractive. There had been her parents' mansion flat in Chiswick, big and cold and pervadingly dark brown, a furnished room in Pimlico, and a furnished room in Shepherds Bush, the little house she had shared with Russell, the basement squat she had shared with Russell's supplanter, her three rooms in Stroud Green. Home to Francesca had never been much more than a place to keep out the rain where there was a table to eat meals off and a bed to go to with someone she liked. But this was another thing. The fourth floor, the penthouse, of Swan Place, Stanhope Avenue, Highgate, was a different matter altogether.

The living room was very large and you went into the dining part of it through an arch. One wall was all glass. The heating made it too hot for even her thin coat; she could have gone naked. Looking out of the big plate-glass windows on to hilly streets and patches of green and snowy roofs, being led into the pastel blue kitchen and the pastel apricot bathroom, Francesca found herself thinking that she would like to live here, she would like it very much indeed. It was a crying shame that she couldn't, or that the price to pay for doing so was too high, because she would like it—oh, wouldn't she! And Lindsay would like it and probably Tim too, though you could never tell with him. It was just too awful that she could have it only by being stuffy old Martin's kept woman. She wondered how much it cost.

"What do you think?" said Martin in the car.

"It's lovely."

"I'm glad you like it, darling, because although you'll think me very high-handed and a real male chauvinist pig, I've actually already told the agent I'll have it and I've put down a deposit."

"What would you have done," asked Francesca curiously, "if I'd hated it?"

"I knew you wouldn't. I think I know you pretty well by this time."

"How much is it, Martin?"

"Forty-two thousand pounds."

Francesca was silenced. She felt quite weak and swimmy in the head at the thought of so much money. Martin said it would be a good investment, house property was the best investment these days, and before they got married he would sell both flats and buy a house. The property market, he had been told, was due for another steep rise in the spring. With luck he ought to make a big profit on both flats.

They went back to Cromwell Court where Martin had got chocolate eclairs and a Battenburg cake in for tea. Francesca partook heartily of both. It was the most miserable shame she didn't find Martin in the least attractive. If only she fancied him she could have put up with the yawning dullness and the accountant's talk and the pomposity for the sake of that lovely flat. But she didn't fancy him, not a scrap, which was odd really because, like Tim, he was tall and dark and though not so good looking, he was younger and cleaner and he didn't permanently stink of Gauloises. Francesca pondered rather regretfully on the anomalies of sexual attraction while Martin lectured her gently on house property and the registration of land and stamp duty and the making of searches and the mysteries of conveyancing.

Francesca ate another chocolate eclair. Martin wasn't the sort of person who would even consider going to bed in the afternoon, he would think it perverse. She let him hold her hand across the spread of sofa cushions.

"I suppose it'll be months and months before you actually own it?" she said.

"Oh, no. I'm paying cash, you see. My friend, Norman Tremlett—you met him here—he'll do a survey for me on Monday. I've already talked to my solicitor—he's another friend, we were all at school together—and he says, provided the survey's favourable there's no reason why the contract shouldn't be ready for my signature by February the twelfth, that's Monday week. Then I'd get completion as soon as possible, maybe three weeks, and you could move in."

Francesca thought how when she and Russell had tried to buy a house, what difficulties and obstacles there had been! The first two they fixed on had been sold over their heads while the building society hesitated over giving Russell a mortgage. Securing the one they had finally lived in took months and months, nearly a year of their hopes being raised and dashed. But they, of course, had had no money and no old-boy network. It no longer mattered, it was history, ten years gone, swept away by oceans of water under the bridge. She smiled at Martin.

"What about furniture, darling?"

"I thought of making a separate deal with the owner for the carpets and curtains and the bedroom furniture and the fridge and cooker. He wants to sell. Of course, if there was anything special you wanted, we could go shopping together next Saturday."

Was there any point now in waiting till February 12? None except that she had given Tim an undertaking. Martin seemed to take it for granted she would now be spending every evening with him. Francesca pointed out that while she was still with Russell she couldn't go out every night and leave him to look after Lindsay. Perhaps she might manage another day in the week as well as Monday...

"I want my parents to meet you," said Martin.

She insisted on going home at six o'clock and he insisted on driving her. This time he didn't drop her a hundred yards away but set her down outside number 54 and there he waited to see her into the house. Francesca stood outside the white iron gate, waving impatiently at him, while he sat in the car, refusing to go till she did. After a few seconds she saw it was useless. She must either make it look as if she were going into that house or else give up the game.

There was a light on in the hall but nowhere else. She unlatched the white gate and walked quickly to the side entrance which was a wooden door set into a six-foot-high fence. It was rather more than dusk and not quite dark. Francesca boldly tried the handle on the wooden door, and when it worked pushed the door open and found herself on a concrete strip of back yard. It would be rather awful, she thought, but rather funny too if someone saw her lurking there and called the police. After a little while she heard Martin's car go, so she opened the wooden door again and got out as fast as she could, running away down the side street on to which the garden of 54 abutted.

It wasn't until her next meeting with him that she learned how Martin had come back to "see if she was all right." How, from a car in the street, he could have known whether she was or wasn't he didn't say. But while there, he said, he had seen Russell Brown come out of the house and walk away towards Coldfall Wood.

First of all he told her that he had felt so happy about the new flat and their future that on Sunday he had decided to rush in (as he put it) where angels fear to tread and had actually called on Miss Watson. There in her employer's house in Hurst Avenue he had explained what his letters perhaps hadn't explained and had convinced her of his good intentions. She had agreed, in tears and some bewilderment, to accept ten thousand pounds with which to buy a small terraced house in the Lincolnshire town where her married sister lived.

"So that's twenty-five thousand disposed of. Do you think it would be wrong of me if I only gave away another twenty? You see, I'm going to have rather more expense than I thought with your flat."

Francesca said with perfect sincerity that she didn't think it would be wrong at all. Every time he talked of giving money away to these people she didn't know and didn't want to know, she had to turn her face away so that he couldn't see her expression of disgust and dismay. She turned her back on him, picking red tulips and blue irises out of the jars on the floor to make a bouquet for his mother.

"And I've got something else to tell you. I've seen Russell."

She turned round slowly, holding the flowers. He smiled, looking triumphant.

"He only waited for you to come in to go out himself, didn't he? I must say, it gave me a strange feeling to see him. He looks older than he is, don't you think?"

"I don't know, Martin."

"More than thirty-five, I thought. D'you like those coneyskin coats on men? They're very 'in' this year. I could get one."

"Was Russell wearing his coneyskin then?" said Francesca with care.

"When I saw him I remembered what he'd done to you and I longed to get out of the car and hit him. But, of course, I didn't. I thought of how upset you'd be. He went off up towards the wood or the North Circular or somewhere."

"He's got friends in Coppetts Lane," said Francesca.

They went out to the car with the flowers.

"I've told my parents a bit about you. I'm afraid I've had to stretch the truth a bit. It seemed politic."

The truth had been stretched so far by now, thought Francesca, it seemed unlikely to snap tonight.

"I've given them to understand you're already living apart from your husband," said Martin. "I refer to you as my fiancée."

"Then I ought to have a ring," said Francesca.

"I'm afraid you wouldn't wear it any more than you wear Russell's wedding ring. But shall I get you one for when your divorce comes through, so you can wear it to the registrar's office?"

The Urbans were very much what Francesca had expected, except that Walter Urban was younger and better looking. She found him rather attractive and speculated as to what it would be like to go to bed with a man twice one's age. Margaret Urban sat making patchwork of the same sort as that with which the cushions were covered. It looked a tedious and intricate task, putting all those hexagons together evenly. Francesca wondered why she did it, for they seemed to have heaps of money, but she would have liked a skirt for herself made in that sort of patchwork. It was a shame really that she wasn't, whatever the Urbans might think, in the running to get one.

They were like the Three Bears, she thought. She had gone to sit down on the right-hand side of the log fire and been told *sotto voce* by Martin that that was his mother's chair. They drank sherry, oloroso for Mrs. Urban, amontillado for Walter, and Tio Pepe for Martin. She felt that, like Goldilocks, she should have tried a little bit of each but settled instead for the Tio Pepe too.

Inwardly, she was amused. How dismayed the two senior Urbans must be at the thought of their only son (a boy brought up with the utmost care) marrying a divorced woman with a child. She tried to read some hint of it in their faces and in Mrs. Urban's tone when she looked up from her sewing to ask questions about Lindsay. But there was nothing. They were playing safe, humouring Martin, in the hope, no doubt, that if they didn't oppose him he might get over her before any irreversible step was taken. It was just the way she envisaged behaving herself if anything so awful was to happen as Lindsay bringing home an accountant or a solicitor and saying she wanted to marry him.

When they were on their second glasses of sherry Martin told them about buying the flat in Swan Place.

"For Francesca and Lindsay," he said.

Where did they suppose she was living now? Francesca wondered. She expected Martin's announcement to be greeted with grave disapproval. In her experience, parents never like you spending money, even your own, but she had reckoned without the passion for wise investment which throbs in the heart of every good accountant. Francesca noticed too that Martin's mother took it very coolly. She had a sensitive awareness of women's reactions, and she understood that Margaret Urban, mother of an only son, would now be able to convince herself that if her son and his fiancée lived under separate roofs before marriage, they wouldn't sleep together before marriage either.

"A very sound idea," said Walter, "buying the place before prices go up again. Of course you'll elect to describe it as your principal residence?"

"It won't be *his* residence at all, Walter," said Mrs. Urban.

Her husband took no notice of this interruption which had made Francesca discreetly smile. "Because if Swan Place is your secondary residence you won't forget, will you, that you'll be liable for Capital Gains Tax when you sell it."

"Do you know," said Martin, "I *had* forgotten. The tax payable would be a third of my profit, wouldn't it?"

102

"Thirty per cent," said Walter.

They talked about tax and tax avoidance all through dinner. Mrs. Urban watched them placidly from under her slate-blue fringe, but Francesca was so bored she couldn't control her yawns.

On Saturday afternoon they paid another visit to Swan Place and saw the owner, a Mr. Butler, and he and Martin went through what Martin called "negotiating a price" for the carpets and curtains and bits of kitchen equipment and bedroom furniture. Afterwards he took Francesca out to tea at Louis' in Hampstead. He said that they would go and buy any other furniture she might want next week-end, and when she said she could do that on her own, he said he thought he would like to be there too. After all, it would one day be his furniture as well as hers. Francesca didn't much care, she had given up, the long drag was nearly over. She would see him on Monday and say she couldn't leave Russell or contrive to have a tremendous quarrel with him, and that would be that.

When Francesca had eaten as many cream slices and rum babas as she could manage—it was too late in the day to worry about sticking to a Victorian lady's appetite—Martin suggested they go across the road and see the Buñuel film at the Everyman. But Francesca wasn't having that. If Goldie upstairs would keep an ear open for Lindsay she wanted to go round the pub with Tim. So she said she had to get back to Lindsay because Russell was having dinner with his publisher and someone who might be interested in doing the *The Iron Cocoon* for television. This was an excuse in which Tim had rehearsed her and she was glad to have an opportunity of using it. Martin, of course, drove her up to Fortis Green Lane. Once more she had to hide in the side entrance. After Monday, she thought, she would never set foot in Finchley again.

February 10, February 11 . . . It would soon be all over. Francesca tried to think of ways of breaking off with Martin that were not too brutal. It was no good discussing this with Tim who would have advised the bald truth, presented as savagely as possible.

Martin walked into the shop at a quarter to six on Monday, February 12. Last time, thought Francesca, last time. She gave him a vague kiss. She hadn't bothered with pink *panne* velvet or burgundy crepe but was wearing *her* favourite collection of garments, a patchwork skirt, a Hungarian peasant top with a long cardigan over it, and her Olaf's Daughters boots, which were heaven to wear in the shop whatever Martin might think of them.

"I'm awfully sorry, darling, but before we have dinner I've got to go round to my solicitor's and see about this contract. You won't mind, will you?"

Francesca didn't particularly mind. She wouldn't have minded if they had spent the entire evening at his solicitor's. All that interested her was how to pave the way for disappearing permanently from Martin's life. Perhaps it would be best to stage a quarrel over dinner or make use of an idea which had come to her earlier in the day. This was to say that she was pregnant and that it was Russell's child, so she would have to stay with him, wouldn't she? Francesca thought she could really enter into the spirit of this. And it had the great merit of not humiliating or even much disillusioning Martin. Francesca was amoral and greedy but she wasn't entirely heartless. Martin sometimes reminded her of a big kind dog, a Newfoundland perhaps, that one might have to abandon at the Battersea Dogs' Home but which one wouldn't kick in the face. She would try to let him down as lightly as possible, for her sake, she admitted, as well as his. She hated scenes, recriminations, fuss.

Martin introduced her to Adrian Vowchurch as his fiancée. There was a Mrs. Vowchurch somewhere, clattering about in the kitchen regions. Francesca sized Adrian up. She didn't like little hatchet-faced men with supercilious eyes and the sort of public school accent so affected as to be a joke. He shook hands with her and said insincerely, she thought, that it gave him really tremendous pleasure to meet her at last. While he and Martin talked more or less incomprehensibly, it was borne in on Francesca that they were there for the express purpose of signing the contract for the purchase of the Swan Place flat. She could see it, or what was probably it, lying on a blotter on a mahogany desk. Adrian saw her looking and said they hoped for completion within a couple of weeks, allowing for searches (whatever that might mean) and would Mrs. Brown like to have a look at the contract? Francesca hesitated. It seemed too unkind to let Martin buy the flat when she hadn't the slightest intention of ever living in it. Somehow the purchase of the flat hadn't seemed real until she saw what, in black and white, it involved.

This agreement is made the Twelfth Day of February, Nineteen Hundred and Eighty, between John Alexander Butler, of Flat 10, Swan Place, Stanhope Avenue, Highgate, in the County of London (Hereinafter called "the Vendor"), and Mrs. Francesca Brown.... Martin had given him her address as 12, Cromwell Court. It was absurd on the strength of that one week-end, but it was rather touching. She read the rest of the first page. She'd thought that he brought her here just to witness his signature. And once this contract was exchanged with Butler's, it would be difficult, if not impossible, for him to get out of buying the flat. Even she knew that. What she ought to do was ask him to postpone signing it, and when they were alone tell him the truth.

She found she lacked the courage to do that. She looked up and met the cold, suspicious eyes of Adrian Vowchurch. He didn't like her. It was far more than that. He distrusted her and resented her presence. He gave an infinitesimal shrug and passed a fountain pen to her.

"Can we have your signature then, Mrs. Brown—er, Francesca?"

She took the pen.

"Not there," he said. "Up here."

Martin gave a soft indulgent laugh. She didn't quite understand, but she signed where Adrian told her to, and then Julie Vowchurch, who had come in and given her a tight smile signed as witness. Francesca felt excited and puzzled and rather frightened. Martin refused the Vowchurches' offer of drinks and they drove up to Hampstead and had dinner at the Cellier du Midi.

"You don't know how relieved I am," said Martin, "that I told you about winning that money. We'll never have secrets from each other, shall we?"

"No," said Francesca, trying furiously to think. She couldn't wait to be home with Tim.

"Now we've got your flat fixed up and the future settled, I want to get the other thing settled too. I mean the philanthropy part or charity or whatever you like to call it. So I'm going to have another go at Mrs. Cochrane, and I really think the last ten thousand had better go to Mrs. Finn. Have I told you about her? She used to be our cleaner and she's a bit crazy, poor old creature, and I'll have to reach her through her son. But I'm sure she's a deserving cause . . . Are you all right, darling? You look as if you're off somewhere in a dream."

"I'm awfully tired. I won't come back with you, if you don't mind. I'll just get a taxi in Heath Street." His face fell. "But I could see you tomorrow, if you like."

"Darling," he said, "if that's a promise I shan't mind letting you go."

Tim was sitting at the kitchen table doing his reporter's expenses, the greatest work of fiction, he sometimes said, since *War and Peace*. He was smoking what smelt like his hundredth Gauloise of the day and drinking retsina out of a bottle. The oven was on and the wall heater and as usual the condensation was running down the walls.

"Oh, Tim," said Francesca, "I feel very peculiar. Wait till I tell you. Can I have some wine, please, and a cigarette?"

"Have you had a heart-rending renunciation scene?"

"No, listen, Tim, we went to his solicitor and he had this contract thing for buying the flat and I read it and it said something about being between John Alexander Butler and Francesca Brown. And I nearly didn't sign it because it seemed a bit mean and rotten making him pay for something I wasn't going to live in, but you needn't look like that, I did sign it, and . . ."

"Thank Christ," said Tim, and his sallow face had become even paler, the red mouth and the black brows standing out like paint. "Think—you're sure it was made just between this Butler guy and you?" She nodded with eagerness. "And you signed it on your own? Livingstone didn't sign it?"

"No."

"When you went to see old Urban didn't he say something about Livingstone having to pay Capital Gains Tax on one of his properties if he sold them both?"

"Yes, he sort of reminded Martin about some law about that. He said if Martin owned two flats and sold them both, he'd have to pay this tax on one of them. Thirty per cent of his profit, he said. What's he done, Tim? He didn't say anything to me, he didn't mention it after we'd left the solicitor's. And I didn't say anything, and I didn't break things off either . . ."

"Break things off?" said Tim. "You'll see that guy every night till completion if it kills you *and* me. Don't you see what he's doing? He's buying it in your name so that he can avoid giving the government two or three grand tax. In other words, in a couple of weeks' time, barring acts of God, that forty-two thousand quid luxury apartment will become the exclusive, undisputed, unencumbered property of mah honey chile."

"Oh, Tim, I really have done it, haven't I? This is better than a ring or a bit of furniture."

"And revenge will be very sweet," said Tim.

He put out his arms and she came into them and they hugged each other.

XV

It was rare for any post to arrive for Finn or Lena. There would be the electricity and gas bills every quarter and the little pension from Finn's father's firm, and at Christmas a card from Brenda. That was all. Months could pass by without Finn's receiving a single item addressed to himself, and it was therefore with the nearest he ever got to astonishment that he picked up the long white envelope from the doormat.

The direction was to T. Finn Esq. and it was typewritten. Finn was on his way to Modena Road where he was papering walls. When he was in the van he took out the letter and read it.

Dear Mr. Finn,

I do not think we have ever met, though our mothers are old friends. Perhaps Mrs. Finn has mentioned to you that they had tea together a few weeks ago. I expect you will be surprised to hear from me, but the fact is that I have a business proposition to put to you and I wonder if we could meet and discuss this. Could you ring me at the above number in the next few days? I shall be there between 9:30 and 5:30.

Yours sincerely,
Martin W. Urban.

Finn started the van and drove off to Parliament Hill Fields. Martin Urban had been wrong in saying they had never met. Finn seldom forgot a thing like that. He remembered Martin quite clearly as a spotty adolescent when he himself was eleven or twelve. Lena had taken him with her to Copley Avenue because it was the school holidays and Queenie was ill with flu. He had opened a bedroom door and seen Martin sitting at a desk, using a protractor and a set square. The older boy had turned on him a look which Finn at the time had taken for outrage and disgust but which later he understood. That look had in fact only been astonishment that Finn had seemed to be attempting to bridge the huge social gulf between them.

What did the grown-up Martin want of him now? If it was true that Mrs. Urban had admired the partitioning of Lena's room, it might be that she had talked about it to her son and he was looking for a builder to do a conversion job for him. Finn was more or less willing, providing the money was right and he wasn't hassled about time. The words "business proposition" seemed to imply something like that. He let himself into the house in Modena Road and walked from room to room, assessing the stage he had reached. Once the paper was up in the ground floor front room and the hall floor retiled, he would be finished and at leisure. But he would see how he got on before making that phone call.

Remembering that look of Martin's all those years ago in Copley Avenue, he was slightly surprised to read that bit about their mothers being old friends. "A few weeks ago" wasn't exactly accurate either. A few months was more like it; it had been November 16, he recalled, his birthday. Just as well, he reflected, that the woman hadn't been back again during the terrible month, the weeks of Lena's sufferings. No wonder he hadn't yet finished the work for Kaiafas . . .

She had said there were maggots coming out of the walls. That had been at the beginning when she could still see colours and smell smells, the real and the imaginary. After that she could only see in black and white and grey and had lain crying all night, all day. He had never left her. If she had gone to the hospital they would have put her in the locked ward. He hadn't dared sleep unless she was drugged and out, for she would spring upon him if she thought he was off guard. Twice she had tried to set the place on fire, and when he prevented this she burned herself instead. There were still burn scars on both her wrists and in the hollows of her elbows.

But she had come out of it at last. She always did, though Finn was afraid the time might come when she wouldn't. She could hear people's voices again and see colours again and remember who he was. On the day she held his hand and asked him if he had worn her birthday present yet he knew she was better and he brought the bird back from downstairs. Mrs. Gogarty started coming in to give him a break and he got back to work. In the past week Lena had twice been up to Second Chance, and this afternoon Mrs. Gogarty was taking her to a street market—somewhere in Islington, he thought it was, miles away from Parliament Hill Fields.

Coming back to Lord Arthur Road at six, Finn found them occupied with the Tarot, not telling fortunes this time but studying the pictures on certain cards. Mrs. Gogarty had just bought the pack off a stall for seventy-five pence. It appeared that the Hermit and Eight of Cups were missing. Lena gave a strong shiver as she picked up and looked at the Ten of Swords. It showed the body of a man, pinned to the ground by the ten sharp blades down the length of his back and lying by the waters of a lake. Finn covered up the card with the pretty Queen of Pentacles, and he thought how if ever he killed again it must look like an accident—it must be taken for an accident, for Lena's sake.

She gave him a tremulous smile and began to produce from a bag for his inspection the things she had bought that day, a man's trilby hat, a pair of wooden elephant bookends, a green china quadruped with its tail missing, half a dozen copies of a magazine called *Slimming Naturally*.

Later on, Mr. Beard, who kept the fur and suede cleaner's shop in Brecknock Road and who had once tried, with some success, to raise up the spirit of Cornelius Agrippa, was coming round and bringing his Ouija board. Finn felt a quiet relief that things were getting back to normal. While they waited for Mr. Beard, Mrs. Gogarty set out the Tarot for Finn and foretold an unexpected accession of wealth.

Finn waited a couple of days before phoning Martin Urban, and then he did so from a phone box by Gospel Oak Station at ten in the morning.

"You wanted me to ring you. The name's Finn."

"Oh, yes, good morning. How do you do? Nice of you to phone. I expect you gathered from my letter that I've got a proposition to put to you that's rather to your advantage. It's not something I'd feel like discussing on the phone. Could we—er, meet and have a word, d'you think?"

"If you want," said Finn.

"A pub? I'll suggest somewhere half-way between our respective homes, shall I? How about the Archway Tavern? If tonight would suit you, we could say eight tonight in the Archway Tavern."

He rang off without asking Finn how he would recognise him or telling him what he himself looked like. Finn wasn't much bothered by that, he knew he would somehow smell out in the man the studious and superior adolescent of long ago. But for a little while he did wonder why, if Martin Urban only wanted him to divide a room into two or make two rooms into one, he hadn't felt like even hinting at it on the phone.

Mr. Bradley was spending the evening as well as most of the day with Lena. His daughter-in-law was having an operation for gallstones, and he couldn't get into the house till his son came back from the hospital at nine. It was a cold, misty evening with

109

not much traffic about and few people. Finn wore the yellow pullover and the black scarf with the coins on, and Lena's birthday present. He walked into the Archway Tavern at two minutes past eight and stood still just inside the door, looking about him. As he had expected, he knew Martin Urban at once, a tallish, square-built man, becoming burly and looking older than his age. He was sitting at a table, reading the *Evening Standard*, and as Finn's pale piercing eyes fixed him he lifted his own. Finn walked up to him and he got to his feet.

"Mr. Finn?"

Finn nodded.

"How do you do? You're very punctual. It's good of you to come. I've been thinking about it. I didn't give you much notice, did I? I hope that's all right." Finn didn't say anything. He sat down. "What will you drink?"

"Pineapple juice," said Finn.

"*Pineapple juice?* What, just by itself? You're sure that's all right?"

"Just pineapple juice," said Finn. "The Britvic."

He expected Martin Urban to drink beer. He was the sort who always would in pubs except perhaps for the last drink. But he brought himself a large whisky, at least a double measure, and a small bottle of soda water. Finn supposed he was nervous about something or someone and that someone was very likely himself. He inspired trepidation in otherwise quite confident people, but he didn't know how to put them at their ease and wouldn't have done so even if he had known. He sat silent, pouring the thick yellow juice from the bottle into a small squat glass. They hadn't been alone at their table, but now the other man who sat there finished his beer, picked up his coat, and left.

"And how's your mother these days?"

"She's okay," said Finn.

Martin Urban turned his chair away from the table and edged it a little nearer to Finn's. "Cheers," he said and he drank some of his whisky. "My mother does see her sometimes, you know. She looks in when she gets a chance." He waited for a rejoinder to this but none came. "I think it was November when she last saw her. She thought—well, she was a bit worried about her."

"Well, well," said Finn.

"She was always very fond of her, you see. They'd known each other for a long time." It was apparent to Finn that he was trying to avoid saying that Lena had been Mrs. Urban's cleaner, a statement about which Finn wouldn't have cared at all. He swilled the juice round his mouth, savouring it. A particularly good batch, he thought. "That stuff you're drinking, is it all right?"

Finn nodded. He watched Martin Urban's face flush to a dark brick-red. "I don't want you to think I'm criticising, finding fault or anything like that. If you don't own your own home these days or have a council place it's pretty difficult to find anywhere to live, let alone anywhere decent. And to buy somewhere you don't just have to be earning good money, you need a bit of capital as well. What I'm trying to say is, when my mother told me the way Mrs. Finn was living—through no fault of anybody's, actually— I thought, well, maybe I could do something to change all that, to sort of benefit you both, because we're all old friends, after all, aren't we?"

Finn finished his drink. He said nothing. He was beginning to be aware that an offer was to be made to him, but for what and in exchange for what he couldn't tell. This man was as shy of approaching the point as Kaiafas was. Reminded of the Cypriot, he seemed to hear a voice saying in another pub, "I give it to my friend Feen instead," and at that recollection, at certain apparent parallels, he raised his eyes and let them rest on the flushed, square, somewhat embarrassed, face in front of him.

"I hope I haven't offended you."

Finn shook his head.

"Good. Then I'll come to the point." Martin Urban looked round to see that they weren't overheard and said in a lower voice, "I could manage to let you have ten thousand pounds. I'm afraid I can't make it more than that. You'd have to go outside London, of course."

Finn's gaze fell and rose again. He was overwhelmed by the munificence of this offer. His fame had indeed spread before him, and it wasn't his fame as a plumber and decorator. Yet one to him were fame and shame; he was without vanity. He drank the remains of his pineapple juice and said, "It's a lot of money."

"You wouldn't do it for less."

Finn did a rare thing for him. He smiled. He spoke one word. "When?"

Martin Urban seemed slightly taken aback. "When you like. As soon as possible. You're going to accept then?"

"Oh, yes. Why not?"

"Good. That's splendid. I'm very happy you don't feel you have to put up any show of refusal, that sort of thing. It wastes so much time. Let's drink to it, shall we?" He fetched another pineapple juice and a second whisky. Facing Finn again, he

111

seemed to become doubtful and his expression took on its former shade of mystification. "I have made myself plain? You have understood me?"

Rather impatiently Finn said, "Sure. You can leave it to me."

"That's fine. It's just that I thought you might not exactly have known what I meant. Would you like me to send you a cheque?"

"I haven't got a bank account. I'd like cash."

"*Cash?* My dear chap, that'd make quite a parcel."

Finn nodded. "Pad it out a bit with newspaper. You can let me have half now and half later. That way you needn't let me have the rest till you know I've done what you want. Right?"

"I suppose so. Are you going to be able to do it on your own? You know how to go about it?"

"Find someone else then," said Finn.

"I'm sorry, I didn't mean that. I *have* offended you. Anyway, it's no business of mine how you go about it. I want to think that once I've let you have the money you're on your own, you're free." Martin Urban swallowed his whisky very rapidly. He wiped his mouth, he sighed. "But you will—you will do it, won't you?"

"Haven't I said?"

He was far worse than Kaiafas, Finn thought. And now, as if it was any concern of his where Lena lived or what Lena did, he began talking once more about buying her a house, moving her out of Lord Arthur Road.

"You can still get small houses for less than ten thousand in the country towns. If you don't mind going a good distance there are still building firms putting up houses for that. I'd get her to decide where she'd like to live—near some relative maybe—and then you and she could have a Saturday out there, calling on the agents."

Finn understood it. Martin Urban wanted him out of the way, a long way away, once the deed was done. He didn't understand how ludicrous it was recommending some country town for Lena, Lena who would go mad, madder, maddest away from her precious tiny segmented home, the only home she could bear to live in, away too from her friends, from Mrs. Gogarty and Mr. Bradley and Mr. Beard. Finn almost felt like telling Martin Urban to shut up, to *think,* to look at reality, but he didn't do this. He sat silent and impassive while the other talked on about surveyors' reports and freeholds and frontages and party walls. For he was understanding more and more. Martin Urban, like Kaiafas, believed that if he talked in this way of mundane, harmless, and practical matters he wouldn't quite have to realise the enormity of the deed for which he was to pay those thousands of pounds.

112

At last he paused for breath and perhaps for some sign of appreciation. Finn got up, nodded to him and left without speaking again. He had been given no further instructions, but he didn't doubt that such would be sent to him in due course.

Over the Archway concourse the snow was dancing down in millions of soft plumy flakes that whirled like fireflies in the light from the yellow lamps.

XVI

The parcel containing the first instalment of the money was brought to Finn by an express delivery service. A man in a green uniform handed it to him at the door. Finn took it upstairs. The house in Lord Arthur Road had its Saturday smell of baked beans and marijuana as against its weekday smell of stale waste bins and marijuana. Finn had unwrapped the parcel and was counting the money when he heard Lena coming down the stairs. Her footsteps were almost jaunty. Mr. Beard was taking her to a meeting of the Tufnell Theosophists. Lena didn't have many men friends so it was an exciting event for her. Finn opened his door.

"Will you be bringing him back with you?"

Smiling a little and bridling, she said she didn't know. She would like to; she would ask him. Her eyes shone. She was wearing the mauve dress with the fringe and over it a red cloak lined in fraying satin. If you half-closed your eyes and looked at her you might fancy you were seeing—not a young girl, never that, but perhaps the ghost of a young girl. She was like a moth from whose wings most of the dust has rubbed away, a faded fluttering moth or a skeleton leaf. She laid her hand on Finn's arm and looked up into his face as if he were the parent and she the child.

"Here," he said, "get something for your tea then." He thrust a bundle of notes, forty, fifty, pounds into her hands.

She smelt of camphor, the mistletoe-bough bride who has been resurrected after fifty years in the trunk. Over the banisters he watched her go down, stuffing notes into her Dorothy bag, into her cloak pocket, miraculously spilling none. Rich now, young again, sane again, down the dirty pavements to her psychic swain. Finn returned to his room.

Putting the money away with the rest in the bag under his

mattress, he reflected once more on Martin Urban's recommendations. At the thought of Lena alone in a small country town, of Lena alone anywhere, he smiled a narrow smile of contempt. For a moment he imagined her removed from Lord Arthur Road, the only place he could remember where she had found fragments of happiness and peace; removed from him and her dear friends and the second-hand shops and her little cosy segmented space. He thought of the terrified feral mania that would overcome her when she smelt the fresh air and felt the wind and had to hunt for sleep, always elusive, in the spacious bedroom of a bungalow.

But Martin Urban, of course, hadn't talked of transferring Lena to the country because he sincerely believed Finn should buy her a house with the money. His talk of prospective house-buying had been the precise equivalent of Kaiafas' references to his homeland and Anne Blake's expressed regret that he had ever left it. They couldn't bring themselves, these squeamish people, to put their desires into plain words. Finn wondered at it. He thought he could simply have said, fixing his water-bright eyes on his listener, "Kill this woman, this man, for me," always supposing he was ever in the unlikely situation of wanting anyone else to do anything for him.

Sitting cross-legged on the floor, he opened a large can of pineapple and ate it with some whole-meal bread and a piece of cheese. He was rather surprised that he hadn't yet been told who his victim was to be. He had expected Martin Urban to bring the money himself and in a note or by circumlocutory word of mouth to give him a name and a description. In the middle of the floor, between the mattress and the pineapple can and other remains of his meal, lay the wrappings from the parcel. They lay in a puddle of sunlight cast by the only sunbeam that had managed to insert itself through the Chinese puzzle of brick walls and penetrate the room. Finn had told Martin Urban to wrap the money up in newspaper, and now his eye was caught by the picture on the front of the copy of the *North London Post* which had been around the notes and under the brown paper covering. He stretched out a long arm, picked up the newspaper and looked more closely at this picture.

He seldom so much as glanced at a newspaper. He had never seen this copy before, but he recognised at once the scene of the photograph. It was the path between the railway bridge and the end of Nassington Road by Parliament Hill Fields. He recognised it because he had been there and because it was there that he had killed Anne Blake—and also because he had seen this photograph

114

in another newspaper, that which Kaiafas had used to wrap *his* payment as a macabre joke.

So Martin Urban knew. Indeed, it must be because Martin Urban knew that he had picked him to do this particular, as yet unspecified, job for him. How did he know? Finn felt a prickling of the skin on his forehead and his upper lip as a little sweat broke. There was no telling how Martin Urban knew, but know he must or why else would he have sent Finn that newspaper with that photograph in it?

The unfamiliar sensation of fear subsided as Finn reflected that Martin Urban would hardly, considering what he was paying for and was about to have done for him, pass his information elsewhere. He shook the newspaper, expecting a note to fall out. He turned the pages slowly, looking for some hint or clue. And there, on page seven, it was.

A paragraph ringed in red ball-point, with a street number inserted and a name underlined. Finn read the paragraph carefully, committing certain details to memory. Then he put on the yellow pullover and the PVC jacket. This was an occasion for covering his distinctively pale hair with a grey woolly hat and his memorable eyes with dark glasses. Both these items of disguise were acquisitions of Lena's. Finn locked his door and went down to the garage in Somerset Grove.

There he replaced his licence plates with a pair bearing the number TLE 315R. These he had two years before removed from a dark brown Lancia which had been left parked in Lord Arthur Road during a day and a night. He had known they would come in useful one day. Slightly disguised and in his slightly disguised van, Finn drove up to Fortis Green Lane and parked a little way down from number 54. It was just on three o'clock.

It was impossible to tell whether the house was at present empty or occupied. The day was chilly, the kind of day that is called raw, with a dirty-looking sky and a damp wind blowing. All the windows in 54 Fortis Green Lane were closed and at the larger of the upstairs windows the curtains were drawn. It was too early to put lights on.

The front garden was composed entirely of turf and concrete, but the concrete predominated. On the strip of it that ran round and was joined to the walls of the house was a dustbin with its lid on the ground beside it. The lid lay inverted with its hollow side uppermost and the wind kept it perpetually rocking with a repetitive faint clattering sound. Finn thought that if there was anyone in the house they would eventually come out to pick up the dustbin lid and stop the noise.

Quite a lot of people passed him, young couples, arm-in-arm or hand-in-hand, older people who had been shopping in Finchley High Road. Their faces looked pinched, they walked quickly because of the cold. Nobody took any notice of Finn, reading his newspaper in his plain grey van.

The dustbin lid continued to rock in exactly the same way until five when a sharper gust of wind caught it and sent it skittering along the concrete to clatter off on to the grass. Still no one came out of the house. Finn gave it another half-hour and then, when he could tell by the continued darkness of the house that it must be empty, he drove home.

Lena was having tea with Mr. Beard. There was a net curtain with scalloped edges spread as a cloth on the bamboo table and this was laden with all the things Lena had bought for tea, lattice pastry sausage rolls and anchovy pizza and Viennese whirls and arctic roll and Mr. Kipling almond slices. Mr. Beard was talking very interestingly about Dr. Dee and the Enochian language in which he was instructed by his spirit teachers, so Finn sat down to have a cup of tea with them. Lena kept giving him fond proud smiles. She seemed entirely happy. He tried to listen to Mr. Beard's account of Dee's Angel, but he found himself unable to concentrate. He kept thinking, turning over in his mind, how was he going to do it? How was he going to kill this stranger he hadn't yet seen and make it look like an accident?

The next day he went back to Fortis Green Lane in the morning. The dustbin and its lid had gone. Finn sat in the van on the opposite side of the wide road this time and watched people cleaning cars and pruning rose bushes. No one came out of or entered number 54, and the bedroom curtains were still drawn.

It wasn't until Monday evening, though he went back again on Sunday afternoon and Monday morning, that his watching was rewarded. First, at about a quarter to seven, a tallish man in early middle age appeared from the Finchley High Road direction, unlatched the white gate, walked up the path and let himself into the house. He was wearing a thigh-length coat of a sleek light brown fur and dark trousers and a dark grey scarf. The appearance of this man rather puzzled Finn who had expected someone younger. He watched lights come on in the hall, then the downstairs front room, then behind the drawn bedroom curtains. The bedroom light went out but the others remained on. After a while Finn went off and had a pineapple juice at the Royal Oak in

116

Sydney Road and then he walked about in Coldfall Wood, in the dark, under the old beech trees with their steely trunks and sighing, rustling boughs. Finn wasn't the kind of person one would much like to meet in a wood in the dark, but there was no one there to meet him.

The lights had gone out in the house when he returned. It was as well for Finn that he was never bored. He sat in the van, on the odd-numbered side of Fortis Green Lane and, putting himself into a trance, projected his astral body to an ashram in the foothills of the Himalayas where it had been before and sometimes conducted conversations with a monk. Such a feat he could now accomplish with ease. The transcending of space was relatively simple. Would he ever accomplish the transcending of time so that he could project himself back into history and forwards into the future?

He slept a little after his astral body had come back and awoke angry with himself in case his quarry had passed by while his eyes were shut. But the house still remained dark. Finn thought he would wait there till midnight, the time now being ten to eleven.

While he had been there cars had passed continually, though the traffic had never been heavy. At just seven minutes to eleven a white Triumph Toledo pulled up outside number 54 and after a little delay a woman got out. She was young and tall with a straight nose and lips curved like the blades of scimitars and hair like a bronze cape in the sulphur light. Finn lowered his window. He expected to see emerge from the car the man in the fur coat, but instead he heard the voice of Martin Urban call softly,

"Good night, Francesca."

That settled for Finn certain questions that had been perplexing him. This was the right place, after all, this was it. He had doubted. He raised his window and watched the woman stand by the gate, then open the gate and walk up one of the concrete strips to a door between the house wall and the boundary fence. She waved to Martin Urban, opened the door and let it close behind her. Finn felt relieved. He watched the white car slowly depart, then gather speed.

As it disappeared into a turning on the right-hand side, his eyes following it, there passed very close to the van's window on the near side, almost brushing the glass, a brown furriness like the haunch of an animal. Finn turned to look. Russell Brown was crossing the road now, unlatching the white gate, walking up the path. Although the woman must now have been in there for at least a minute, no lights had yet come on. Though, since she had

117

entered by the back way, she might have put lights on only in the back regions. Russell Brown unlocked the front door and let himself into the house. Immediately the hall light came on.

Finn switched on his ignition and his lights and drove away.

XVII

It saddened Francesca to have to give in her notice. She had liked working for Kate Ross, being among flowers all day, arranging flowers in the window and in bouquets, delivering flowers and seeing on people's faces the dawning of delighted surprise. Tim had once said that there was something especially flower-like about her and that—he was presumably quoting—her hyacinth hair, her classic face, her naiad airs had brought him home from desperate seas. He had been rather drunk at the time. But there was no help for it; she had to leave. February 24 would be her last day at Bloomers, and Adrian Vowchurch had promised completion of the purchase of the Swan Place flat two days later.

"You'll be too grand, anyway, to work in a flower shop," said Tim, and he put his mouth to the soft hollows above her collar bone. Francesca made purring noises. The air in the room was so cold that their breath plumed up from the bed like smoke. "Why don't you ask Livingstone to buy you a garden centre?"

"That would be pushing it," said Francesca primly. "I think I've done marvels actually. I shan't be getting any more out of him because I shan't be seeing him. Not after he's paid for the flat and that Adrian person has done the what-d'you-call-it. He won't know where to find me when I've left Bloomers."

"He'll be able to find you in delectable Swan Place, though perhaps mah clever honey chile won't give him a key?"

From the electric blanket came up waves of heat that made them both sweat, but that morning Francesca had found ice on the inside of the windows. The atmosphere held a bitter and quite tangible dampness. Tim lit a Gauloise and smoked it in the darkness. The glowing tip of it was like a single star in a cold and smoky sky.

"I don't think I'm going to go there at the beginning. I did think of moving in like he expects me to and after I'd been there a few days stage a tremendous irrevocable sort of row with him and say I never wanted to see him again. But I don't think I could. I'm not good at rows. So what I think now is I'll just stay home here very quietly for two or three days and then I'll write him a letter.

118

I'll tell him in that what I'd have told him in the row, that it's all over but that I know the flat's mine and I need it and I'm going to live in it. How's that? Shall we go and live in that lovely place, Tim, or shall we sell it and buy another lovely place?"

"That will be for you to say."

"What's mine is yours, you know. I think of you as my common law husband. Can you have a common law husband if you've already got an uncommon law one?"

Tim laughed. "I'm wondering what steps, if any, Miss Urban will take when she discovers your *coup*. You'd better not count on keeping the furniture." He drew on his cigarette and the star glowed brightly. "I must say I shan't be sorry when mah honey chile isn't deceiving me every night with another woman."

"You must feel like a ponce," said Francesca. "Ponces never seem to mind, do they?"

"The minding, as you call it, fluctuates in direct proportion to the immoral earnings." He stubbed his cigarette out and turned to her. "It has nothing to do with the activities. Personally, I hope you're giving Livingstone a good run for his money."

"Well, yes and no. Oh, Tim, you've got one warm hand and one icy cold one. It's rather nice—it's rather fantastic...."

Francesca brought Martin a large specimen of *xygocactus truncatus* from the shop. It had come late into flower and now, at the end of February, its flat scalloped stems each bore on its tip a bright pink chandelier-shaped blossom. Martin was childishly, disproportionately, pleased by this gift. He put it on the window sill in the middle of the window with the view over London. It was snowing again, though not settling, and the flakes made a gauzy net between the window and the shining yellow-and-white city.

That was Wednesday and Martin let her go home in a cab, but on Thursday she spent the day and stayed the night in Cromwell Court. Martin took the day off and they bought bed linen and towels, a set of saucepans and a French cast-iron frying pan, two table lamps, a Japanese portable colour television, and a dinner service in Denby ware. These items they took away with them. The three-piece suite covered in jade-green and ivory velvet, the brass-and-glass dining table and eight chairs would, of course, have to be sent. Francesca said she would be bringing her own cutlery and glass. She was bored with shopping for things she doubted she would be allowed to keep.

They had dinner at the Bullock Cart in Heath Street. Martin

said he had heard from John Butler and that he and his wife would move out of Swan Place first thing Monday morning. He would give the key to the estate agent, or if Martin liked he could call in and fetch it himself during the week-end.

"We could collect it on Saturday," said Francesca who could foresee the difficulties of any other course.

When Mr. Cochrane rang the bell at eight-thirty in the morning Francesca opened the door to him. She was wearing the top half of Martin's pyjamas and a pair of blue tights. Martin had come out of the kitchen with the Worcester sauce apron on. His expression was aghast. Mr. Cochrane came in without saying anything, his eyes perceiving the flowering cactus, his nostrils quivering at the scent of Ma Griffe. He closed the door behind him, said, "Good morning, madam," and walked into the kitchen where he put his valise down on the table.

"How's your sister-in-law?" said Martin.

"Home again," said Mr. Cochrane. He looked at Martin through the bi-focals, then carefully over the top of them. Then he said, "Yes, home again, Martin, if you can call it home," and, carrying a tin of spray polish and two dusters, he went into the living room where he scrutinised the cactus and, lifting up each item and examining it, the sheets and towels and saucepans and lamps they had bought on the previous day. At last he turned to Francesca, his death's head face convulsed into a smile.

"What a blessing to see him leading a normal life, madam. I like a man to *be* a man, if you know what I mean."

"I know what you mean all right," said Francesca, giggling.

"Is there anything special you'd like me to do, madam, or shall I carry on as usual?"

"Oh, you carry on as usual," said Francesca. "I always do," and she gave him her best and most radiant smile.

It was her last day at the shop since Kate had said she needn't come in on Saturday morning. Next week, when she had disappeared, would Martin come to the shop and ask Kate about her? It wouldn't really matter what Martin did after Monday, after the deal was completed and the money handed over. Perhaps she should screw up her courage and really move in on Monday afternoon as Martin thought she was going to, move in, invite him that evening—and tell him the truth, that legally the flat was hers and she intended to live in it without ever seeing him again. She would never summon up that courage. The only way was to do as she had told Tim she would do, disappear, write to him, when he made a fuss let Tim explain to him, finally take possession

120

when it had all blown over. The flat is *yours*, hang on to that, she told herself. It's yours in the law and nothing can shake that.

Martin called for her at ten to six and they went back to Cromwell Court where he cooked the dinner. At about eleven he drove her up to Fortis Green Lane and Francesca was again obliged to take refuge in the back garden of number 54. Tonight the house was in darkness. She stood against the stuccoed wall, listening for the car to go. As it happened, she came out too soon. It hadn't been Martin's car but a small grey van pulling away. Martin was still there, still watching the house—watching for lights to come on?

She told him she had left her key in the house and would have to wake Russell to let her in.

"Please go, darling. I'll be all right."

Reluctantly, Martin did go. Francesca was actually trembling. She had to sit down on the low wall for a moment. When she got up and turned round to look warily at the house she half-expected to see its occupant glaring at her from an upper window. But there was no one. It was colder tonight than it had been for a week, the sky a dense unclouded purple and the air very clear. She really needed something warmer on than the red-and-blue-striped coat over her corded velvet smock. Each time Martin landed her up here she tried walking in fresh directions to find a taxi, but now she had exhausted them all. So was it to be down to Muswell Hill or across the Finchley High Road? Martin had headed for Muswell Hill . . . Francesca, who wasn't usually very apprehensive or given to improbable fantasies, found herself thinking, suppose his car broke down and I walked past it and he saw me . . .? Now that her task was so nearly accomplished, she was growing hourly more and more frightened in case anything should happen at the eleventh hour to stop her getting the flat. People said it was virtually impossible to withdraw from such a deal once the contracts were exchanged. He wouldn't have to withdraw, though, he would only have to have a new contract made with his name on it instead of hers.

Nothing must happen. She only had Saturday to get through now. They had agreed not to meet on Sunday, she would be too busy packing. She pulled up the hood of her coat and set off along wide, cold, empty Fortis Green Lane for Finchley High Road. A taxi picked her up just before she reached it.

"I don't usually ever feel nervous about anything, you know," she said to Tim. "I suppose anyone can get nervous if there's enough at stake. While I was sort of lurking in that garden I kept thinking how awful it would be if that man came out of his house. I mean, he might have chased me and Martin might have hit him, thinking he was my husband. I imagined the most fearful things."

Tim laughed. "The most fearful thing about that would have been the outcome, the loss of our future home. Otherwise I can't imagine anything funnier than Livingstone having a punch-up with a complete stranger in the middle of the night in darkest Finchley."

Francesca thought about it. Then she laughed too and helped herself to one of Tim's cigarettes. "What made you pick on that funny house, anyway? What made you pick on that man?"

"Me? I didn't pick on him. I didn't pick on the house. That was your fiancé. Remember? I didn't even know there was anyone called Brown living in Fortis Green Lane. The idea of writing that par for the *Post* was solely to give verisimilitude to your story. People say newspapers are full of lies, but they believe everything they read in newspapers just the same. Fortis Green Lane is a long road and Brown is a common name. There may be half a dozen Browns living there for all I know. Livingstone happened to find this one in the phone book."

With a giggle Francesca said, "It would be most awfully unfair then if Martin had hit him."

"You'll have to take good care he doesn't. He truly is that mysterious individual, the innocent bystander."

There was a heavy frost that night and the roof tops were nearly as white as when they had been covered with snow. Francesca and Tim lay late in bed and Francesca brought Lindsay in with them. They talked about the flat in Swan Place while Lindsay sat on the pillow and braided Francesca's hair. Tim said they would probably have to sell the flat and buy one that wasn't in Highgate, it would be so awkward if they ever ran into Martin. That would be all right, Francesca said, she would quite like to live up near the Green Belt or out towards Epping Forest, she wasn't wedded to London. Nor to the distinguished author of *The Iron Cocoon*, said Tim, and they both laughed so much that Lindsay pinched their lips together.

Tim drove her as near as he dared to Cromwell Court. Martin wanted to know what arrangements she had made for Monday. Had she booked a car? Was Lindsay going to the nursery that day or not? Could she manage all her clothes at one journey? And what about Russell? Had she told him there should be a fair division of their property and had he agreed? Francesca answered these questions as best she could while they were on their way to Swan Place to pick up the key from Mr. Butler. She felt elated when the key was in her possession. A key gives such a secure feeling of rights and privacy and ownership. Mrs. Butler took her round the flat once more, and Francesca could hardly contain her excitement. How different it was to view all this, to tread these soft, subtle-shaded carpets, finger stiff silky curtains, feel the warmth, turn on a tap, press a switch, in the knowledge it was going to be all her own!

"Will you ask me to supper on Monday evening?" Martin said.

"Tuesday. Give me just one day to settle in. Lindsay's bound to be difficult, you know."

"Yes, I suppose so. Tuesday then." His face wore the hurt look that blurred his features and made it dog-like. "Adrian hopes to complete by mid-day on Monday, so you can come any time after. I expect the Butlers will still be moving out."

Francesca didn't see much point in talking about it when she wasn't going to move in at all. She wished she had the nerve to ask Martin what was to be done with the deeds or lease or whatever it was. Deposited in his bank maybe. Not for long, she thought, not for long. Tim would deal with all that, she had done her part, she had almost done it. She held Martin's hand in the car, held it on her knee and said, "Let's not go out to dine, let's have a quiet evening at home on our own."

XVIII

Most of the time there was nobody in the house, but the man was there more often than the woman. This was a reversal, Finn thought, of the usual order of things. He had never seen them together, though he had been to Fortis Green Lane on five evenings now, each time parking in a different place. He had seen the woman twice and the man three times, and once he had seen the man with another woman. This didn't trouble him, nor was he perplexed about the relations of these people to each other or that of Martin Urban to them. Emotions, passion, jealousy, desire, even hatred, were beyond or outside his understanding. They bored him. He preferred magic. He longed now to be able to wield practical magic, to conjure his victim out of the house and into his trap.

But he had lost that power even before the death of Queenie. Sitting in the van, watching, he thought of how, in Jack Straw's, he had concentrated on that reporter and made him get out and light a cigarette. Or had he? Such doubt is the enemy of faith, and it is faith that moves the mountains.

Come out of the house, he said in his mind to the darkened windows, the closed front door, the indestructible stucco. He said it over and over again like the mantras he repeated for his meditation. He had no idea, and no means of knowing, if the house was empty or not. There might be a light on in the downstairs back room or in the kitchen. He had been there since five, since before the dark came down, but there had been no sign of life from the house and no flicker of light.

It was a cold evening, the air already laying frost in a very thin silvery glitter on the tops of fences and the crosspieces of gates, on twigs and laurel leaves and on the oblique rear windows of parked cars. The sulphur light showed tiny early spring flowers in some gardens, pale or white or no-colour buds and bells. Finn didn't know the names of flowers. The frost wasn't heavy enough to whiten the grass much. Inside the van it was cold. Finn wore the yellow pullover and the grey woollen cap and the leather coat and sat reading Crowley's *Confessions*. Back in Lord Arthur Road he had left Lena and Mrs. Gogarty indignant because Mr. Beard, proposing to raise up for their edification Abremelin the Mage, meant to do so by indefencible methods. In fact, by the sacrifice of a pigeon, the emanation from whose blood would provide the material for the seer to build a body out of. Pigeons were commoner than flies in Brecknock Road, Mr. Beard had said. Lena and Mrs. Gogarty shuddered and twittered and sent Mr. Beard to Coventry. Finn wished he was back there with them and the innocent pleasures of Planchette to which they had retreated, scared by Mr. Beard's sophistication.

A light had come on in 54 Fortis Green Lane, a not very strong light as from a sixty-watt bulb, in the hall. It showed through the slit of a window on the right-hand side of the door and through the small diamond-shaped pane of glass in the door itself. No one came out, no one went in. It was ten o'clock. Finn didn't think anything was going to happen tonight. Again it would have to be postponed. That he had taken Martin Urban's money and as yet done nothing to earn it vaguely oppressed him. But because it was a waste of time sitting there any longer, he drove down to Muswell Hill, to the Green Man, and drank two bottles of Britvic pineapple juice.

Sitting alone at a table, he fixed his thought on a fat man in a checkered sports jacket, willing him to get up and go <u>outside to</u>

124

the gents. After about five minutes of this the fat man did get up and go outside, but a smaller thinner man sitting with him had gone out a moment or so before. Finn didn't know what to think. As he came out into the street he was visited by a premonition so intense as almost to blind him. He felt it like a pain in his head.

Tonight *was* the time for it. If he would only seize his opportunity and go back to Fortis Green Lane now, all would be well. In his mind's eye, as on a screen, he saw the house quite clearly, the light shining through and alongside the front door, the front garden with its alternating turf and concrete. He stared into this vision and silently commanded Martin Urban's enemy to appear. At once this happened and Finn seemed to be staring into a pair of puzzled and dismayed eyes. He got into the van and drove back to Fortis Green Lane as fast as he could go.

There was no need to watch and wait. As in his vision, Martin Urban's enemy was in the front garden, unlatching the white iron gate. But this time there was no meeting of eyes.

Finn hadn't even switched off the engine. He watched the figure in the fur coat close the gate and turn immediately left into the side street. For what purpose would anyone go out alone at this time on a Saturday night? Finn knew it was no good judging by himself. He might go out to commune with the powers of darkness but others lacked that wisdom. They would be more likely to visit some friend, a nocturnal person who had no objection to late callers.

He allowed his quarry two minutes' start and then he followed. Martin Urban's enemy was nowhere to be seen. The street was deserted. Coldfall Wood, grey and still under the indigo sky, lay ahead of him. He turned right along the edge of the wood and then he saw the figure in the fur coat ahead of him, a long way ahead, casting an attenuated black shadow as it passed under a lamp. There was scarcely any other traffic; parked cars everywhere but only one that moved, a sports car that passed him, going towards Finchley.

Finn lagged behind, stopped for a while. When he started again, driving slowly, it wasn't long before he came to a sign that indicated the nearness of the North Circular Road. The houses had stopped. Soon the parked cars had stopped. On either side of the road he had turned into stretched open land. Not woods, though, or heath or anything that remotely approximated to real countryside except that grass grew on it. It was a vast acreage of tips, of heaps of rubble, dismantled cars, rusty iron, stacks of wood that looked like collapsed huts, and the overgrown remains of abandoned allotments. The whole of this wilderness was weirdly but brilliantly lit by lamps on tall stems which coated the sky with a shimmering brownish fog and gave to the ground a look of total desolation.

There was no dwelling of any kind in sight. Finn knew that most new approach roads to motorways or trunk roads look like this, that the land only had this appearance of nightmare violation because heavy construction work had not long since taken place on it. Yet knowing this, he still had the feeling of having entered a different and uncanny world, a place where the ordinary usages of life were suspended and the occult reigned. In it he felt alone, he and the bobbing shadow in the distance ahead. He felt too that he might even be invisible, had perhaps discovered unwittingly the secret of invisibility which since the beginning of time magicians had sought for.

A thrill of power ran through him. The clear brown sky seemed to be meshed all over with a dazzling veil of gold. But for a distant throb there was silence. Finn made the van glide slowly along. On the left-hand side, ahead of the moving figure, the pavement petered out. It would be necessary, inevitable, soon to cross that wide curving roadway, white and gold and glittering at close on midnight.

The head above the fur collar turned to the right, to the left, to the right again. The black shadow dipped into the road. Finn was in second gear. He rammed his foot hard down on the accelerator, changed in one movement up into fourth, and shot towards the shining, moving pillar of fur. Now, at last, he saw the eyes, round, gleaming, dark with terror. He had to swerve in pursuit, to make sure. A shattering scream rang through the glittering empty air, arms were flung up in a desperate useless defence, and then, when it seemed as if the suddenly huge, screaming, animal-like shape must flatten and paste itself against his windscreen, he felt it under the van, the wheels crunching flesh and bone.

Finn reversed over the thing he had crushed and then drove over it once more in bottom gear. There was a lot of blood, dark and colourless as Anne Blake's had been, splashed blots of it on the white road. He made a U-turn and drove back the way he had come up. For a yard or so his tyres left their imprints in blood. He would clean those tyres when he changed the licence plates, before he went home to Lena.

XIX

As yet the wood showed no sign of greening but it had grown sparkling brown and the beech trunks silver. Their myriad delicate fronds, for twigs was too solid a word, fanned against a mother-of-pearl sky. Martin was inescapably reminded of Tim. He had a feeling, utterly absurd and one to which he wouldn't have dreamt of yielding, that he should park the car here on the winding bit up to Highgate, and go on a pilgrimage through the wood to find the spot where he had met Tim. The dying day—not so different from a day just born—and the coming spring recalled to him the warmth of that encounter and that other curious feeling which he had felt for no one, not even for Francesca, either before or since.

He drove on. The sky was deepening to lavender and the sunset had brushed it with pink and golden strokes. What had Tim been doing in the wood that morning? Strange that he had never asked himself that question before. While he had come in from Priory Gardens and was walking north, Tim seemed to have entered from the Muswell Hill Road as if he had come from the junction where the Woodman was. Martin was approaching this junction now and it occurred to him that he might go into Bloomers and buy Francesca some spring flowers. Of course he had promised not to see her today, but he would phone her when he got home and if she really didn't want to see him tonight, he would take the flowers to her on his way to work in the morning.

Bloomers, however, was closed and its lights off, though the time was only twenty to six. Martin drove up Southwood Lane and down the High Street to Cromwell Court. No letters had come by the second post. He had written again to Mrs. Cochrane on Friday but perhaps it was too soon yet to expect a reply. In the living room, part on a chair and part on the floor, were still stacked the saucepans, the frying pan, the apricot-and-brown-and-cream-patterned towels, the brown-and-white sheets and pillowcases, and the Denby ware dinner service. Francesca might be in need of those things.

In the flat on Saturday afternoon he had noted the Butlers' phone number. He dialled it now and got the unobtainable signal. The Post Office presumably hadn't let her keep the old number when they came in today to reconnect the phone. Perhaps you always had to have a new number. Should he now phone Tim?

It was three months, more than that, since he had last spoken to Tim. There was nothing really that he would like more tonight, since he couldn't be with Francesca, than to spend a couple of hours with Tim. They hadn't even quarrelled. They had parted because of his own absurd guilt over nothing. He had broken their friendship over that money. And it was nearly all gone now, would all be gone when he had settled with Mrs. Finn and Mrs. Cochrane.

Tim wouldn't be home yet. Martin phoned Adrian Vowchurch and thanked him for getting completion so promptly.

"Francesca move in all right, did she?"

"Oh, yes," said Martin.

"By the by, I had a message, heaven knows why, that there are two more keys with the agents. Okay?"

Martin said it was okay and that he had wondered why there had only been one key. He kept Adrian talking for a while in the hope that he might invite him and Francesca round one evening, but Adrian didn't. He said he must fly because he and Julie were going out to dinner with the senior partner and his wife. Martin thought it likely that Francesca would phone once she had got Lindsay to bed and off to sleep. He drank some whisky, he made himself an omelette with four eggs and two rashers of bacon and a lot of mushrooms, and when he had eaten it and washed up it was half-past eight.

The phone rang at nine. It was Norman Tremlett. Norman lived at home with his parents, and he wanted to know if Martin would bring Francesca to dinner on the evening of Saturday week. Martin didn't much want to dine with the Tremletts, but he felt excited at the idea of having the right to accept for himself and Francesca just as if they were already a married couple, so he said yes, they'd like to.

Just as it had previously been too early, it now seemed too late to phone Tim, too late anyway for them to arrange to meet and go out anywhere that night. He would phone Tim tomorrow or the next day. For the first time since the autumn Martin unlocked the glass door and went out on to the balcony. The night was cool but the sky was so unusually clear that you could see the stars, though so tiny and faint that it was as if the gloomy pall of London had pushed them even greater distances into space. Francesca wasn't going to phone tonight. He realised it with resignation, but it was silly to feel such intense disappointment. She would be tired after her long day, which had started perhaps with a final quarrel with Russell and ended with Lindsay's tantrums, and by now she might well be asleep.

128

The post brought a letter, not from Mrs. Cochrane, but from her brother-in-law. The tone was that of Mr. Cochrane's notes, clipped and censorious. It began "Dear Martin," and the gist of it was that he and Mrs. Cochrane would come to Cromwell Court that evening, eight o'clock if this was convenient. Martin looked in the phone book to see if Mr. Cochrane was on the phone and found, to his surprise, that he was. But when he dialled the number there was no answer. He would have to try again later. This evening he was to dine with Francesca in Swan Place, so of course he couldn't see Mr. and Mrs. Cochrane.

He drove to work via Shepherd's Hill, thus passing close by Stanhope Avenue, but Francesca's windows weren't visible. It was a nuisance having no phone number for her. He had an appointment with a client at eleven, which eventually lengthened over lunchtime, and it was half-past two before he got back.

Francesca hadn't phoned.

"Are you positive there haven't been any calls for me?"

Caroline, with black-varnished fingernails today and red hair cropped to a crew cut, said that of course she was positive; he ought to know she didn't make mistakes like that.

"Okay, well, would you like to get hold of directory enquiries and find if they've got a number for Brown of Flat 10, Swan Place, Stanhope Avenue, Highgate?"

She came back after about five minutes. "No, they haven't, Martin, and I'm quite *positive*. He was a very nice man at directory enquiries, got a voice just like Terence Stamp."

So the Post Office hadn't yet got around to fixing Francesca's phone. She was probably waiting in for them, which could be why she hadn't phoned him from a call box. It didn't matter particularly, he would just go straight there on his way from work.

He left at five-thirty sharp. Swan Place was, if anything, more attractive than Cromwell Court. The block was newer and there were lifts and carpet on the stairs. Martin smiled to himself to think he had spent more on Francesca's home than he had on his own. He went up in the lift and rang the bell of number 10.

No one came. He rang again. She was out. What on earth was she doing out now? Wasn't she expecting him? He wondered where she could have gone at this hour when nearly all the shops were closed. Perhaps to tea with some friend who had a child of Lindsay's age? Martin had never heard of any friend of Francesca's apart from Annabel. He hung about outside the door, wishing he had thought of calling in at the estate agents to collect those other keys. They would be shut now.

He waited nearly half an hour for her. Then he wrote a note on the back of an envelope he found in his pocket and put it through the letter box. The note said to phone him as soon as she got in.

It began to worry him thinking something might have happened to her. Suppose Russell had asked her to go back and have a talk with him and was preventing her from leaving again? He drank some whisky, not too much because he was sure to have to drive again that evening. There was nothing to eat in the flat apart from bread and cheese and things in tins.

The phone didn't ring but at just before eight the doorbell did. Martin was sure it was Francesca who had thought that if she had to go out into the street to find a call box, she might as well get in a taxi and come straight to him. On the doorstep stood Mr. Cochrane and a very small woman in a scarlet coat and black fur pixie hood. He had forgotten all about them.

"Evening, Martin. This is Mrs. Cochrane, Martin. Rita, this is Martin."

Mr. Cochrane was in casual gear, denim jeans, a fairisle pullover and a kind of anorak with fur trimmings. Martin felt bereft of ideas and almost of speech by the sight of them. But there was no help for it. Mr. Cochrane hadn't waited to be invited in or asked to sit down. He had gone in, taken his sister-in-law's coat and hat, seated her on the sofa, hung up her coat and his own in the hall cupboard, and was now alternately rubbing his hands and warming them on a radiator.

"Would you like a drink?" Martin said.

"Whisky for me, Martin, and Mrs. Cochrane will have a lemonade with a drop of port in it."

Martin had neither port nor lemonade. Every bottle had to be removed from the drinks cupboard before Mr. Cochrane could decide on a substitute. His sister-in-law hadn't opened her mouth. When she was at last given a wine glass containing a mixture of sweet red vermouth and soda she nodded her head very fast and on and on as if she had a spring where her neck should be. Her mouth had set into a pinched, tight, and intensely nervous smile.

Mr. Cochrane, now sitting on the radiator, launched into a speech. His attitude was one which Martin hadn't met before in his dealings with the objects of his charity. His sister-in-law was prepared to accept Martin's offer—here Mrs. Cochrane, who hadn't ceased to smile, began nodding again—provided she was allowed absolute freedom of choice as to where she lived and what kind of dwelling she lived in. Also Martin must understand

130

that one must move with the times, things had changed out of all knowledge in the past few years and you couldn't buy anything worth considering in the London area for less than fifteen thousand pounds. At this point the phone rang and Martin leapt for it. It was a wrong number. Mr. Cochrane said that he supposed it was all right to help himself to more whisky, did so, and terminated his speech with words to the effect that now they understood each other and had cleared the air he would start house-hunting in the morning.

Martin felt he only wanted to get rid of them. If it cost him his last five thousand did it so much matter? He realised that that was what it would do, it would all be gone. Deliberately and methodically he half-filled his glass with whisky and drank it at a gulp.

"I'm glad to be of help," he said. "It's good we've been able to arrange things so easily."

The phone rang. It was Norman Tremlett to ask if Martin and Francesca could make it Saturday fortnight instead of Saturday week. Martin said yes and he would call Norman back. Mr. Cochrane had got himself into his anorak and his sister-in-law into her coat and pixie hood and was staring piercingly at the stack of saucepans and china and towels and bed linen.

"If I don't see madam on Friday, Martin, you can tell her I mean to commence the spring cleaning. Subject to her approval, of course."

Martin didn't know what to say to this.

"Come along, Rita."

Martin closed the door on them and finished his whisky. There was only about an inch left in the bottle so he had that too. After the phone had rung the second time he had made up his mind to drive round to Swan Place as soon as the Cochranes had gone. But he couldn't go now, he had drunk too much. He slept heavily and dreamlessly that night, awakening early with a headache.

But a quarter to nine he was ringing Francesca's doorbell. He continued to ring it long after there was no point. Then it occurred to him that she might still be taking Lindsay to the nursery and he wrote her another note, on the back of the bill for the sheets and towels this time, asking her to phone him before lunch.

When it got to twelve, to half-past, and she hadn't phoned he began to feel real anxiety for the first time. He excused himself to Gordon Tytherton with whom he had said he would have lunch, and went back to Swan Place. Francesca was still out. He simply didn't know what to do, and then he remembered the two spare keys. He drove up to Highgate Village and was given the keys without demur by the estate agent's receptionist.

His notes were still on the doormat. That was the first thing he absorbed. The second—though this took some time fully to register—was that no one had occupied the place since the departure of the Butlers. There were the carpets on the floors and the curtains at the windows, the chairs and tables, the fridge and the cooker and an electric kettle, but there was no food in the kitchen, the fridge door still stood open after Mrs. Butler's final defrosting, and in the bathroom there was no soap, no toothbrush. Martin went into both bedrooms to find that the beds hadn't been made up. The cupboard in the main bedroom was empty but for five wire coat hangers.

For a while he was nonplussed. He sat down in the penthouse living room by the window that was even bigger than his own in Cromwell Court. But almost immediately he jumped up again. The first thing he must do, obviously, was phone her at home in Fortis Green Lane. For some reason, because she was ill or Lindsay was ill or Russell had intervened and used force, she had been prevented from leaving home on Monday.

Rejecting the idea of phone boxes, which he had hardly ever in his life had occasion to use, he drove home to Cromwell Court. There, for the first time, he dialled the number the directory gave for H. R. Brown of 54 Fortis Green Lane, N. 10. The bell rang unanswered. She couldn't be at home ill. He felt rather sick, with a hangover perhaps or hunger. He made himself a cheese sandwich but he couldn't eat it. The idea of taking the afternoon off to look for Francesca didn't cross his mind. He tried the phone again and then he went back to work, remembering a fear that had come to him during the first days of their acquaintance when she had told him nothing of her circumstances or history and had withheld from him her address. He had wondered what he would do if she left her job, for the flower shop had been the only place where he could be sure of finding her.

Bloomers was again closed and unlit when he drove past it just before six. He went home and poured himself a stiff brandy because all the whisky was gone. He thought inconsequentially how a week ago he could have afforded cases of whisky without thinking about it, but not now. He had no more money now than on the last occasion he sent in Tim's pools perm.

No one was answering the phone at 54 Fortis Green Lane. He tried it four times between six and seven. Immediately after he put the phone back for the fourth time it rang. Norman Tremlett. Why hadn't he rung back last night as he had promised? Martin dealt with Norman as best he could, trying not to lose his temper at facetious questions about his "lovely betrothed" and when the "happy day" was to be. As soon as he could terminate the conversation he did. He grilled the steak he had brought in with him and ate it without enjoyment. The brandy bottle beckoned him, but he knew that if he drank any more he wouldn't dare drive up to Finchley.

He could tell the house was empty before he even got out of the car. What now? Enquire of the neighbours as he had enquired for Annabel? After sitting in the car for an aeon of minutes, after some painful soul-searching, he tried number 52.

A girl of about fifteen came to the door. He might have been speaking to her in Hausa or Aramaic for all her comprehension.

At last she said, "You what?"

He realised he had asked questions which, in these lawless times, give rise to deep suspicion. The girl went away to fetch her mother. Martin rehearsed in his mind better ways of eliciting information, but they weren't much better. The woman appeared, drying her hands on a tea towel.

"I'm sorry," Martin began, "I know you must think this very odd, but I only want to know if Mr. and Mrs. Brown next door are away. I'm"—it wasn't exactly true but what else could he say?—"a friend of theirs."

It was as if he had demanded payment for goods she hadn't bought or even wanted. She gave a humourless, cynical laugh.

"That's not true for a start. There is no Mrs. Brown. He's a widower. He's been a widower for all of five years."

Martin couldn't speak.

Perhaps she sensed that he had had a shock. Her manner softened. "Look, you could be anybody, couldn't you, for all I know? Such a lot of funny things go on these days. He's not in, you can see that. I haven't seen him since Saturday, but that doesn't mean a thing. He keeps himself to himself."

She had closed the door before Martin was half-way down the path. His hands shook when he got hold of the steering wheel. He flexed them and took deep breaths and tried to blank out his mind. When he tried again his hands were steady. It wasn't more than a couple of miles down to Highgate, though he was slowed up by the rain which had suddenly begun and now was lashing down.

The phone was ringing as he walked into the flat. He thought that if it was Francesca he wouldn't know what to say, he would be able to find no words in which to speak to her, to ask, even to begin. What she had done to him he didn't know, only that it was terrible.

He picked up the phone. There were pips, six of them.

A voice said, "This is Finn speaking."

XX

"Yes," Martin said. "yes?" He had forgotten who Finn was and the flat low voice meant nothing to him.

"I thought I'd have heard from you by now."

Heard from him? Oh, yes. Finn was Mrs. Finn's son and Mrs. Finn was... He was surprised to hear his own voice sounding so normal, so characteristic even. "You've been successful, have you?"

A short toneless "Yes."

Martin was getting used to ingratitude. He no longer cared. "I'll send the rest round like I did the first lot, okay?"

"In cash again," said Finn and put the phone down.

It was still only nine o'clock. Martin poured himself some more brandy but he couldn't drink it, the smell of it made him feel sick. Was it possible that the woman in the house next door had been lying? Why should she, except from madness or motiveless malevolence? Francesca didn't live there, had never lived there. But he had seen her go into the house... No, he had never quite seen that. He remembered little things, that insistence on taxis, her refusal ever to invite him into the house. Where was she now?

She must have a home somewhere. She hadn't come to him like some fairy woman out of the sea or from another world. Surely she had loved him...? There must be some motive for the lies she had told him, but that motive might not in itself be evil. He tried to think of reasons for it, sitting there in the chair by the window long into the night. At last he drank up the brandy and went to bed. London went on glittering down there as if nothing had happened.

Next day the world had become a different place. The day was cold and wet, a high wind blowing. He awoke to some sense of indefinable misery. A moment later it was no longer indefinable but had settled into the knowledge that Francesca had deceived him.

The wind was blustery and sharp. He saw it blow someone's umbrella inside out as he crossed the Archway Road. The lights weren't on in Bloomers but it wasn't yet nine-thirty. Stuck up on the door, on the inside of the glass, was a notice that hadn't been there last week. *Closed till Monday, March 5*. He turned away. Kate Ross could be ill or just taking a holiday. He went back to his car and drove to work.

Kate would be bound to have Francesca's true address. There were a dozen or so people in the phone book called K. Ross but none in Highgate where Kate lived. Or where Francesca had said she lived. Could he believe anything Francesca had told him?

Her parents lived in Chiswick. Her maiden name had been Blanch. But was that true? There was an E. Blanch in a place called Petrarch Court, Barrowgate Gardens, Chiswick. She had said they lived in a flat, an old mansion block. She had said, she had said . . . He dialled the number, tried to resign himself to hearing a voice say she had no daughter, had never even been married.

A man answered. He sounded elderly, as if he might be retired.

"I'm trying to get in touch with your daughter, Francesca Brown."

There was a dense silence. Then, "I might say I don't have a daughter."

Martin didn't know what to say. He nearly put the receiver down. But the old voice, very dry now, said, "I haven't seen Francesca for five years." There came a crackling chuckle. "She was never very filial. A cold-hearted girl. I can give you her husband's phone number, though God knows when she left him. She leaves everybody."

Martin said he would have the number. He wrote it down.

"That's right," said Mr. Blanch. "Russell Brown's his name, but he'll be out now. At work. She hasn't by any chance left *you*, has she?"

The exchange was an East London one, Ilford or Stratford. Had Francesca given him the Fortis Green Lane address because she was ashamed of her real one? He seemed to hear the dry rasping voice again, "God knows when she left him. She leaves everybody." There had been a bitter cynical amusement underlying Mr. Blanch's words. For the first time Martin felt the absurdity of his position, the humiliation. How was he going to explain to his parents, to Norman and Adrian, that he had bought Francesca a flat and she had left him without even living in it. "She leaves everybody. . . ."

He couldn't think of an excuse for getting out of dinner with his parents. His mother, drinking oloroso, said she had half-expected Francesca too, though she supposed that would have meant a baby-sitter for the little girl. Mr. Urban leant against the mantelpiece with his amontillado. Martin had three glasses of Tio Pepe, wondering where Francesca was now and who Lindsay's father was and why she had lied to him so that it seemed almost everything she had said was a lie.

"Do you think Francesca would like me to make her a patchwork skirt?" said Mrs. Urban.

Martin said he didn't know, which was the answer he would have been obliged to make to any question put to him about Francesca.

"I don't care for them myself," said his mother, "but she looks the type to wear them."

Martin left early, having taken from the bathroom cabinet one of the sleeping pills his mother had for when she went on holiday. He was home by half-past nine. What did he hope to learn, anyway, by phoning Russell Brown? According to her father, "God knows when" Francesca had left him, years ago perhaps; he couldn't be Lindsay's father. At last he did try the number that Mr. Blanch had given him, but there was no answer. He took the Mogadon tablet and washed it down with brandy and went to bed.

Mr. Cochrane, arriving at eight-thirty in the morning, made no reference to the events of Tuesday evening. He had brought Martin's letters up with him, having encountered the postman on the way in. Martin didn't open them, didn't so much as glance at them. He was in no mood for bills or for querulousness from Miss Watson or the Gibsons which he felt those envelopes might contain.

He carried the saucepans and the frying pan, the dinner service, the two lamps, the bed linen and towels into his bedroom and stuffed them into the bottom of the clothes cupboard. They would come in useful one day, he thought with dry anger, for other people's wedding presents.

Mr. Cochrane, in his ironmonger's coat, was emptying cupboards and shelves on to the kitchen floor, the first stage of his spring cleaning. On the table were the two piles of newspapers, the broadsheets and the tabloids.

"Beats me what you want all this muck for, Martin," said Mr. Cochrane. "Hoarding up rubbish like an old woman."

Martin took no notice. He was looking through the *Posts* for the copy of December 8, the one that had contained the paragraph about Russell Brown. Surely it had been on the top because it was

136

the last one he had ever received; after that he had stopped taking the *Post*. Then he remembered. He must have used it to wrap up Mrs. Finn's money. Naturally he had used the paper that was on top of the pile. Mrs. Finn. Some time today, he thought, he had better go to the bank and draw out the other five thousand, phone them first maybe as he had done last time . . .

He had been at work ten minutes when Adrian Vowchurch phoned. He said it was rather embarrassing (he didn't sound embarrassed), but he simply had to know whether his account for the conveyance was to go to Francesca or to Martin.

Martin hadn't expected an account at all. It was true that Adrian had charged him for the conveyance of his own flat, but since then he, Martin, had put in a whole lot of hours sorting out some family trust muddle for Julie and he wouldn't have dreamt of expecting payment for that. He said shortly,

"To me, of course. Who else?"

"My dear old chap, I only asked. Ladies get very uptight these days if their equality isn't respected. Francesca is a property owner now and a ratepayer. It can go to their heads, you know, and you do rather . . ."

"Adrian . . ." he interrupted but he couldn't finish.

"What? I was merely going to say—if merely is the word—that you do rather talk as if her flat was sort of yours. You can't have it both ways, avoid your tax *and* keep a foot in the door."

The flat was hers. Did she know that? He had never exactly explained this to her but she must know it, she was no fool. If she knew it was hers, surely she would come to it. He put his head round his father's door to say he was going out for an hour. Walter Urban was preoccupied with a client's letter. He looked up, irritability making him more than usually dog-faced.

"Extraordinary chap," he said, tapping the letter. "Calls himself the chairman of a financial PR company and he doesn't know the first thing about finance. Here he is telling me he's given away— *given*, if you please—ten thousand pounds to his sister to start some sort of business and can he get tax relief on it? He won't find the government giving anything to him, he'll be giving it to them. Hasn't he ever heard of CTT?"

"CTT?" repeated Martin, although he knew perfectly well what those initials stood for.

"Capital Transfer Tax. Wake up, Martin. His sister's not a charity. Why didn't he consult me before he started throwing his money about?"

Martin asked himself why he too hadn't consulted Walter or

even consulted his own knowledge. Was it because he hadn't wanted to know and have his noble-hearted schemes spoiled? Just as he hadn't wanted to know of the true relations between Francesca and her husband? Now, in both cases, he was going to have to pay for wilfully shutting his eyes. Almost all his money was gone and he was presumably going to have to pay tax at least on what he had given Miss Watson and Mrs. Cochrane, though perhaps not Mrs. Finn since that was cash...Was he planning on being dishonest about it as well? He pushed all thought of money out of his mind—did he really care about it at this juncture?—and drove to Swan Place. The flat was just as it had been on Wednesday, empty, waiting, the fridge door open, the carpet marked with circular depressions where furniture legs had stood.

He had wanted to tell Adrian about it but he hadn't been able to. Adrian's voice had been too cool, too mocking and urbane. He thought of those friends of his whose advice he could ask—Norman, the Tythertons. They couldn't help him any more than he could help himself, and behind his back, because they were deeply conservative and unshakeably conventional, they would laugh nervously.

Back in the office, he reverted to that paragraph in the *Post*. He could remember perfectly what it had said. Russell Brown was thirty-five, was a teacher in a technical college who had written a book about the fourteenth century and the Black Death, wife, Francesca, daughter, Lindsay. Martin sighed and dialled the Ilford number Mr. Blanch had given him. There was no answer.

Could the *Post* have got it wrong? Could it have been Fortis Green Road or Fortis Green Avenue instead? That wouldn't explain how Francesca had seemed to live, had repeatedly said she lived, in Fortis Green Lane. The *Post* must have some sort of clue to all this and he knew someone who worked on the *Post*...

Tim Sage.

Tim might not know the answer, but Tim would be able to help him. Journalists always knew how to go about finding elusive addresses and phone numbers, and elusive people, come to that. And it was foolish to think of himself and Tim as enemies. Why did he do that? There had been no quarrel except in his own mind and in his dreams.

He dialled the *Post*'s head office in Wood Green. No, Mr. Sage wasn't there but he could try their Child's Hill office. Martin tried Child's Hill and was told Mr. Sage hadn't been in all day. It was always hard to get hold of Tim. In the old days—he thought of pre-November as the old days—it was nearly always Tim who had phoned him. A feeling of desolation crept over him. He sat at his desk, unable to work for the first time in as long as he could remember.

It was about an hour later that Caroline came in to say that an Indian family had arrived and were asking for Mr. Urban.

"A man and a woman and a little boy and an old man and an old woman who looks just like Mrs. Gandhi."

He stared at her.

"What do they want?"

"You," said Caroline. "They've just got back from India today, or some of them have, and they've been in Australia first and they want to see you and thank you for something. That's what they said."

The Bhavnanis.

For months he had hoped to see them, had longed, though never quite admitting it to himself, for some crumb of gratitude from someone. And now they had come he knew he couldn't face them.

"Take them in to my father," he said. "He's called Mr. Urban too." Although it was only four he walked out of the office and drove back to Swan Place where he sat by the window, waiting for Francesca to come, although he knew she wouldn't come.

Samphire Road. Martin found it in the London Atlas he kept in the glove compartment of his car. It was Finsbury Park really, North Four. He didn't think he had ever been there or known anyone else who lived there.

If Tim was out he would sit in the car and wait for him. He would wait till midnight if necessary, he had nothing else to do. But he probably wouldn't have to wait like that because the man Tim lived with would be there. Why had he ever worried about having to meet this man, about seeing him and Tim together? He couldn't have cared less now.

It was getting on for six when Martin left Swan Place. If Tim had had an afternoon job he would be home by now, and if he had an evening job it was unlikely he would go out before seven. He and his friend might be eating their evening meal. Martin recalled the big red sofa he had dreamed about, red velvet, sponge-like yet dusty. It embarrassed him even to think of it.

He drove up Crouch End Hill and down Hornsey Rise. The sky was like a thick grey veil which the sunset had torn open to show through the rents radiant flesh colours. He would tell Tim everything, he thought, and the prospect of being able to be open and candid with Tim at last filled him with a joy so intense that his hands actually trembled on the wheel. For a moment he forgot the loss of Francesca and the bitter, growing disillusionment. The secret he had kept from Tim for three months had weighed upon him—how heavily he was only now realising—and at last, within a few minutes perhaps, he was about to unburden himself. That his purpose in coming here was to question Tim about the paragraph in the *Post* had receded and dimmed in the fierce light of the confession, the money and its source, Francesca, his long silence and coldness, he was going to make. He longed for it as the devout sinner longs for the confessional and the exhausted tormented prisoner for a chance to admit his guilt.

He had entered a desolate wilderness where streets, walled in wooden barricades, traversed a grassless, treeless, and almost building-less waste. A few new houses, in strange colours of brick, lemon, pasty white, charcoal, rose here and there in straggling lines. The old streets of old brown houses clung to the perimeter like low cliffs surrounding a crater in a desert. Martin found Samphire Road quite easily, even though his map no longer gave a very clear idea of the lay-out. It was a gorge in the brown cliff with shabby houses which made Martin think of the living quarters in some aged and perhaps abandoned garrison. Compared to it, Fortis Green Lane was paradise.

He walked up broken concrete steps to the liver-coloured front door and pressed the bell marked Sage. Nothing happened for a moment and then a light came on behind the green-and-yellow glass transom over the door. He was aware now that he could smell Gauloise smoke, as if Tim hadn't long come in.

The door opened and Tim stood there. He wore jeans and an old grey, heavy, stringy sweater that made him look thinner than ever, gaunt almost. His face was very pale, his mouth as red as fresh blood. Had he always been so pale? He took the cigarette out of his mouth and said,

"I thought you'd turn up. It was only a matter of time before you cottoned on."

Martin stared at him. He didn't know what he meant. Then something so strange happened, so amazing really, that temporarily he forgot all about Tim. The door at the end of the passage opened and a child came running out and towards them. The child was, must be, but couldn't be, Lindsay.

She came to an abrupt halt and looked at Martin. Her look was full of anger and dislike. She threw herself against Tim's legs, holding up her arms. Tim lifted her up and held her against his shoulder, black hair against black hair, sallow velvet skin touching sallow waxen skin. Four blue eyes looked at Martin. He felt the earth move under his feet, the walls tilt, the dark, frowsy, un-carpeted passage rock back and forth and steady itself.

"You'd better come in," said Tim.

Martin came in and felt the door closed behind him. He was unable to speak. He took a few steps down the passage, then turned, shaking, to contemplate again Lindsay and her undoubted father. But Francesca was her undoubted mother...

"I don't understand," he began. "You and Francesca...Where's Francesca?"

Tim put the child down. He leant against the door, his arms folded. "She's dead. You didn't know? No, I reckon—well, how could you? She was killed last Saturday night, run over, the car didn't stop."

Lindsay, clinging to his legs, began suddenly to cry.

XXI

Lindsay's screams seemed to express the grief of both men; Tim's sorrow, Martin's stunned, incredulous dismay. They were both silent, oblivious of the sobs and howls, the stamping feet, the fists beating at Tim's legs. They stared at each other, but Martin was the first to let his gaze drop and to turn away. Slowly Tim reached down and picked Lindsay up. She stopped screaming but continued to sob, her arms and legs clamped against him like a starfish.

A door opened upstairs and a woman's voice called,

"Everything okay, Tim? God, she was making a racket."

Tim went to the foot of the stairs with Lindsay in his arms. "Could you have her for half an hour, Goldie?"

"Sure, if you want. She'll have to watch telly, though, it's my serial on."

"Lindsay wants Goldie!" The child scrambled down her father's body and up the stairs on all fours.

"You'd better come in here and have a drink," said Tim. "We could both use a drink."

He led Martin down the passage into the room from which Lindsay had emerged. It was a kitchen, modernised in skimpy patches round the sink area and unit of cupboards, but otherwise dismally old-fashioned with a defunct boiler in one corner and, in the wall facing them, a fireplace whose flue was blocked up with red crepe paper. The oven was on and so was a wall heater.

On the table, which was littered with newspapers and Gauloise packets, were the remains of a meal and a half-empty bottle of Dominic's Military gin.

Martin moved as if in a daze. Tim motioned him to one of the small shabby fireside chairs that flanked the wall heater, but Martin sat, or sank, into a bentwood chair at the table and put his head in his hands.

"D'you want it neat or with water?"

"Doesn't matter."

Martin had never before drunk gin without tonic or martini or some other fancy mixer. He had never drunk it warm which this was. It tasted so disgusting that he gave a strong shudder, but the fiery stuff bolstered him. He turned to look at Tim with haggard eyes. Tim was watching him with something that might have been despair or just indifference. When he spoke it was in a cool detached voice, such as a sociologist might use, reporting on failure, misery, defeat.

"I'll tell you what the police told me and fill in the gaps from my own knowledge. After you'd dropped her at that place in Finchley she went to look for a taxi to take her home. It wasn't the first time. It's not easy to find taxis up there. She walked a long way, nearly up to the North Circular." Tim paused, resuming in the same flat voice. "You can't see how anyone could have failed to see her crossing the road, it's so brightly lit. Maybe the guy was drunk or just not looking. Another motorist found her ten minutes afterwards—or that's what they think. She wasn't dead. She died in hospital on Sunday evening."

Martin said softly, "She lived all that time . . . ?"

"She wasn't conscious. Have some more gin?"

Tim refilled their glasses. He lit another cigarette. The only sign of emotion he gave was the way he drew on that cigarette, with nervous, greedy gasps.

"Right," he said. "Question time."

The gin was making Martin hot and dizzy and brave. "Were you *married* to Francesca?"

Tim laughed, a sound that had nothing to do with amusement. "You know better than that. You're my accountant. Wouldn't I have had to tell you if I'd been married? Francesca was still married to a guy in Ilford. He's called Russell Brown, *he* really is."

"But that piece in your paper . . ."

"Pieces in the paper are of human origin. They're not messages from some infallible source of truth." Tim shrugged. "I made it

142

up, bar the names. You found the house yourself. I didn't tell you she lived at 54 Fortis Green Lane and, incidentally, neither did she. You fabricated it. You made conjecture into truth just as you did when you saw those bruises on Francesca and thought Russell had put them there. In fact, she'd fallen over on the ice like several thousand other people did that day."

Martin was silent. Then he said slowly, "Do you mean that it was all a conspiracy between you and Francesca? All of it?" The enormity of what had been done to him was now breaking over Martin in waves. He could feel a pulse drumming in his head. "You both of you set out to con me, to get"—he understood now—"a flat out of me? You were two—criminals who did that?"

"At the beginning," said Tim, "Francesca set out only to get money or a piece of jewellery. I knew about your pools win, of course. I've known from the first. You must have forgotten that though I'm not much of a success at things I've got a spectacularly good memory." He took a gulp of gin and it made him shudder. "You aren't the soul of generosity, are you? I got nothing and she got nothing until you hit on your bright idea of a tax dodge. By that time, as you accountants might say, she was in for a penny, in for a pound."

Martin had got to his feet. He swayed and steadied himself. There was one thing still, one last thing. If she had been unfaithful to Russell Brown with Tim, she had been unfaithful to Tim with him. He looked into Tim's eyes and the voice which he meant to be defiant, spitting revelations, came out falteringly.

"She slept with me! Did she ever tell you that?"

Tim had half-risen, his mouth smiling, his eyes dead. He shrugged. "So? It was hard work. There was no question of mixing pleasure with business."

Without thought or preparation, Martin hit him. He doubled his fist and swung and struck Tim on the jaw. Tim let out a grunt and fell back into the chair, but he was up again straightaway, leaping on Martin with both hands raised. Martin ducked and struck out again and fell across the table, knocking over the lamp which rolled on to the floor and went out.

The room was dark but for the fierce red glow from the wall heater, so that redness lay on the air and on the furniture and on Tim, backed against the door, a demon, a fallen angel, painted with red light. He came at Martin again, punching to his face, but this time Martin seized him by the shoulders, by his thin hard rib cage. For a moment they remained upright, locked together, struggling, then they tumbled to the floor and rolled, clutching each other, into the deep dark shadows of the floor and across the thick, old, rumpled rug.

Tim was trying to grab his shoulders so as to beat his head against the ground. Martin was stronger. He was bigger and heavier than Tim, and more powerful. He got hold of Tim's wrists and held them behind his back, wrapping him in his arms.

With this success, this subduing of Tim, a tremendous excitement seized him. He was wrestling with Tim, he was doing what he had longed to do in those dreams. And in the pressure of Tim's hard flesh, the friction of his body writhing and turning so that they rolled this way and that, embraced so tightly that each body seemed to penetrate the other and fuse with it, he felt himself charged and stiff with desire. He felt a passion which made his relations with Francesca seem thin and cold.

Whether Tim realised or not he didn't care. He was lost to all caution and all inhibiting restraint. He spoke Tim's name in a hoarse whisper and the struggling slackened. There was a moment in which Martin hardly seemed to breathe and then, because he couldn't help himself, he put his mouth over Tim's and gave him a long, enduring kiss. The release that came with that kiss seemed to take with it the repressive burdens of a lifetime. He rolled away from Tim and lay on his face.

Tim got up first. He did what he would do on the gallows or at an H-bomb early warning. He lit a Gauloise. His mouth quirked up on one side at Martin and he gave a sort of half-wink. Martin was flooded with shame, the burdens of a lifetime were still there. He got to his feet and sat, hunched, in one of the fireside chairs.

"Don't put the light on."

"Okay, not if you don't want."

"I'm sorry about that. Just now, I mean." Martin tried not to mumble. He tried to look at Tim through the red gloom, to meet his eyes and speak lucidly. It was nearly impossible. "I don't know why I did that."

"It was the military gin. The fact is, it's meant for guardsmen and you know what guardsmen are."

"I'm not queer, gay, whatever you call it."

"It was the gin, love," said Tim.

He had perched himself on the edge of the table. Martin managed to focus on him now, and if he was flushed it didn't show in that light. "Perhaps I am, though," he said in a low voice. "Perhaps I am really and I never knew it. Why have there been so many things I didn't know and couldn't see, Tim?"

" 'Humanity treads ever on a thin crust over terrific abysses.'

I remember I said that to you before all this started. We've both fallen in with a crash, haven't we?"

Martin nodded. He was embarrassed still and ashamed still, but a warmth that had nothing to do with the heater was slowly engulfing him. He loved Tim, he knew it now. Nothing that Tim had done to him mattered any more. He said,

"That flat, the one Francesca was going to move into, you can have it. I want you to have it."

"Is it yours to give, my dear?"

"Well, I..." Technically, legally, it wasn't. It was the technical, the legal, aspect which mattered, though.

"It'll be shared between four people, I should think. Francesca had a husband and a child and parents. Lindsay will get some of it and I suppose Russell Brown will get most of it."

"Tim, I'll give you..." What? He had nothing left to give. "I want to do something. We've both lost Francesca, that ought to bring us together, it ought to... what are you smiling at?"

"Your naïvety."

"I can't see that it's naïve to want to help someone because you feel you owe it to them. Look, I could sell my flat and buy a small house somewhere—well, not so nice, and you could bring Lindsay and come and live there with me and... We have to be friends, Tim."

"Do we, my dear? I've injured you and we dislike those we've injured." Tim walked across the room and switched on the central light. It was bright, glaring, uncompromising. "I'm sorry for what I did now, I bitterly regret it, but being sorry doesn't make me like you any more. I wouldn't dream of sharing a house with you, and if you offered me money I should refuse it." He stubbed out his cigarette, coughing a little. "It's time you went home now. I have to fetch Lindsay and put her to bed."

Martin got up. He felt as if he had been hit in the face with something cold and wet, a wet glove perhaps.

"Is that all?" he stammered. "Have we said it all?"

Tim didn't answer. They were out in the icy dank hallway now and from upstairs, distantly, came a wail, "Lindsay wants Daddy."

Tim opened the front door. "The inquest was today. Accidental death. Cremation Monday, three o'clock, Golders Green. A hearty welcome will be extended to all husbands, real, imaginary, future, and common law."

Martin walked down the steps and into the street without looking back. He heard the door close. His head was banging from bewilderment and incredulity and gin.

It was a quarter past seven. He had been with Tim for less than an hour. In those forty-five or fifty minutes his whole life, the past as well as the present and the future, had been changed. It was as if the world had tilted and he been thrown sliding down the slope of it to hang there, breathless, by his hands. Or as if, as Tim said, the thin crust had given way.

His head was hurting him now. He had drunk a lot of that gin, probably a tumblerful. But he didn't feel drunk, only sick and headachy and drained. He was tired as well, but he didn't think he would sleep; he felt as if he would never sleep again.

For a long time he sat in the car in Samphire Road. He only drove away because he was afraid Tim might come out and find him still there, and even then he parked again almost immediately, in one of the streets that had been turned into a cul-de-sac by the crater of devastated land.

It was quite dark now and the rubble-covered waste was totally unlighted. The edges of it only were visible, a horizon of black jagged roofs, punctured with points of light, against the crimson-suffused sky. Francesca had lived here, come from here every morning, returned here each night. It seemed to him infinitely strange, something he would never fully understand. She was dead and had been dead for nearly a week now. In her dying she had somehow come back to him—there had been no terrible betrayal. How could Tim know how she had felt? How could Tim tell that for all her early motives she hadn't, at the end, come to prefer the new man to the old?

From taking a vicious pleasure in the fact of her death—he had felt like that when he first began to understand—he found he could now think of her with a pitying tenderness. They would never have been happy together, or not for long, he could see that. He was getting to know himself at last, he thought.

His head wasn't going to get any better just sitting here. If the place had been more attractive—less downright sinister, in fact— he would have gone for a walk, walked to clear his head, for it was a mild evening with that indefinable smell and charge in the air that heralds spring. But he couldn't walk here. He started the car and drove away into Hornsey Rise.

Someone walked across a pedestrian crossing ahead of him. He braked and waited rather longer than usual. He thought of the manner of Francesca's death. Who could do such a thing? Knock someone down and drive away to leave her dying? She had taken a night and a day to die. He shivered uncontrollably. Whoever

146

was, the police would find him, the police would be relentless . . . Martin reflected that he shouldn't be driving at all, he had had far too much to drink, a lot over the permitted limit. Perhaps Francesca's killer had also been drinking, had sobered up in terror when he saw what he had done, and terror had made him flee. Martin drove home over the Archway, the road in its deep concrete gorge flowing northwards beneath him.

He put the car on the hard-top parking in front of Cromwell Court, parking it between an orange-coloured Volvo and a small grey van. The Volvo belonged to a doctor at the Royal Free who lived on the ground floor. The grey van was probably some tradesman's, though Martin felt obscurely that he had seen it somewhere before, and recently, and in a context he couldn't at the moment recall. It couldn't be of the slightest importance. He walked across the asphalt to the entrance of the block, aware that someone had got out of the van and was also coming in.

But he didn't hold the door open. He let it swing shut and made for the stairs, wishing not for the first time that there was a lift here as there was in Swan Place. Should he get Adrian to fight for Swan Place against that family of Francesca's? Was there any chance of success? At least, he thought as he climbed the third flight, he could now tell Adrian and Norman and his parents the melancholy truth, that Francesca was dead.

The soft but regular footsteps which, lower down, he had heard coming behind him he could now hear again. They were coming up to the top. The driver of the grey van must be calling at one of the other three flats on this floor. Martin got to the top and crossed the corridor to his own front door. There, standing on the threshold of his home, he was suddenly and sharply visited by the memory of himself and Tim embraced in Tim's red-lit kitchen, and of kissing Tim and holding him in his arms. What would become of him if this was what he wanted? What must he look forward to? He released his pent-up breath and put his key into the lock.

As he did so he heard a low cough behind him. It made Martin jump and he wheeled round. Standing about a yard from him, in grey woolly hat, yellow pullover, black-velvet waistcoat and a black scarf with coins sewn round it, was Finn. Martin hadn't really noticed before what extraordinary eyes the man had. They were almost silver. The man with the silver eyes . . .

"Well, well," said Finn. "I've been waiting long enough."

He pushed past Martin and into the flat.

147

XXII

The flat was warm and very stuffy. For most of the day the sun must have been shining on that big window. It was rare for Finn to be a guest in anyone's home. He could count on the fingers of his large, splayed hands the number of times it had happened: twice at Mr. Beard's, once at Mrs. Gogarty's, three or four times in girls' rooms.

He stood looking about him. At the structure and the paintwork mainly; he had a business interest in things like that. He took off his woolly hat but kept his gloves on.

Martin Urban was getting a brandy bottle out of a drinks cabinet. You would think he had had enough, he stank of gin. Finn could tell that something had frightened or upset him. His hands trembled and made the bottle chatter against the glass.

"Brandy? There's no whisky but there's vodka and martini and sherry."

"I don't drink," said Finn.

The voice sounded both weary and awkward. "Look, I'm sorry about the money. I've had a lot on my plate and I'm afraid I forgot all about you. I could give you a cheque here and now only you will insist on cash."

Finn didn't say anything.

"Sit down, won't you? I'm sorry you've come all the way here for nothing. You should have phoned." He sat down and drank his brandy at a gulp as if it were medicine. Finn watched him curiously, watched a flush mottle his skin. He wasn't going to sit down. What would be the point?

"I haven't come here for nothing," he said.

"Well..." Into the glass slopped more brandy. "Not in the sense that you've reminded me. I can get it for you sometime next week. Cash is difficult, you know, that sort of cash. I'll have to phone my bank first, I'll have to..."

Finn took a step forward from the position he had taken up by the balcony door. "You can get it for me Monday morning," he said. "And I don't want it sent, not this time. Put it in your car on the front passenger seat and leave the car in the park outside the palace."

"The palace?" repeated Martin Urban, staring at him.

"Alexandra Palace." Finn was getting impatient. "Have you got that? Put the money in a carrier on the front seat of your car and leave it there between one and two Monday, okay?"

Martin Urban had flushed a dark crimson. His eyes had become very bright, his features blurred and thickened. He set down his glass and stood up. Very deliberately he said, "No, it is not okay. It is very much not okay." He passed a hand over his forehead, and when he took it down Finn saw that his face was working with fury. "Just who the hell d'you think you are, coming here, barging in here, telling me what I should do with my own money? You haven't got some sort of right to it, you know. You people, you're all the same, you think anyone with a bit more than you've got owes you a living. It's purely out of the kindness of my heart I'm making it possible for your mother to have a decent place to live in. But I'm damned if I'm going to break an important appointment on Monday morning to go to the bank for you or do without my car for an hour. Why should I? Why the hell should I?"

Finn thought the man was going to fall. He watched him get hold of the back of a chair and hang on to it and draw a long breath and seem to get a grip on himself. Enough control, at any rate, to say coldly now, "You'd better go," and then, pushing past Finn to unlock the balcony door, "Excuse me, I must have some air."

Martin Urban went out on to the balcony. Finn watched him standing there, looking down on London and then up at the clear, faintly starry, purplish sky. After a moment or two he came in again, appearing partially recovered, and stood staring with a curiously pained expression, like a hurt dog, at the big cactus which stood on the window sill, at its pink, waxen flowers. Without turning to Finn, he said,

"I thought I told you to go."

Finn didn't reply to this rhetorical question. He said, "I don't want the money sent. Is that understood? I don't want those delivery people knowing."

"Knowing what, for God's sake?" Martin Urban turned round and said sharply, "I'm sick of this. I'm tired. I've had a bad day. If it wasn't that I promised and I don't like to break my word, I'd tell you you can forget the money. Right, so you can have a cheque or nothing."

"Well, well," said Finn. "Now we know."

"Indeed we do. And when that's over I think I'll have done quite a favour to you and your mother." He went to the writing desk, though none too steadily, and fumbled about inside it for cheque-book.

"Haven't I ever done anything for you?" said Finn.

Without looking at him, Martin Urban said, "Like what? Like making a damned nuisance of yourself. What have you ever done for me?" He began to write the cheque. Finn went up to him, laid a heavy hand on his arm and took the pen away. Martin Urban jumped to his feet, shouted, "Take your hands off me!"

Finn held him by the upper arms and looked searchingly into his face. The square, flushed, puffy face was resentful and indignant—and utterly bewildered. Finn could read faces—and minds too sometimes.

"You don't know about it," he said flatly. "It wasn't in the papers. Well, it's done. Last Saturday."

Martin Urban struggled to free himself and Finn let him go. "How dare you touch me! And what the hell are you talking about?"

It was a strange thing, but now that he had to do it Finn found it as hard to put the act into words as his clients had done. He looked around him, he cleared his throat.

"Last Saturday," he said gruffly, "I did for the girl. Like you wanted."

Martin Urban stood quite still.

"What did you say?"

"You heard."

"Last Saturday you..."

"I did for that girl, like you're paying me for. I've done it and now I want my money."

The sound he made was a kind of ghastly groan, the like of which Finn had only previously heard from Lena, and he fell back on the sofa, covering his face with his hands. Finn regarded him as he rocked backwards and forwards, pushing his fists into his eyes, beating them against his temples. Finn stepped away and sat down on an upright chair, understanding now that he had made a mistake. Things, details, fell gently into place like the silver balls in Lena's Chinese puzzle dropping into their slots.

"Give me some more of that brandy."

Finn poured some brandy and pushed the glass at Martin Urban' mouth. The brandy was drained and there was a shuddering and a kind of sob and the thick broken voice said,

"You were—in the car—that—didn't—stop?"

"I've said so."

"What am I to do? My God, what am I going to do? You thought I'd paid you to do that? What sort of a monster *are* you?" He got up shakily and stood with his hands pressed to his head

"I loved her," he said. "She loved me. We were going to be married. And you . . ."

He turned towards modern man's succour, lifeline, first aid—the phone. He took an uncertain step towards it. Finn calculated how to get there first, take him by surprise, wrench the wires out of the wall. And then? There was only one way to make certain no one was ever told what Martin Urban knew.

Swaying, holding his head, he stood staring hypnotically at Finn. Finn began to get up. Sweat beads had started to prickle his face. Somehow he must get Martin Urban out of here, into a car, away from this place into some lonely place. In order to silence him he must put on an act, make promises, play along . . . He didn't know how to do these things, he was powerless, bereft of energy, as if a fuse had blown in him and there was no current to power his limbs.

Martin Urban took down his hands and turned away from the phone. The attack he made on Finn was entirely unexpected. One moment he was standing there in the middle of the room, his fists clenched, his arms gradually falling to his sides, the next he had sprung upon Finn, flailing out, using his hands like hammers. Finn toppled backwards. It was the first time in his life he had ever been knocked down by another.

He rolled over on to his front, pressed himself up with a violence that sent the other man staggering back, and leapt like a panther. Martin Urban ducked and stumbled out on to the balcony. London glittered out there like the window of a tourist souvenir shop. Finn stood poised in the doorway, his arms spread, his body quivering. And the man who had given him five thousand pounds from some quixotic altruism Finn couldn't even begin to understand, stood against the low parapet, convulsed, it seemed, with some kind of passionate need for revenge. He leapt forward again, deceived perhaps by Finn's white thinness.

But Finn was there a split second before him, to smash with his right arm harder than he had ever smashed before. And a strange thing happened. Martin Urban raised his arms hugely above his head in some exaggerated defensive gesture. He staggered backwards in an almost comic, tiptoe slow motion, bathed in the shining night air, against the spangled backdrop, staggered, teetered until the parapet wall, that reached lower than the tops of his thighs, was just behind him. Finn could see what would happen and he jumped to catch the man before he fell. He jumped just too late. Martin Urban made contact with the wall, doubled over backwards, and with a low cry, fell.

Forty feet into a pit of blackness. There was a concrete well down there, an area that perhaps gave access to a porter's basement. Finn stood, looking down. No other windows opened, no one appeared, no one had been alerted by the groaning sound the man had made as he starfished to earth. Finn went in and closed and locked the balcony door. He turned off the lights and stood listening for movement in the corridor outside, for doors opening and footsteps. There was nothing.

He had been a fool to lock that door. It must look like suicide. It must look as if Martin Urban had killed himself over the death of the woman he was to have married. Finn unlocked the door again. He didn't touch the brandy glass. A man might well drink brandy before he committed suicide. The irony of it struck Finn, though, as he moved towards the front door of the flat, the irony that now, at this moment, in this place, he was at greater risk through this man's accidental death than he had ever been when he had done murder.

When he was satisfied that all was quiet and still he passed stealthily out of the flat and pulled the front door softly shut behind him. He went downstairs very fast, passing no one, hearing nothing. The van was waiting for him in a deserted car park. And deserted too Cromwell Court and its environs would have seemed but for the lights which shone with tranquillity in most of its broad rectangular windows.

Still, it was only a matter of time, of short time, before that body would be found. He must get away, not linger, not yield to the temptation to steal softly around to the other side of the block and peer into that dark well, check what light must go on or which door open to reveal its occupant . . .

He resisted. As he was driving down Dartmouth Park Hill, coming up to the traffic lights at Tufnell Park Station, he heard the wail of a siren. But there was nothing to say it was an ambulance summoned for Martin Urban, it could just as well have been a fire engine or a police car. He put the van away in the garage at the corner of Somerset Grove and walked home along the street where the sulphurous light laid a pinchbeck gleam.

The house smelt of cannabis and wastebins. Finn went on up to the top, taking two stairs at a time with his great loping stride. He felt a surge of confidence and contentment. This time it really had been an accident, he could face Lena without dread. And there was no possibility now of anyone suspecting Martin Urban might not have been alone in the flat, not a soul who would know of any connection between himself and Martin Urban. He was sure no one had seen him or would know him if they had. Yet Martin Urban was out of harm's way, silenced, taking the secret of Finn's mistake with him into the dark spaces or losing it in oblivion as he began on a new cycle of life.

The green bird began a shrill twittering when he came into the room. Mrs. Gogarty, who had been making forecasts with the aid of the Tarot, got up and threw the shawl over its cage.

"Well, well," said Finn, "we *are* cosy."

He pulled off his gloves and put them in his pocket and took Lena's hand. She was as transparent as an insect tonight and dusty like a moth. Her dull leaden eyes met his silver eyes and she smiled.

"The picture of devotion!" said Mrs. Gogarty with admiring sighs. She studied the cards, laid out now for Finn. "There's a lot of death here . . ." she began.

Over Lena's head Finn gave her a warning look.

"Ah!" She slid the cards together and the Death card, Scorpio's Death card—Death cloaked and riding a pale horse—came out on top. She covered it with the Queen of Wands. In her mechanical gypsy voice she said, "There's money here, my darling, a lot of money. But wait . . . no, it's not coming your way, you'll have a disappointment."

The hand that held Lena's grew cold and limp. He bent down, he looked unseeing into the soothsayer's face.

"What? What did you say?"

"A disappointment over money . . . Why are you looking at me like that?"

Finn saw, not the cards which Mrs. Gogarty's hands now covered in fear, not Lena's face, apprehensive, growing stricken, but a cheque that lay on a writing desk, locked up in Martin Urban's flat. The date had been written—had his name?

The women's eyes fearfully upon him, he stood upright yet trembling in that tiny room, listening to the distant sound of a siren crying through the dark, a herald of the one that must cry for him.

ABOUT THE AUTHOR

RUTH RENDELL decided early in her life to be a writer. Unfortunately, her first efforts, short stories for women's magazines, were all rejected. And so, after the birth of her son, she dedicated herself to motherhood. Nine years later she tried again, only to have her serious novel rejected. However, a mystery that she tried her hand at just for fun was accepted and published. She has now written nineteen mysteries and has had numerous short stories published. She consistently receives excellent reviews and wins awards both here and in England. She was awarded the annual silver cup presented by *Current Crime*, a British mystery publication, for the best British Crime Novel of 1975 (*Shake Hands Forever*). The Mystery Writers of America presented her with their Edgar for her short story "The Fallen Curtain." *A Demon in My View* was given the Golden Dagger Award for the best Crime Novel of 1976 in England. Furthermore, her readers agree with these accolades. *Current Crime* took a poll in which for that year Ruth Rendell's *Shake Hands Forever* easily surpassed every other contender, Christie and Deighton among them. Ruth Rendell lives outside London and also has a thatched cottage which was the site of a famous nineteenth-century murder.

Dear Reader,

*There is nothing unusual in having two Christian names,
but perhaps it is less common to be called by each of them
equally. This is what happened to me. Ruth was my
father's choice of name for me, Barbara my mother's.
Because Ruth was difficult for my mother's Scandinavian
parents to pronounce, her side of the family called me
Barbara, and since this sort of duality was impossible in
one household, my father finally started calling me Barbara too.*

*I tend to divide friends and relatives into the "Ruth
people" and the "Barbara people." Both names are equally
familiar to me, equally "my" names. If either were called
out in the street I would turn around. And I don't mind
which I am called so long as people don't try to change in,
so to speak, midstream. There is for me something grotesque in a Barbara person trying to become a Ruth
person, or vice-versa. Only my husband knows as well as
I do into which category each friend falls. He can write the
Christmas cards and always get them right. But he never
calls me by either of my Christian names.*

*It has always interested me—I don't think my parents
realized this—that both my names mean or imply "a
stranger in a strange land," Ruth who was exiled into an
alien country, Barbara that signifies "a foreigner."*

*Growing up with two names doesn't make you into two
people. It does give you two aspects of personality, and
Ruth and Barbara are two aspects of me. Ruth is tougher,
colder, more analytical, possibly more aggressive. Ruth*

has written all the novels, created Chief Inspector Wexford. Ruth is the professional writer. Barbara is more feminine. It is Barbara who sews. If Barbara writes it is letters that she writes.

For a long time I have wanted Barbara to have a voice as well as Ruth. It would be a softer voice speaking at a slower pace, more sensitive perhaps, and more intuitive. In *A DARK-ADAPTED EYE* she has found that voice, taking a surname from the other side of the family, the paternal side, for Vine was my great-grandmother's maiden name. There would be nothing surprising to a psychologist in Barbara's choosing, as she asserts herself, to address readers in the first person.

The novel itself is the story of Faith Severn, and her exploration of circumstances that led to a terrible murder in her family more than thirty years before. I hope you will enjoy reading this book, as much as Barbara Vine enjoyed writing it.

Sincerely,

Ruth Rendell

1

On the morning Vera died I woke up very early. The birds had started, more of them and singing more loudly in our leafy suburb than in the country. They never sang like that outside Vera's windows in the Vale of Dedham. I lay there listening to something repeating itself monotonously. A thrush, it must have been, doing what Browning said it did and singing each song twice over. It was a Thursday in August, a hundred years ago. Not much more than a third of that, of course. It only feels so long.

In these circumstances alone one knows when someone is going to die. All other deaths can be predicted, conjectured, even anticipated with some certainty, but not to the hour, the minute, with no room for hope. Vera would die at eight o'clock and that was that. I began to feel sick. I lay there exaggeratedly still, listening for some sound from the next room. If I was awake my father would be. About my mother

I was less sure. She had never made a secret of her dislike of both his sisters. It was one of the things which had made a rift between them, though there they were together in the next room, in the same bed still. People did not break a marriage, leave each other, so lightly in those days.

I thought of getting up but first I wanted to make sure where my father was. There was something terrible in the idea of encountering him in the passage, both of us dressing-gowned, thick-eyed with sleeplessness, each seeking the bathroom and each politely giving way to the other. Before I saw him I needed to be washed and brushed and dressed, my loins girded. I could hear nothing but that thrush uttering its idiot phrase five or six times over, not twice.

To work he would go as usual, I was sure of that. And Vera's name would not be mentioned. None of it had been spoken about at all in our house since the last time my father went to see Vera. There was one crumb of comfort for him. No one knew. A man may be very close to his sister, his twin, without anyone knowing of the relationship, and none of our neighbours knew he was Vera Hillyard's brother. None of the bank's clients knew. If today the head cashier remarked upon Vera's death, as he very likely might, as people would by reason of her sex among other things, I knew my father would present to him a bland, mildly interested face and utter some suitable platitude. He had, after all, to survive.

A floorboard creaked in the passage. I heard the bedroom door close and then the door of the bathroom, so I got up and looked at the day. A clean white still morning, with no sun and no blue in the sky, a morning that seemed to me to be waiting because I was. Six-thirty. There was an angle you could stand at looking out of this window where you could see no other house, so plentiful were the trees and shrubs, so thick their foliage. It was like looking into a clearing in a rather elaborate wood. Vera used to sneer at where my parents lived, saying it was neither town nor country.

My mother was up now. We were all stupidly early, as if we were going away on holiday. When I used to go to Sindon I was sometimes up as early as this, excited and looking forward to it. How could I have looked forward to the society of Vera, an unreasonable carping scold when on her own with me and, when Eden was there, the two of them closing ranks to exclude anyone who might try to penetrate their alliance? I hoped, I suppose. Each time I was older and because of this she might change. She never did—until almost the end. And by then she was too desperate for an ally to be choosy.

I went to the bathroom. It was always possible to tell if my father had finished in the bathroom. He used an old-fashioned cutthroat razor and wiped the blade after each stroke on a small square of newspaper. The newspaper and the jug of hot water he fetched himself but the remains were always left for my mother to clear away, the square of paper with its load of shaving soap full of stubble, the empty jug. I washed in cold water. In summer, we only lit the boiler once a week for baths. Vera and Eden bathed every day, and that was one of the things I *had* liked about Sindon, my daily bath, though Vera's attitude always was that I would have escaped it if I could.

The paper had come. It was tomorrow the announcement would be, of course, a few bald lines. Today there was nothing about Vera. She was stale, forgotten, until this morning when, in a brief flare-up, the whole country would talk of her, those who deplored and those who said it served her right. My father sat at the dining-table, reading the paper. It was the *Daily Telegraph*, than which no other daily paper was ever read in our family. The crossword puzzle he would save for the evening, just as Vera had done, once only in all the years phoning my father for the solution to a clue that was driving her crazy. When Eden had a home of her own and was rich, she often rang him up and got him to finish the puzzle for her over the phone. She had never been as good at it as they.

He looked up and nodded to me. He didn't

smile. The table had yesterday's cloth on it, yellow check not to show the egg stains. Food was still rationed, meat being very scarce, and we ate eggs all the time, laid by my mother's chickens. Hence the crowing cockerels in our garden suburb, the fowl runs concealed behind hedges of lonicera and laurel. We had no eggs that morning, though. No cornflakes either. My mother would have considered cornflakes frivolous, in their white and orange packet. She had disliked Vera, had no patience with my father's intense family love, but she had a strong sense of occasion, of what was fitting. Without a word, she brought us toast that, while hot, had been thinly spread with margarine, a jar of marrow and ginger jam, a pot of tea.

I knew I shouldn't be able to eat. He ate. Business was to be as usual with him, I could tell that. It was over, wiped away, a monstrous effort made, if not to forget, at least to behave as if all was forgotten. The silence was broken by his voice, harsh and stagy, reading aloud. It was something about the war in Korea. He read on and on, columns of it, and it became embarrassing to listen because no one reads like that without introduction, explanation, excuse. It must have gone on for ten minutes. He read to the foot of the page, to where presumably you were told the story was continued inside. He didn't turn over. He broke off in mid-sentence. 'In the Far,' he said, never getting to 'East' but laying the paper down, aligning the pages, folding it twice, and once more, so that it was back in the shape it had been when the boy pushed it through the letterbox.

'In the far' hung in the air, taking on a curious significance, quite different from what the writer had intended. He took another piece of toast but got no further towards eating it. My mother watched him. I think she had been tender with him once but he had had no time for it or room for it and so her tenderness had withered for want of encouragement. I did not expect her to go to him and take his hand or put her arms round him. Would I have done so myself if she had not been there? Perhaps. That family's mutual love had not usually found its expression in outward show. In other words, there had not been embraces. The twins, for instance, did not kiss each other, though the women pecked the air around each other's faces.

It was a quarter to eight now. I kept repeating over and over to myself (like the thrush, now silent), 'In the far, in the far'. When first it happened, when he was told, he went into paroxysms of rage, of disbelief, of impotent protest.

'Murdered, murdered!' he kept shouting, like someone in an Elizabethan tragedy, like someone who bursts into a castle hall with dreadful news. And then, 'My sister!' and 'My poor sister!' and 'My little sister!'

But silence and concealment fell like a shutter. It was lifted briefly, after Vera was dead, when, sitting in a closed room after dark, like conspirators, he and I heard from Josie what happened that April day. He never spoke of it again. His twin was erased from his mind and he even made himself—incredibly—into an only child. Once I heard him tell someone that he had never regretted having no brothers or sisters.

It was only when he was ill and not far from death himself that he resurrected memories of his sisters. And the stroke he had had, as if by some physiological action stripping away layers of reserve and inhibition, making him laugh sometimes and just as often cry, released an unrestrained gabbling about how he had felt that summer. His former love for Vera the repressive years had turned to repulsion and fear, his illusions broken as much by the tug-of-war and Eden's immorality—his word, not mine—as by the murder itself. My mother might have said, though she did not, that at last he was seeing his sisters as they really were.

He left the table, his tea half-drunk, his second piece of toast lying squarely in the middle of his plate, the *Telegraph* folded and lying with its edges compulsively lined up to the table corner. No word was spoken to my mother and me. He went upstairs, he came down, the front door closed behind him. He would walk the leafy roads, I thought, making detours, turning the half mile to the station into two miles, hiding from the time in places where there were no clocks. It was then that I noticed he had left his watch on the table. I picked up the paper and there was the watch underneath.

'We should have gone away somewhere,' I said.

My mother said fiercely, 'Why should we? She hardly ever came here. Why should we let her drive us away?'

'Well, we haven't,' I said.

I wondered which was right, the clock on the wall that said five to eight or my father's watch that said three minutes to. My own watch was upstairs. Time passes so slowly over such points in it. There still seemed an aeon to wait. My mother loaded the tray and took it into the kitchen, making a noise about it, banging cups, a way of showing that it was no fault of hers. Innocent herself, she had been dragged into this family by marriage, all unknowing. It was another matter for me who was of their blood.

I went upstairs. My watch was on the bed-side table. It was new, a present bestowed by my parents for getting my degree. That, because of what had happened, it was a less good degree than everyone had expected, no one had commented upon. The watch face was small, not much larger than the cluster of little diamonds in my engagement ring that lay beside it, and you had to get close up to it to read the hands. I thought, in a moment the heavens will fall, there will be a great bolt of thunder, nature could not simply ignore. There was nothing. Only the birds had become silent, which they would do anyway at this time, their territorial claims being made, their trees settled on, the business of their day begun. What would the business of my day be? One thing I thought I would do. I would phone Helen, I would talk to Helen. Symbolic of my attitude to my engagement, my future marriage, this was, that it was to Helen I meant to fly for comfort, not the man who had given me the ring with a diamond cluster as big as a watch face.

I walked over to the bedside table, stagily, self-consciously, like a bad actress in an amateur production. The director would have halted me and told me to do it again, to walk away and do it again. I nearly did walk away so as not to see the time. But I picked up the watch and looked and had a long, rolling, falling feeling through my body as I saw that I had missed the moment. It was all over now and she was dead. The hands of the watch stood at five past eight.

The only kind of death that can be accurately predicted to the minute had taken place, the death that takes its victim,

> . . . feet foremost through the floor,
> Into an empty space.

*A Bantam paperback
coming in September 1987.*

50 YEARS OF GREAT AMERICAN MYSTERIES
FROM BANTAM BOOKS

Stuart Palmer

"Those who have not already made the acquaintance of Hildegarde Withers should make haste to do so, for she is one of the world's shrewdest and most amusing detectives."　　　　　　　　　　*—New York Times*
May 6, 1934

☐ 25934-2 THE PUZZLE OF THE SILVER PERSIAN (1934) $2.95

☐ 26024-3 THE PUZZLE OF THE HAPPY HOOLIGAN
(1941)　　　　　　　　　　　　　　　　$2.95

Featuring spinster detective Hildegarde Withers

Craig Rice

"Why can't all murders be as funny as those concocted by Craig Rice?　　　　　　　*—New York Times*

☐ 26345-5 HAVING WONDERFUL CRIME　　　$2.95

"Miss Rice at her best, writing about her 3 favorite characters against a delirious New York background."
—New Yorker

☐ 26222-X MY KINGDOM FOR A HEARSE　　$2.95

"Pretty damn wonderful!"　　　*—New York Times*

Barbara Paul

☐ 26234-3 RENEWABLE VIRGIN (1985)　　　$2.95

"The talk crackles, the characters are bouncy, and New York's media world is caught with all its vitality and vulgarity."　　　　*—Washington Post Book World*

☐ 26225-4 KILL FEE (1985)　　　　　　　　$2.95

"A desperately treacherous game of cat-and-mouse (whose well-wrought tension is heightened by a freakish twist that culminates in a particularly chilling conclusion." *—Booklist*

For your ordering convenience, use the handy coupon below:

Special Offer
Buy a Bantam Book
for only 50¢.

Now you can have Bantam's catalog filled with hundreds of titles plus take advantage of our unique and exciting bonus book offer. A special offer which gives you the opportunity to purchase a Bantam book for only 50¢. Here's how!

By ordering any five books at the regular price per order, you can also choose any other single book listed (up to a $4.95 value) for just 50¢. Some restrictions do apply, but for further details why not send for Bantam's catalog of titles today!

Just send us your name and address and we will send you a catalog!

☐ 25789-7 **JUST ANOTHER DAY IN PARADISE,**
      Maxwell $2.95

Fiddler has more money than he knows what to do with, he's tried about everything he'd ever thought of trying and there's not much left that interests him. So, when his ex-wife's twin brother disappears, when the feds begin to investigate the high-tech computer company the twin owns, and when Fiddler finds himself holding an envelope of Russian-cut diamonds, he decides to get involved. Is his ex-wife's twin selling high-tech information to the Russians?

☐ 25809-5 **THE UNORTHODOX MURDER OF**
      RABBI WAHL, Telushkin $2.95

Rabbi Daniel Winter, the young host of the radio talk show "Religion and You," invites three guests to discuss "Feminism and Religion." He certainly expects that the three women, including Rabbi Myra Wahl, are likely to generate some sparks . . . What he doesn't expect is murder.

☐ 25717-X **THE BACK-DOOR MAN,** Kantner $2.95

Ben Perkins doesn't look for trouble, but he isn't the kind of guy who looks the other way when something comes along to spark his interest. In this case, it's a wealthy widow who's a victim of embezzlement and the gold American Express card she gives him for expenses. Ben thinks it should be fun; the other people after the missing money are out to change his mind.

☐ 26061-8 **"B" IS FOR BURGLAR,** Grafton $3.50

"Kinsey is a refreshing heroine."—*Washington Post Book World*

"Kinsey Millhone . . . is a stand-out specimen of the new female operatives." —*Philadelphia Inquirer*

[Millhone is] "a tough cookie with a soft center, a gregarious loner." —*Newsweek*

What appears to be a routine missing persons case for private detective Kinsey Millhone turns into a dark tangle of arson, theft and murder.

Look for them at your bookstore or use the coupon below: